The Scoundrel's Son

Frederic Fahey

Goose River Press
Waldoboro, Maine

Copyright © 2024 Frederic Fahey

All rights reserved. No part of this book may be reproduced in any form without written permission from the publisher, except by a reviewer who may quote brief passages in a review to be printed in a newspaper or magazine.

Library of Congress Card Number: 2024941021

ISBN: 978-1-59713-273-2

First Printing, 2024

Design and art direction by Scott Nash.
Cover illustration by Douglas Smith.
Interior art by Chris Harper-Fahey.

Published by
Goose River Press
3400 Friendship Road
Waldoboro ME 04572
email: gooseriverpress@gmail.com
www.gooseriverpress.com

To Chris, my loving partner in creativity

In the ancient city of London, on a certain autumn day
in the second quarter of the sixteenth century,
a boy was born to a poor family of the name of Canty,
who did not want him. On the same day another
English child was born to a rich family of the
name of Tudor, who did want him.

The Prince and the Pauper
Mark Twain

Part I

She lifted the frog again, but this time she was careful not to touch the release mechanism. "How does it work?" she asked as she examined it from every angle.

Chapter 1

I had the adventures of a lifetime by the time I was ten years old, but the events around my sixteenth birthday were even more astounding and more than a young man should have to bear. Now that more than twenty years have passed, and I have found you, my lady, the time is right to share this tale. Whether you believe me or not, I still have the desire—no, the need to tell it to you as best I can.

Tom Canty is my name and maybe you remember me. When I was nine years old, I found myself embroiled in one of the great masquerades of English history along with my good friend, Edward. By some stroke of fortune, Edward and I were born on the exact same day and looked remarkably alike, and so I came to often refer to him as my "twin." But our birthdays and physical appearances were where our similarities ended.

I was born in Offal Court, a vile and disreputable part of London not far from Pudding Lane. The children there, including my sisters and me, were very poor and exceedingly hungry at practically all times. On the other hand, the birth of my twin, Edward, was the most celebrated event of the time since he was born to King Henry and Queen Jane. Yes, Edward was born the Prince of Wales. On the day of his birth, bells throughout the kingdom rang with joy and throngs took to the streets to sing, dance, and revel in the most wonderful news.

One day, when I was nine years old and wandering about London, I found myself at Whitehall Palace in Westminster, hoping to catch a glimpse of the royal family, and there was Prince Edward in the courtyard right before my eyes. There was so much excitement to see the young prince that the crowd pushed me too close to the gate, and one of the royal guards proceeded to scold me and handle me a bit roughly. The prince took

Frederic Fahey

notice of this and objected to my harsh treatment. Before I knew it, I was within the palace walls in the presence of the prince. As we talked, I was surprised to find that Edward's fascination with me and my simple life was at least as great as mine with his bestowed life. It also occurred to us that we looked amazingly alike.

A wild idea hatched. Edward proposed that we switch places temporarily so that we each could experience the other's life. Certainly, it would be wonderful to be the prince for even a short time; however, I could not understand why Edward would want to spend even a minute in my sorry place. Still, like many schemes construed by nine-year-old boys, at that instant, it seemed like a marvelous idea.

We exchanged clothes, and Edward made his way out into the world while I remained at the palace pretending to be the prince. We spent about a fortnight living each other's life. However, during that short time, King Henry died, and, for a brief while, I became the king! As he would later relate to me, Edward's adventures were quite harrowing. Luckily, he was befriended by a gallant soldier by the name of Miles Hendon, who rescued him on more than one occasion. On the very day of the coronation, good fortune prevailed, my twin and Miles found themselves back in the royal court, and Edward was crowned instead of me. He named me a ward of the king, and assigned my care to Father Andrew, a kindly priest I had known all my life. Being the king's ward afforded me both protection and opportunities beyond those typically available to the sons of Offal Court.

This is truly a marvelous tale, and I hope that some good storyteller, one perhaps better than me, will one day happen upon this adventure and relate it in a way that does it justice. But, as extraordinary as this story is, it is not the one I intend to share with you today.

And so, my lady, I will tell you my tale from the beginning. I have waited a long time for this chance. The painful events of that time are as vivid in my mind's eye as if they occurred yesterday. I share with you long-kept secrets of the wonder and fragile nature of young life and love. The words may stick in my throat or tear at my heart as I try to release them after all this time. Please be patient as I strive for the best way to relate it all to you.

***

The Scoundrel's Son

"Please come with me. His Majesty will be with you soon," said the king's head groom as he directed me through the door to the royal sitting room. Richard, his name as I recalled, had been kind and patient with me when I posed as prince during the masquerade, as I have come to refer to our earlier adventure.

"Thank you very much, sir," I answered. I had not seen His Majesty or been to Whitehall Palace since the day of his coronation, over a year previously. Since then, our shared tenth birthday had passed in the fall, and winter was now reluctantly giving way to a burgeoning spring. My heart was jumpy. I was not sure what may lie ahead. For me, it would be wonderful to see His Majesty again, but I had to wonder why he would want to see me. The letter I received inviting me to meet with the king offered little clue except to say that he had something to ask of me. When His Majesty asks, is it truly a request or, in fact, a command? Was my fortunate position as ward of the king coming to an end? Was I going to be asked to train to serve in His Majesty's army or be part of the royal guard? Or had I been chosen to serve as His Majesty's new whipping boy?

In hopes of calming my reeling mind while I waited for His Majesty, I paced about and reacquainted myself with the royal sitting room. I had forgotten how large rooms in the palace were. This single room was almost as big as a church, and at least four times the size of an entire house in my parish of Offal Court. The walls were covered with a richly decorated purple tapestry. There were several portraits of the king's ancestors hanging from the walls. The portrait of His Majesty's mother, Queen Jane, had been there when I was here last, but the one of his father, King Henry, had been added since then. A display of crossed swords above a battle shield with the Tudor crest gave the room a regal and a bit of an intimidating feel. But the brightly painted figure of an armored knight next to an open book of tales of chivalry next to His Majesty's seat was a reminder that the king was still a boy.

Just then the door opened, and Richard and a regimen of servants escorted His Majesty into the room. At first, I could barely see the ten-year old king amidst the collection of grown men about him.

"Behold His Royal Majesty, Edward, by the Grace of God, King of England, France and Ireland, Defender of the Faith and of the Church of England," Richard announced. I stood still, not entirely sure how to respond. Several servants looked at me and abruptly bent at the waist. I then understood and made a rather awkward bow towards His Majesty.

The king immediately broke with formality rushing to me and grasping my hand with both of his. A broad smile beamed across his face.

"It is so good to see you, Tom," he greeted me. The breath I had been holding made a happy escape. "Richard, provide a chair for my ward, and place it close to mine. And bring some refreshments."

"Certainly, Your Majesty," Richard responded as he signaled to one of the many servants behind him. As if by magic, a chair appeared and was placed as His Majesty had commanded.

"Come, Tom. Please have a seat while we visit." I allowed him to sit first. He gestured to the other chair, and so I sat. Richard excused himself and directed the many servants out of the room so that we might have a more private visit.

Once settled, I tried to ask a question but, in my nervousness, it sputtered forth like bubbled water from a faucet.

"Your Majesty ... umm ... is that right? ... How should I refer to you? I mean Your Majesty? By Your Majesty?"

"Well, Tom, probably best for you to refer to me as 'Your Majesty' when in the company of others, I suppose. But in more private settings such as this, 'Your Royal Majesty, defender of the realm and master of this humble servant' might suffice." He cleared his throat as he tried to maintain a straight face, but once he exploded in laughter, I knew he was joking with me. "Refer to me as Edward. We are merely Edward and Tom, two good chums."

"Edward it is," I responded, smiling back. I could sense my spine starting to loosen and my hands unclench. This was indeed to be a friendly visit. One of the servants brought some cider and gingerbread topped with cream. Edward took a nibble of the treat, but I devoured mine in two bites. He told me of his fencing lessons and how he loved to play a game called tennis. I spoke of my mother and sisters and thanked him for his kindness in providing for their care. My heart calmed as I gazed upon my twin. I hadn't realized how much I had missed seeing him in the past year.

Right then Edward's eyes darted about the room as if to make sure we were alone. My ears perked when he put his finger to his lips.

"Tom, I have a thought." he leaned forward and spoke in a voice bare-

The Scoundrel's Son

ly above a whisper. "I would like you to take my place again."

"Are you serious, Edward?" was all I could think to say.

"Tom, you might remember," he continued, "that I have many meetings that merely require my presence and little else. I think it would be fun for you to take my place again. For me, it would afford a bit of a break. I listen to people's requests of me all day, and after a while, I sometimes get numb to it. Besides it will give me the chance to complete my assignments before my lessons tomorrow. Doctor Cheke can be quite stern if I fall behind."

"Would you also take my place as before?" I asked.

"Goodness no! Last time, I thought it would be fun to be in your place, to have the freedom to go anyplace and do anything without all the trappings of being the prince, but I certainly learned otherwise. If not for Miles Hendon, I am afraid I would not have survived. As you have found, my life is quite simple in comparison to yours.

"It would only be for an hour or so. Usually, I just sit upon the throne, listen, and wave my hand once in a while in response. One doesn't really have to speak very much as king. I have some audiences with subjects as soon as our visit is over today.

"In the meantime, I will make myself scarce in my chambers dressed in your clothes until you return. I will pretend that you, I mean the king, offered me, I mean you, the opportunity to select a book to borrow from my library. So, you stayed behind to select one. After you return, we will switch back. I think it is a splendid plan!"

Edward's request took me totally by surprise. Our previous masquerade had put Edward's life in true danger. I certainly did not want to make the same mistake twice. However, as reluctant as I was, the way Edward presented the notion made it seem almost harmless. I have to say, I was a bit excited by the secret nature of the endeavor. Also, the audiences with the subjects were some of the more enjoyable parts of the masquerade, while I found dressing up, all the pomp and being waited upon to be a drudgery. Of course, some of the petitions before the Crown were incredibly boring but I liked trying to help people in some way.

"All right," I finally relented, as if I had a choice when being asked by His Majesty. "This one time to see how it goes. And for only an hour! If it goes too long, you must promise to rescue me!"

Frederic Fahey

Edward's face shone with delight. "Yes! Yes! Thank you, Tom! By the way, let me show you this." He rolled up his right sleeve to reveal a rather nasty scar. "This is the result of an unfortunate fencing lesson. You can imagine my instructor was quite upset, but my uncle, Lord Somerset, noted that a lesson learned with blood is a lesson learned well. My head groom, Richard, as well as my doctor know of this scar and so, if necessary, I can be easily distinguished from you."

"That is wonderful! I don't mean your injury…"

"By the way, I have not lost a fencing match since."

"Splendid!" I responded, although I wondered how many of his opponents would be willing to risk injuring their king a second time.

Edward and I exchanged clothes once again. I had forgotten how many layers of clothes a king dons. I started by putting on a long-sleeved white undergarment and hose that fit rather tightly. I then pulled on short trousers that I thought were shaped like large melons around each of my thighs. A tunic was then worn with a belt around my waist, letting the ruffles from the undergarment show both at the collar and at the end of the sleeves. A loose jacket with broad shoulders on top gave the appearance of a manly frame to my otherwise slender build. I slipped on Edward's shoes that were stunning to view and as uncomfortable as can be. Mine, on the other hand, were ugly to the eye but at least practical. And, of course, this was all topped by the flat hat with a plume that Edward favored as he felt it made him look like his father. My usual dress was quite simple, a tunic worn with a belt over loose-fitting hose. I had worn a coat on that day to guard against the brisk March wind.

"I must say," Edward commented as he was putting on my last bit of clothes. "Your manner of dress has improved dramatically! Last time, after I left the palace grounds, I realized that your garments were infested with fleas! I itched for weeks even after I returned to the palace!"

I looked down at myself. "I must say that your manner of dress has not improved one bit! When I returned, I smelled of perfume for weeks! My sisters were quite jealous!" We both laughed.

"Are we ready?" Edward asked.

"I suppose so," I said. "Remember, one hour at most!"

While I walked towards the chamber door as regally as I could muster, I started to appreciate the gravity of what I was about to undertake. We had

The Scoundrel's Son

gotten away with it once, but Edward was merely the Prince of Wales at that time. Now I was going to impersonate the King of England! This had to be a serious crime although I kept telling myself that it had been requested of me by His Majesty himself. My knees started to shake, and my palms to sweat the more I thought about it. Could I convince those about me that I was the King of England?

Edward called to Richard, who entered the room.

"Yes, Your Majesty?" Richard asked as he looked straight at me and not at Edward. It was too late to back out now.

I gathered my wits and tried to mimic Edward's manner of speech as best I could. Certainly, Edward's accent was different than in Offal Court. His cadence was more pronounced with each word being clearly annunciated. During the masquerade, I had practiced speaking like those in the royal court for many hours to the point I had gotten quite good at it, at least I thought so.

"Master Tom has asked if he could borrow a book from my shelf," I said with my royal accent. "So, he is going to stay and select one while I am gone. Escort me to the great hall," I commanded.

"Certainly, Your Majesty," Richard replied. He and another servant covered my wardrobe with a royal cape of red and fur and replace my hat with a crown of many jewels. His Majesty was ready to be seen publicly. Richard and a guard walked with me to the great hall, leaving the king, dressed as me, behind in the chamber. As we approached the great hall, my anxiety started to mount again. Perhaps the noble members of the Council would not be so easily fooled as the servants. My legs felt unsteady, and my heart was pounding rapidly. I took one last deep breath and entered the hall.

I strode to the dais and took my place upon the throne. I was immediately surrounded by a bevy of advisors. I recognized Edward's uncle, Edward Seymour, the oldest brother of his mother, Queen Jane. During the masquerade, I had dealt with him when he was known as the Earl of Hertford on several occasions. He was there on the day of Edward's coronation when our prank was finally revealed. Since then, he had been named Duke of Somerset. All Edward had told me in preparation was that Somerset was his closest advisor and ruled in his stead as Edward was not yet of an age to rule in his own right. Later I would come to know that

Lord Somerset had been named Lord Protector of the Realm and Governor of the King's Person, and that he presided over the Council established by King Henry's will to serve as the closest advisors to the young king.

"Your Majesty," Somerset greeted me as he approached and took his place, perched behind my right shoulder. Again, my anxiety rose as I hoped he would not realize that I was not Edward.

"Uncle," I responded, as Edward had instructed me to refer to him. I relaxed just a tad as it appeared, at least for the time being, that my impersonation was working.

"Your Majesty," another advisor I did not recognize greeted me as he approached with a smile and a wink. Just when things seem to be going well, my uneasiness was back! Did this man think I was Edward, or did he realize that I was not? I then noticed that he shared a resemblance to Somerset although he was younger, and his manner was much friendlier and easygoing. I concluded that he must be another uncle that Edward had mentioned in our earlier chat, Thomas Seymour, Lord Sudeley, and Somerset's younger brother. Sudeley apparently also served on the Council. Later I would learn that he was also the Lord Admiral of the King's Navy. I smiled at him in response.

"Let the first subject approach," I announced. Over the next hour I sat and listened to a number of subjects who came forward with their requests and petitions. All the cases were simple, and Somerset or another advisor decided how best they should be dispensed. I considered sharing my thoughts or opinions in some instances but decided to stay silent and merely give my assent as the session went on. I did not want to push my luck.

"That is all for today," I announced after receiving a prompt from one of the royal servants, bringing the session to an end.

"Well done, Your Majesty," Somerset responded.

I informed the Council that I would return to my chambers to prepare for dinner. At that point, Sudeley approached and asked if he could walk back with me. I wasn't sure of what was proper, so I glanced at Somerset who nodded, and so I agreed.

As we walked, Sudeley passed along greetings from Queen Kateryn, King Henry's widow and Edward's stepmother, to whom he was now married. He also noted that Edward's sister, Lady Elizabeth, and his cousin, Lady Jane Grey, were staying with them in Chelsea at the time. Sudeley's

The Scoundrel's Son

tone then turned a bit more serious.

"My brother keeps a tight rein on Your Majesty as well as on the realm. I feel it would be better to split my brother's duties between presiding over the Council and directing your education. The queen and I could take a more active role in guiding your maturity," he concluded.

I was not sure what to say. "Thank you, Uncle, for this brief but very pleasant visit," was all I could think to say. As soon as I uttered it, I realized how silly it sounded, but Sudeley merely nodded with a grin. We had reached the door to Edward's chambers.

Sudeley withdrew from his pocket a small bag of coins and handed it to me.

"You are a king without resources because of my brother's control. Maybe this will ease your burden," he said with a whisper and a wink. "Have a pleasant dinner and I will see you very soon," he said and hurried away. Richard, who had been walking a few paces behind us, informed me that servants would soon arrive to help His Majesty prepare for dinner.

"How did it go?" Edward inquired looking up from his book as I entered the chamber. He was sitting in the seat that had been provided for me. Now he seemed to be the nervous one, as his fingers were frantically drumming and his left leg shaking.

"It went rather smoothly. Perhaps being king would be a good job for me!" I joked.

"Perhaps," Edward smiled back.

"Lord Sudeley walked me back to your chambers."

"My Uncle Thomas is quite charming, isn't he? Not at all like Somerset."

"No, not at all. He gave me these," I said as I handed the bag of coins to Edward.

"Splendid!" Edward looked inside the bag and quickly counted the coins. "Uncle Thomas is always trying to get closer to me. Last summer he had me sign a paper giving him permission to marry Queen Kateryn, just a few months after my father had passed. That did not sit well with Somerset, believe me!" He handed me two coins. "For your troubles." I thanked him with a broad smile. I was surprised a few coins could delight Edward so. However, these two coins would allow me to buy some very nice things for my mother and sisters.

Frederic Fahey

As I ambled home after my royal visit, I hoped that I would have the opportunity to visit Edward often. I wondered if he would continue to want me to take his place. After all my worrying, today seemed to go quite well. But could I continue to fool the members of the royal court with my portrayal of their king? As I recalled the interaction between Somerset and Sudeley and how they vied for his attention, I thought Edward's life may not be quite as simple as he had stated. When given the opportunity, I would keep a keen eye open in the hopes that what I observe could someday be of help to my twin.

Chapter 2

After my royal visit, I returned to the house I shared with Father Christian. Perhaps I should explain, my lady. Following the masquerade, I had been placed in the care of Father Andrew, a priest whom I had known and who had been kind to me since I was a small child. It was he who had taught me to read and gave me my love of books. He also taught me what little Latin and history I knew. But when I arrived at his house, I found Father Christian instead who informed me that Father Andrew had died unexpectedly during my absence. Father Christian, also beyond his time serving in a parish church, had decided to continue Father Andrew's good work in Offal Court.

"I saw the note to Father Andrew that you had been named ward of the king and put in his care. Would you consider sharing this home with me?" Father Christian asked as he spoke of needing help from someone who knew the parish well. Since I had nowhere else to go, and Father Christian offered to help me with my studies, I accepted his invitation. I have never once regretted that decision. Father Christian was a beacon who guided me along rocky shores during the stormy days that lie ahead.

The next day, Father Christian said to me, "Come, I would like you to meet Mr. Nobson, a gold and silversmith who lives in the parish. I know how much you like to make things, and I thought he might be looking for an apprentice." I had always been good with my hands. I would fashion dolls out of old cloth and carriages from scrap metal. Also, I would whittle horses and dragons from any piece of wood I might find. My sisters' eyes lit up when I revealed my newly made treasures for them. On my way out the door, I stuffed a few items I had made into my pocket.

When Father Christian pointed to a building across the square, I knew it immediately. I had stopped by the display window many times to gaze at all the marvelous metal objects. There would be pots and mugs as well as broaches and pins. But most of all, I was fascinated by the toys that were sometimes shown: soldiers, knights, and animals painted wonderfully in every color. Father Christian rapped on a window that had a counter for customers. At first, there was no reply. Then I heard a voice from inside.

"I'm comin'!"

Suddenly, the window slid open, and a tuft of white hair rose above the counter, then two friendly eyes, and lastly a pair of spectacles perched on the end of a long, slender nose.

"Oh, hello, Father. Is today the day? I thought you were comin' on Tuesday. Oh, today is Tuesday, and here you are."

Father Christian beamed. "Good morning, Robert! Yes, today is Tuesday. We can come another day if it would suit you better."

"Today suits as well as any. And it's Tuesday."

"So it is, and here we are."

"Where else would you be? It's Tuesday after all. Come in! Come in!"

The door between the counter and display windows slowly creaked open, and we entered Robert Nobson's workshop, or simply "the shop" as he referred to it. Once inside, I couldn't believe the wonder of it all. Bright metals of all colors were strewn everywhere. There were new things as well as older items that had been repaired on practically every available flat surface. On one shelf was a dazzling necklace with matching earrings. On another there was a repaired pot that looked as good as new. Father Christian had described Mr. Nobson as a gold and silversmith, but he was clearly adept at working with practically all metals. I would come to realize that Mr. Nobson's work was of the highest quality, even compared to what I would see at Whitehall. There were also pieces from a mechanical object of some sort that I noticed on a workbench. Metalworking tools hung from hooks on every available space on the back wall.

"Robert, let me introduce to you Master Thomas Canty. He is the fine young man I told you about."

Robert, or, as I referred to him in the early days of my apprenticeship, Mr. Nobson, inspected me from head to toe. In one hand, he held a tinker's hammer as he ran his other hand through his mop of snowy hair. "Hmmm," he murmured as he licked his lips. "I thought you said he was ten. This lad looks much younger than ten. I can't handle a boy younger

The Scoundrel's Son

than ten!"

"I am ten as of my birthday last October!" I blurted.

"He speaks!" Robert's eyes went wide. "And it seems he can count as well. So, what brings you here, Young Sprout?"

I glanced at Father Christian, worried that I had spoken out of turn, but he gave me a reassuring smile. I sheepishly replied, "Well, I like to make things."

"Pardon? Speak up! I can't hear you if you whisper!"

"I said I like to make things," more loudly this time. I walked over to him and brought from my pocket a carriage I had formed from a scrap of metal I had found on the street along with a horse I had whittled from a piece of wood.

"Hmmm. Pretty rough. Crude for sure. But I see where you're goin' with these." He lowered his head and peered at me over his spectacles, right into my eyes. "And you say you are ten? I can't work with a boy younger than ten! I'm not a nanny you know!"

"I am ten for sure," I said.

"We have the baptismal records to prove it," Father Christian affirmed with a wink.

"All right! All right!" Robert conceded. "Can you start today? There is much to learn!"

This was my introduction to Robert Nobson. He was a man of great energy, even though he was perhaps the oldest man I knew at the time. He would flitter about his workshop from project to project and item to item like a mother sparrow attending to the needs of a nest of hungry chicks. Was this kettle properly formed? Was this hair clasp well fashioned? Was the ring ordered for a special occasion going to please a loving wife? How his mind kept track of so many projects all at the same time always astounded me. His spectacles were balanced on the tip of his pointed nose which he seemed to look over, around, under and occasionally through. As the years went on and his eyes began to fail, his spectacles became of less use, and he would rely on the touch of his fingers and my eyes for the examination of his objects. I was blessed to work with Robert until the end of his years.

***

Frederic Fahey

I whistled the bright melody of my favorite tune as I walked through Offal Court after my first day working for Robert. He told me to be on time the next day, but I knew I would be there before him, even though he just lived upstairs.

"Tom, dear boy," my father's voice called as he spotted me from across the square.

"Hello, Father." I said as I continued to walk. Just the sight of him darkened my spirit.

"You're looking good, aren't ya? You had a turn of good fortune. That's what I heard anyway."

"Ah ya, I'm blessed." I tried to quicken my pace so as to spend as little time with him as possible.

"How's your mum and those daughters of mine? The magistrate, he won't let me near them. I don't understand it. They're my family, isn't that right?"

"They're doing good," I responded as my anger started to rise. He knew all too well why he was not allowed to see them. During the masquerade, Edward had witnessed my father's cruelty firsthand, and so it was his instruction that my father and my grandmother were not allowed to stay or even visit my mother's cottage at Christ's Hospital.

"Anyway, I got a prospect, son. I need your help. This rich gent comes this way every so often, and I hear he walks with his pockets full. He wears jewelry fit for an earl. You've grown to be a strong lad, I see. I think the two of us could handle him without a lick of trouble. We could relieve him of some of his coin and bobbles. What ya think?"

I stopped and looked at him straight.

"Father, I want none of your trouble. Leave me be! Please!" I said directly.

Without a moment's warning, he fiercely seized my collar and shoved me into a small lane between two houses and up against the wall. His fist pressed against my neck making it impossible for me to speak.

"I find myself down on my luck, boy! I need your help to get back on my feet! You owe your own father this much!"

I reached in my pocket and took out what coins I had. As he snatched them from my hand, several went bouncing in the street. He released me while he frantically gathered the coins from the ground. I tried to regain

The Scoundrel's Son

both my breath and my spirit.

"You're a good lad," he called as he hurried off to spend the coin on drink, I was certain.

From the earliest time I could remember, my father was very cruel to me, my sisters, and my mother. His mother, my grandmother, who lived with us at the time, also treated us poorly. When I was four or five years old, he would send me into the streets to beg. I would sit in a doorway or on a stone and plead with tears in my eyes to any passerby. Even though I was very young, I could spot someone who might give a coin if I pleaded my best. I would also try to spot folks who were not from the parish, as I felt they were more likely to give. If I was not as successful as my father or my grandmother had wished, they would beat me in the hopes that this would convince me to do better the next time. And so, they beat me to tears almost every day.

I did the best I could, and my guess is that I did bring in a bit of coin for them, not motivated by the beatings but my desire to do well for my family. I thought that if I raised more money, we would have more food, better clothes, and a warmer home. But I soon learned that this was not the case. Even on days when I came home with my pockets full, our food was never more plentiful, and our home was never warmer. My father would take the coins and head to his favorite drinking spot. This was a cruel lesson to learn at such a young age.

My father did not limit his bad ways to the treatment of his family. He was mean and conniving in all his dealings, always looking for some unfortunate or vulnerable soul from whom he could steal, cheat, or otherwise take advantage. And so, I vowed that my life would be different. I did not want to grow up being the scoundrel's son. I wanted to work hard and be good at what I did. I wanted to ease the burdens of those I loved and to help even those I did not know. I wanted a good life, an earned life. Now I would be working and learning from Robert Nobson, and the opportunity for that desired life shone bright. But in a dark corner of my being lied a creature in wait determined to drag me back to my father's nasty ways.

I decided that this would be a good time to visit my mother and sisters and so I headed directly for the cottage at Christ's Hospital that Edward had arranged for them. By the end of the masquerade, I had become complacent in my portrayal of Edward the King. I didn't mind so much the

Frederic Fahey

fancy dress and all the preening, the pomp, the elaborate dinners, or even the dreadfully boring meetings. I might have even started to believe I could be king. On the day before the coronation, as the procession neared Offal Court on its way from the Tower of London to Westminster for the ceremonies, I saw my mother approach to get a better glimpse of the young king, not knowing that it was her own son riding by. However, as she was forcefully turned away by the royal guards, my first thought was to say, "I do not know you, woman." But as that thought was forming in my head, my heart broke, and the farce of my portrayal was fully revealed to me. I was not the king, I was Tom Canty of this very parish. The shame of the near denial of my own dear mother still haunts me, and so I was determined to be a more caring person who understood who he was.

Several cottages had been built on the grounds of Christ's Hospital to house poor families. All the cottages looked the same with white-washed clay and mud exterior walls accented by dark colored timber along the corners and at the window and door frames. But even if I didn't already know, I could tell which was my family's cottage by all the hustle and bustle inside.

"Well, look who's here! Isn't he a sight!" my mother exclaimed. "Sit yourself down, Tom. I'll pour you some cider, and I will toast some fine bread I have."

The interior of the cottage was one room with a fire pit in the middle for both cooking and warmth. There was a table with four chairs and three sleeping cots arranged around the room. My mother along with my twin sisters, Nan and Bet, about six years older than me, had done a wonderful job making this place feel like home. No matter where she resided, my mother ruled over the kitchen as if she were royalty. During the masquerade when I was king briefly, I had toyed with the notion of naming her Duchess of Offal Court. The small cottage was even more crowded on this day as my sisters had a couple of guests.

"Izzy," Nan said, "you remember our brother, Tom."

"Indeed, I do. But this can't be him! He's grown like a weed, hasn't he?" said Isabel Brown, Izzy as she was called, a good friend of my sisters for as long as I could remember. She was a tall girl with a bunch of curly, light brown hair amassed on the top of her head and blessed with a friendly smile and a joyful way about her. "Last time I saw you, you were a wee

The Scoundrel's Son

thing! You remember my sister Alice?"

I did remember Aly as we called her, though I had not seen her in a while. She was about a year younger than I was. Small for her age, she loved to play games with the boys. I remembered that she was the fastest runner of all the children in Offal Court. She would not back down from any bully and could throw a punch as well as any boy. Her hair was fairer than her sister's, both in color and texture. She had blue eyes and a freckled smile.

I said to Aly, "When we played tag, no one could ever catch you. That's what I recall. You were so fast!"

"You were fast as well!" she responded. "And you could climb like it was nothin'. You'd scoot right up the side of a tree like a frightened squirrel. I can climb but not like you!"

My mother brought us all some cider as well as toast with berry jam.

"Jam! Mother brings out the best when Tom's here!" Bet noted playfully.

"You hush!" my mother shot back. "It's just a little treat for our company."

"Company?" Izzy said, getting in on the joke. "I'd be in this house every day practically, and I never seen berry jam before!"

"Enough! All of you!" my mother said, good naturedly turning to Izzy. "You too Isabel! You'd think I don't treat you girls right! Fine! I'll keep the jam for another day." She reached for the jam dish.

"No!" we all cried in unison. My mother put her hands on her hips and laughed. "These children! What am I to do!"

"I do have good news!" I proclaimed. "Mr. Nobson has agreed to take me on as his apprentice! You know the goldsmith in the square?"

"That's some happy news, isn't it!" my mother responded. "I know how good you be at making things. I knew something special was in the air. The jam is to celebrate Tom's new job!"

"A toast!" Nan proclaimed raising her toast and jam, which made everyone smile.

"A toast to Tom!" they all joined in. I sat back without a word, but my heart was singing.

"I must be goin'," I then said. "Father Christian is expecting me." I hugged my sisters and turned to my mother, who gave me a vigorous hug.

Frederic Fahey

"Now go!" she said. "Father Christian, he'll wonder where you be! Then he'll come by the cottage and ask why I wasn't at church on Sunday!" And with that she practically pushed me out the door.

Chapter 3

One thing metal work does is make a lot of grimy filings and shavings and, as much as one might try to contain them, the metal scatters everywhere. "The filings can be sharp and easily cut a person," Robert explained one day. So I found myself constantly wiping surfaces and sweeping the floor. I gave particular attention to the area near the door where customers may enter to talk with Robert. "We certainly don't want our customers to hurt themselves while they are in the shop. We would prefer they buy something and spend their coin." He made a good point.

So, one day a couple of weeks later, I was sweeping the floor when I heard a man's voice coming from outside the counter window speaking with Robert.

"Good morning, sir. I hope you can help me. My wife has this hair pin that she loves, and the back has come detached. I am hoping, perhaps beyond hope, that you can repair it. It looks so stunning in her auburn hair. Can you fix it? Is it …?"

"Slow down, kind sir," Robert said as if trying to calm a wild horse. "Let me look at it."

"Oh, thank you so much!"

"Hold your thank you's for later. All I am doing is looking at it. Hmm."

I peered over Robert's shoulder and immediately recognized the engaging smile of the man at the counter. There stood Lord Miles Hendon, the kind soldier who had rescued my twin time and time again during the masquerade. Recently, Edward had spoken in awe of the soldier's bravery even though he never seemed convinced that Edward was the King of England. We hadn't truly met but I had seen him from across the hall at Edward's coronation. Edward told me that Lord Hendon and the Lady

Edith, his love from before he had gone to war, had been married and lived at Hendon Hall in Kent, south of the city. Lord Hendon took a quick look in my direction and, at the sight of my face, took a second look.

Robert said that the pin was indeed repairable but that it would take a few days for him to get to it. Lord Miles thanked him profusely, reached right through the window, grasped Robert's hand, and shook it vigorously.

"Yes! Yes! But if you injure my hand, it will take a bit longer," Robert noted as he snatched his hand back. I put my broom aside, left the shop, and approached the man on the street as he was preparing to leave.

"I beg your pardon sir, but are you Lord Hendon?"

"Why yes," he answered as he stared at my face. "I am sorry, young sir, but you so remind me of a young man I know. Well, not just any young man. He is actually …"

"Are you referring to His Majesty the King?" I responded with a smile. Now he really seemed perplexed.

"I'm Tom Canty," I blurted out. "Do you remember me?"

"Tom Canty? Tom Canty?" Lord Miles repeated as if to retrieve my being from the stacks of an overstuffed bookshop. Suddenly, the light of recognition dawned. "Oh! You're the boy who traded places with …!"

"Yes! The very same!" I bowed quickly. "It is a pleasure to see you again, Lord Hendon."

"Enough with the formality! I must admit the title is a bit tight around the collar for me. You can call me Miles."

"It would make me a little uncomfortable to be quite so informal. Perhaps, we can settle on Lord Miles?" I offered.

He smiled and nodded. "Lord Miles it is. I like the sound of that much better."

I told him about my apprenticeship with Robert and living with Father Christian. He told me how he and Lady Edith had made a good home for themselves in Kent at Hendon Hall. It appeared that both of our lives had been blessed in this past year.

"Have you seen my little friend recently?" he finally asked. "It's probably disrespectful to refer to His Royal Majesty the King as 'my little friend' but I'm still getting over the fact that he really is the king." I told him I had visited Edward a couple of times and that he was doing well. Lord Miles indicated that he had not seen the king for several months but

The Scoundrel's Son

planned to see him very soon.

As he continued on his way, he turned and said, "And if you need me, you know where I live. Just come to Kent and ask for Hendon Hall."

***

I received another invitation to visit Edward the following week. The walk from Offal Court to Whitehall takes less than an hour, but, in many ways, it was on the other side of the world. Offal Court was dark and dingy even at midday as the buildings seemed to be built on top of one another, and the second floor of many of the buildings extended over the first to provide more living space. One had to be ever watchful as garbage was often heaved out the door or from an upstairs window into the street. Dirty water and worse ran along in the gutters. I left the stench-filled streets of Offal Court and followed the river toward Westminster. On my right, I could see St Paul's Cathedral, on the far side of which was Christ's Hospital and my family's cottage. I walked along the Strand by the splendid houses of the nobility. I strolled by a magnificent home that Lord Somerset was having built along the banks. Around the river bend stood Whitehall Palace, the size of which was that of an entire parish onto itself.

I presented my letter at the gate and was escorted to Edward's private chambers.

"Good day, Master Tom," Richard welcomed me. He was thin with only a wisp of hair atop his head. He always stood as straight as a flagpole giving him the appearance of being much taller than he truly was. As expressionless as his face was, there was a gentleness in his eyes that portrayed a kind spirit. He tended to Edward like a mother hen. Over the years, I would come to know Richard quite well.

He announced my arrival as we entered the royal sitting room.

"Splendid!" Edward said. "Please be seated, Tom. I am just finishing my dinner. Would you like something to eat?"

I took my seat as directed and indicated that I had just eaten. Edward asked about my family and my apprenticeship. I told him a particularly funny story regarding a proper couple trying to control their mischievous child when they visited the shop. As the father was chasing the child about the shop, his feet became tangled, and the three of them, father, mother, and child, went sprawling on the floor! At the conclusion of the story, we both burst into laughter, which brought a surprised look to Edward's face.

"Oh my! That laugh put milk in my nose!"

"Well, then that story makes me very proud!" I exclaimed, which made us laugh all the more. I must say that the thought of His Majesty with milk in his nose brought happy satisfaction to me for weeks to come!

Edward then rose, walked across the room, and retrieved a table with small statuettes carved of ivory on top. He placed it between our two chairs.

"Have you ever played chess?" he asked as he started to arrange the "pieces" as he called the statuettes on certain squares of the tabletop.

"No, I haven't," I said, transfixed by the beauty of the arrangement.

"Your pieces are white and mine are black. The goal is to capture your opponent's king," he instructed as he held up the largest of the black pieces, "while protecting your own." He then explained how the various pieces moved differently. It was all quite fascinating and confusing at the same time.

"We will go slowly at first until you learn how the pieces move and some of the strategy." And so, we started to play with Edward patiently teaching me along the way.

"Is that priest of yours treating you well?" Edward asked as we played.

"Oh, yes, very well. He is very interested in my schooling. We read every day, and my writing is getting much better. After dinner, we sit in our little reading place and discuss all sorts of topics from history and stories to how the city and kingdom work. And, of course, as you can imagine, we talk about God and being a good Christian."

At the mention of God, Edward's brow furrowed. "I must admit," he stated, "that his approach to religion gives me a bit of pause. My own instructors have been speaking to me about the new ways to worship God beyond the old Church. I worry that perhaps a priest was not the right choice for your guardian, but you spoke so kindly of his influence on your early life and your obvious regard for him." I understood then that Edward was speaking of Father Andrew rather than Father Christian. I was starting to explain the situation when we were interrupted.

Richard entered and announced, "My apologies, Your Majesty, but

The Scoundrel's Son

you have another visitor. Lady Jane Grey has arrived."

"My goodness!" Edward exclaimed. "I did not realize my sweet cousin was back in the city! Please have her come and join us!"

"Edward, perhaps I should take my leave so you may visit with your cousin," I suggested, not wanting to intrude on their visit. I was also nervous of visiting with a member of the royal family beyond Edward, particularly a young lady.

I had met Lady Jane on several occasions during the masquerade. Her grandmother was the younger sister of Edward's father, King Henry. Lady Jane had visited the palace once alone and several times with Edward's sister, Lady Elizabeth. I tended to be uncomfortable when around girls when I was young, but the Ladies Jane and Elizabeth were particularly intimidating. In their royal dress, they looked unbelievably beautiful to me. When I first met the two young ladies, it was at a point in the masquerade of frustration for me, so I was trying to convince everyone that I was not Edward. They probably left our visits a bit confused, but I think their only thought was that Edward was not well that day and acting quite strangely. I don't believe Lady Jane ever knew of our masquerade, but I did recall her kindness and concern towards me when she thought I was Edward and that I was ill.

"Nonsense!" Edward responded. "I would love for you to meet my cousin."

Lady Jane Grey entered. Although she was about our same age, she moved with a graceful step that belied her youth. Certainly, the young girls of Offal Court did not walk with such a confident air. She was thin with very fair skin. Her face was framed with the same red hair possessed by practically all the royal family. I had red hair as well, but I had always associated mine with the color of rust while hers added a radiance to her visage. By royal standards, her dress was simple but still stunning to my eye. It was of a rose-colored silk brocade, somewhat fitted above the waist and fuller below with very wide sleeves. She wore a bonnet towards the back of her head that was adorned with elaborate beads or perhaps they were pearls.

"How kind of my dear cousin to visit today," Edward greeted her. He also instructed Richard to provide another chair and to bring some refreshments. "Jane, I would like you to meet my ward, Master Thomas Canty.

Frederic Fahey

He is also my good friend. Tom, this is the Lady Jane Grey."

I was not sure how one greeted a royal cousin. I rose from my chair. "It is an honor to have your acquaintance…I mean to make your acquaintance, Your Royal Highness." I stumbled in my speech as I greeted her with an awkward bow.

"It is a pleasure to meet you as well, Master Thomas," Lady Jane smiled and bowed her head.

"Enough!" Edward proclaimed with a happy grin. "When it is just the three of us, we are Edward, Jane, and Tom. I command it."

"As you command, Your Majesty," I was relieved by Edward's relaxing of formality.

"I suppose that would be acceptable if it is only the three of us." She glanced between Edward and me and smiled. "My, my, Tom, you certainly have quite an effect on my sweet cousin. He often seems overwhelmed by his royal duties. I have not seen his spirit this bright in a long time."

Edward gave me a very warm glance. "Tom and I have been having a most wonderful visit. We've spoken of things from the childish to the profound." He paused slightly. "But mostly the childish. I believe I spend too much of my time considering the profound. And I am teaching Tom to play chess!" he said as he gestured towards the table.

Servants arrived with several platters of sweetened fruits, gingerbread, and beverages. In Offal Court, this would have been enough food to feed several families for a week. I thanked the servants with the level of politeness I had been taught by Father Christian. Both Edward and Jane looked at me quizzically, then at each other, shrugged their shoulders and laughed.

"I was just trying to be polite," I attempted to explain.

"I think it is very sweet," Jane said with a smile.

I waited for Edward and Jane to take some gingerbread before I decided to try the fruit. It was incredibly sweet and delicious.

Our friendly conversation continued for a bit longer. I was taken by how comfortable Edward and Jane made me feel, a boy from Offal Court. Finally, I announced, "Father Christian will be upset if I am not home for supper. I should probably be going. I have had such a wonderful time this afternoon."

"So have I," Jane answered.

The Scoundrel's Son

Edward beckoned me to approach and then grasped my hand. "Tom, thank you so much for coming. Your visits always brighten my day."

As I was walking back to Father Christian's house, it occurred to me that Edward had asked me many questions regarding my new life. He asked about Father Christian, about my mother and sisters, about Robert and the shop. But in all that, I had never asked Edward about his life. I never asked about what it was like to be a king, truly a king, not just pretending as I had done. I never asked about his sisters or if he missed his father. I did not even ask how his day had gone. His look at the end as he took my hand seemed to show that our visit had provided him some needed relief from the pressures of being king. Jane had commented on this as well.

During the masquerade, I had learned that everyone's attention was always on the king. Has His Majesty risen from bed? Has he eaten properly? Is he dressed? Is he too warm? Is he too cold? The list went on. However, during our visit, the roles had been reversed. All his attention was on me. Perhaps he found the role of caretaker enjoyable for a change. I realized then that if we were to truly be good friends, I had to become more sensitive to his concerns and needs. Not his concerns of state, how to deal with France or Spain, or even his physical wellbeing, but his more human interests and concerns. What did he like to do? What fascinated him? Did he prefer sunrise or sunset? What was his favorite music? What scared him? What made him sad? He had plenty of advisors like Somerset who were more than happy to help him rule. But I was an expert in being a ten-year old boy. Going forward, I intended to share this expertise with him.

Chapter 4

After what had seemed a particularly cold winter, a warm spring day finally arrived in the middle of April. For the first time in months, folks of the parish were able to spend time out in the square in the evening with their neighbors. It was a good time to catch up on what had happened over the winter—whose child had gotten married, whose cousin had a new baby, whose mother had gotten ill and passed—while the children played in the streets for the first time since the autumn. Someone had started a bonfire. As pleasant as the evening was, it was still early spring, and there was a bit of a chill in the air.

"Tom! Tom Canty! Over here!" In the glow of the bonfire, I could see the smiling face of Aly Brown. It had been a couple of months since I had seen her at my mother's cottage. She was standing with several of her friends, children from the parish I had known my whole life. We had all played games like tag and hide-and-seek in our younger years. Over the past few months, while I had been working in Robert's shop, I had less time for play. I joined her and the others by the fire's edge.

"Hi, Aly. Quite a night, isn't it? What's everybody doin'?"

"Nothing really. Just tryin' to get warm by the fire."

"Well, if it isn't Tom Canty!" Another voice entered the conversation.

"Hi Jem, you seem as chipper as ever," I responded. I had known Jem Riley all my life. He was a year or so older than me and a bit taller. He had a full head of bushy brown hair and a grin with a missing tooth, likely the result of a fist fight with one of the older boys. Jem was always trying to prove his mettle.

"Not seen you in a bit. Figured you'd been arrested along with your crook of a father."

The mention of my father and his recent arrest bristled me, but, on this

The Scoundrel's Son

occasion, I let it pass.

"No. Been workin' for Mr. Nobson. His shop's down a piece," I said, pointing across the square. "He keeps me busy, I gotta say."

"Oh? Doin' what?" Jem inquired.

"He's teaching me a lot! How to work with metals and such. Maybe I'll have my own shop someday."

"Hmm. Sounds like a bit more work than I fancy!" Jem paused. "I bet Mr. Nobson keeps lots of pretty things in his shop."

"Not that many and locked up mostly." Jem's interest with what was in Robert's shop was starting to make me nervous. At that instant, someone threw a large piece of wood into the fire, which led to a burst of ashes and glowing embers.

"Wow!" Aly exclaimed; her freckled face highlighted by the fire's glow. "Let's find a place to sit." I was pleased that this had diverted Jem's attention from Robert's shop. We walked a short distance from the bonfire to a bench under a large oak tree surrounded by a plot of grass. There were six of us. Besides Aly, Jem, and myself, there were Willy Smith, Ben Baker, and Margy Cummings. I could sense that Jem was the leader of the group, perhaps a little more adventurous than the rest. Willy and I made ourselves comfortable on the bench while Aly and Margy sat on the grass under the tree. Ben, being the shy one, sat on the grass a few feet away. Jem remained standing leaning against the tree right behind Aly. He picked up a dead branch. As he stripped the leaves from it, he dropped them in Aly's hair.

"Stop it!" she protested and moved a little from Jem. Jem reached into his pocket and pulled out some cards made from thick paper.

"Let's play Primero!"

"Where'd you get the cards?" I asked.

"I made them myself," Jem responded. He had done a good job making all the cards close to the same size, and I was impressed by his drawing skills. I thought the knave and the queen cards were particularly nicely drawn.

"But I don't have any coins for bettin'," Willy noted as Primero was a popular game for gambling.

"We'll just play for fun. Look around and gather twenty small stones as money," We all did as Jem directed.

Frederic Fahey

Jem dealt each player four cards and spread another eight cards face down. Then the bidding began. We took turns deciding whether we wanted to drop out of the hand, exchange one of our cards for an unknown card on the ground, or to "knock" meaning to keep our hand. After two players knocked, the rounds were over, everyone's cards were revealed, and the winner of the hand determined. After a few rounds, I was the second knock. I thought I had a good hand with two sixes, a five, and a four, but Jem beat it with three sevens and a two. Seven was the high card in Primero as the eight, nine and ten cards were not used, and picture cards and aces only counted for one.

"Good luck for me, isn't it!" Jem announced with a laugh as he pulled the betting pool into his pile.

A few hands later, Ben was the second knock. He had three fives and a four, which seemed like a wonderful hand, but again Jem won with three sevens and a three.

"Jem, you dog!" Aly yelled. She sprang to her feet and pushed Jem over to reveal he was sitting on a pile of extra seven cards. Even in a game for fun, Jem had been cheating.

"Ya caught me, Aly!" Jem confessed as he burst out laughing. Aly's face turned red, and she punched him in the arm.

Jem continued to laugh loudly. "Got quite a wallop there, don't ya!" The rest of us just shook our heads. I must admit, Jem's cheating bothered me, even though we were only betting stones.

A group of young folks were starting to sing together by the bonfire.

"I wanna have a listen," Margy announced. Jem gathered up his cards and off we went. There were six in the singing group, four girls and two boys, all with very pleasant voices. One man was playing a horn, and another joined in with a lute that he had made himself. A third man was keeping time by rapping on a log with a stick. They were singing songs we all knew, and soon we were all singing along. Margy and Ben sang the loudest of our group. They were not quite in key, but they were enthusiastic. Willy, surprisingly, could sing quite sweetly. Aly was singing along while Jem just smiled with his arm around her shoulder which she didn't seem to mind. The sour feeling in my gut that had resulted from Jem's cheating was quelled by the sweet singing. I looked on from the edge of the crowd as the community of neighbors came together on this clear night

The Scoundrel's Son

under the vernal moonlight.

    A day or so later, I walked by Aly's home on my way to the shop. Besides Izzy, Aly, and their mother, there were three younger brothers. Bet had told me that Aly's mother had a bit of trouble with the drink since the passing of their father the year before in an accident with a horse and carriage. So, Izzy and Aly shared raising the young boys. Aly was barely ten years old, a child herself, but such responsibilities were not uncommon in girls so young in Offal Court. I had put a few things in a bag including some of my old clothes that were now too small and a few toys I had made over the years: a horse, a bear, and a dragon. I placed the bag on Aly's doorstep and left without being seen.

Chapter 5

A few weeks later, I was again called to Whitehall. I had decided to keep my dealings with Edward a secret from most people. I did not want the added pressure of folks expecting special favors because I personally knew the king. I decided to tell Robert so he would understand why I had to leave the shop some afternoons. After I told him all about the masquerade and my visits to the palace, he only had one question.

"What do a boy from Offal Court and the king of all England talk about?" Was that honestly his only question after such an incredible tale? My answer that we talked about anything and everything seemed to suffice as he immediately returned to his work. "Much to do. Much to do."

On the morning of my next visit with Edward, I spent more time than is typical for a ten-year-old boy deciding what to wear in the hopes that Jane might be there. The clothes I decided upon were what I considered to be my best, a blue tunic I would wear if I attended Sunday services. I even tried to comb my hair, which was rare for me. My usual grooming involved running my fingers through my hair to flatten it a bit. I was also carrying a satchel with a surprise for Jane should she be there.

It was a fine spring day, and my mood was high, as I made my way to the palace. The foul stench of Offal Court soon gave way to fresh air smelling of spring as I passed the glorious gardens along the Strand. The flowers were in bloom and summer was at the doorstep. It was early May, and this might be my last visit with Edward for a while as he, along with much of the nobility, would soon flee the city's heat and disease. It was customary for the king to go on his annual "progress," a summer tour of the realm that provided the king an opportunity to see the beauty of the land as well as to be seen by many of his subjects.

When I arrived at the palace, I realized I was early and decided to

The Scoundrel's Son

amble around Whitehall's outside wall. I happened upon an entrance where merchants were delivering their wares. I thought it would be fun to try entering the palace grounds on my own. I still had my letter of invitation in my pocket, which I would show, if necessary, with the excuse that I had merely gotten lost. The guards seemed to be familiar with most of those making the deliveries and so were not as attentive as they might be. I acted as if I was also making a delivery and eased through the entrance. One of the guards looked at me as I entered. My heart started to rush.

"Good day, young Sir," was all he said. I returned his greeting and quickly moved on.

Once inside the gate, I looked around to get my bearings. On several occasions during the masquerade, I had secretly roamed the palace grounds wearing an outfit I had obtained from one of the servant boys. I had become quite skilled at wandering either unnoticed or ignored. I recognized the building that contained Edward's chambers across the courtyard and snuck over to it. I finally arrived at Edward's chambers with a satisfied stride. I had made it here all on my own. Richard greeted me at the door.

"Greetings, Master Tom. His Majesty is ready for your visit. He is not alone. Lady Jane is here."

"Splendid!" I responded with a grin and a slight blush. As I entered the room, Edward glanced my way.

"Wonderful! Tom is here! Now the festivities may begin!" Edward announced.

"Good day, Edward. Hello, Jane. I am good ... I mean it is good to see you again." Today her dress was a light blue that suited the season and complimented her reddish-brown eyes.

"Hello, Tom. It is good to see you as well," Jane responded.

Edward asked how the folks in Offal Court entertained themselves, and I spoke of the evening we all sang in the square by the bonfire. Jane thought it sounded lovely.

"How have you been spending your time, Edward?" I asked, trying to turn the conversation more towards him.

He spoke of his schooling and all the studying he had to do.

"I am reading all the time and yet I am still behind!"

Then he told us of his fencing and archery lessons, and how he hoped that someday he would be allowed to participate in a joust.

"Everyone seems to be too concerned that I might get hurt. But isn't that possibility part of the excitement of it all?"

"I feel a bit different than you," Jane commented. "My family loves silly endeavors such as hunting and dancing, in which I have no interest. I love horses but I do not care to ride one to chase furry little animals through the woods. I'm much more content sitting in the garden with a good book that stretches my mind."

"I love you dearly, sweet cousin," Edward remarked, "but it would warm my heart to see you have fun once in a while."

"I suppose reading is fun for me, but in a different way. Edward, you are the only member of my family that respects my thoughts. My parents certainly don't understand. I will say that my youngest sister, little Mary, is quite bright for only being four years old. She always wants me to read to her. Katherine, on the other hand, is most concerned with the look of her smile. And she certainly loves to dance!"

"Does your family have a place near the city?" I inquired.

"Yes, but these past few months, I have been staying with Edward's uncle, the Lord Admiral, and Queen Kateryn, sometimes in Chelsea and sometimes at Sudeley Castle in Gloucestershire. I, along with Lady Elizabeth, have been attending to Her Majesty."

"And how is my sister?" Edward asked.

"She's doing well. Lord Thomas seems to have grown quite fond of her," she smirked. "Anyway, your sister is a smart girl! She considers all things, the sacred and the worldly. She thinks more than I do about how the kingdom runs and other happenings in the world, such as the relationships between the realm and Spain and France. I could learn some things from her."

At that point, Edward and Jane struck upon a discussion of religion and how the church should best serve God's mission. This was clearly an essential theme in both of their educations, and a conversation to which I could contribute very little. Most of my chats with Edward had been more typical of those of young boys. We pondered what one should do to survive, if one happens upon a dragon in the woods, for instance. However, I was struck by Jane's sincere concern for the common folk whereas Edward seemed to be trying to better understand his role as leader of the Church.

The Scoundrel's Son

At this point, my mind was like a whirling wagon wheel as this was all a bit beyond my understanding. I thought it might be a good time to lighten the conversation.

"Oh! I almost forgot! Jane, I've made a gift for you...with help from Mr. Nobson." I reached into my satchel and removed a toy a little smaller than the size of my hand.

"What is it?" Jane asked, perplexed. Suddenly, I was anxious that this might not be the proper gift for a girl like Jane. Perhaps she would think it too silly.

"It's a frog."

"A frog?" She gave me a quizzical look.

It was made of tin and painted bright green with bulging eyes and a friendly grin. I brought out a small key, placed it in a hole underneath the toy, and gave it a turn. I then placed the frog on the floor in front of them. "Go ahead, Jane. Give its bottom a little push."

Jane knelt next to the frog. She glanced up at Edward as if for approval, but he seemed as confused as she was.

"All right." She gave the toy the slightest of nudges and nothing happened.

"A bit harder than that."

She nodded and did as instructed. The frog leaped forward.

"Oh, my goodness!" she squealed, eyes wide as both of her hands went to her cheeks. In that moment, I saw the wonder of childhood in Jane's face, a rare and marvelous sight. She was always so serious but for just a few seconds, she was a joy-filled child. A broad smile broke across her face like the rising sun warming my heart. In my life, I've had many experiences, a good many typical of most folks and some beyond belief, but this one moment is still one of my most cherished memories.

"Will it jump again?" she asked with a look of delight.

"I think so! Give it another push!" She did and the frog leaped again.

"That is so marvelous!" Edward shouted.

Jane went to pick up the frog to examine it, and it leaped from her hand, startling her. She let out a marvelous, uncontrolled laugh and then a snort as she tried to catch her breath. Her eyes went wide at the outburst only to be followed by more laughter. This made Edward and I howl even more. She lifted the frog again, but this time she was careful not to touch the release mechanism.

"How does it work?" she asked as she examined it from every angle.

"There are very small wheels that engage as they turn." I tried to think of an example. "It's something like a clock but smaller. The key winds the mechanism and the push on the bottom releases it for the leap. Edward, I'm working on something for you, too. I hope to have it completed by our birthday in October."

"I will certainly look forward to it!"

At that point, Richard announced the arrival of the Lord Admiral, who entered the room with a big smile. "Here is Lady Jane and my favorite nephew!"

"Hello, Uncle," Edward greeted Lord Sudeley. "I would like you to meet Master Thomas Canty, Tom as we call him, ward of the king."

"Tom Canty? That name sounds familiar," Sudeley pondered. "Weren't you the one involved in that incident just before my nephew's coronation?"

"My, you have a good memory, Uncle," Edward responded. "That is all behind us now."

"Interesting," Sudeley responded as he looked upon me intently. "It is good to see you back at Whitehall, Tom." I could sense that his mind was continuing to turn.

"Tom is my very good friend," Edward glanced in my direction. "He is always welcomed at court."

"It is probably best I take my leave," I offered. "Lord Sudeley, it was a pleasure to meet you. Your Highness and Your Royal Majesty, I so enjoyed my visit," I said, bowing to all three of them, and I started to leave.

"Your Majesty, would you mind if I have a brief word with Tom?" Sudeley asked.

"Not at all. Tom, I hope to see you once more before I leave for the summer." I acknowledged that I would enjoy that.

"I am sorry to bother you," Sudeley began once we were in the hall outside Edward's chambers, "I care deeply for my nephew as well as for my wife's stepdaughters, Lady Mary and, of course, Lady Elizabeth. I see that you and His Majesty are close and that he is quite fond of you. You and I must keep an eye on his wellbeing. My brother, Lord Somerset, is often distracted by other concerns regarding the realm and can't always give His Majesty the attention he deserves. I am sure you agree."

I said yes as I wasn't sure how else to respond.

"Good! Good! Let me know if there is ever a way you see that I could better serve His Majesty. A time may come when we might need to take some steps to ensure that His Majesty is receiving a proper education. I am glad we had this chat," he said as he patted my shoulder and returned to Edward and Jane. Then he turned and said in a whisper, "And keep this between you and me." He then winked at me. I was taken aback by this brief encounter. I did not understand what sort of influence he felt I had over Edward, or how he might benefit from it. I decided to follow Sudeley's direction and keep this exchange to myself for the time being in the hopes that it might just end there.

When I exited the palace, I realized that a spring drizzle was falling on the city. In all my concern about what to wear, it hadn't occurred to me to bring a coat even though it was not uncommon for the weather to change quickly at this time of year. As I hurried along in the rain, the look on Jane's face when the frog first leaped was enough to keep me warm against the elements.

Chapter 6

"Tom, it is your move," Edward prodded from the other side of the chess board. As promised, one more visit had been arranged before Edward left London for the summer.

"Oh, I guess I am a bit distracted. I received some disturbing news that my father was killed while in prison."

"My goodness! I am so sorry, Tom. What happened?"

"As I understand it, he found himself there after a raucous dispute over a gambling debt with a man with more influence than him."

"I know he did not treat you and your family well, but it must still sadden you." He was right, and I was surprised that it did sadden me. As much contempt as I had for my father, I still felt an emptiness within. Without thinking, I swiped at my nose with my sleeve. Edward handed me a table linen that had come with the refreshment tray.

"Do you think of your father often?" I asked Edward as I dabbed my nose with the linen.

"Yes. Almost every day. I so miss him," he replied after reflecting on my question. "When I was very young, I could not wait until I was older, and he could show me how to joust or we could go on hunts together. However, as I grew, he became more frail with illness. Now he is always in my prayers. I ask him for guidance as I prepare to rule on my own. I so want to be like him. Strong, brave, determined. I want the respect of all men." I knew his answer was genuine. One just had to look at Edward's dress. Even though he was only ten years old, he dressed almost exactly like his father.

"You knew my father," I reflected. "He was cruel, not just to our family but to all. I want to be nothing like him." Although true, the boldness of my statement rendered me quiet for a moment.

The Scoundrel's Son

"I do remember your father," Edward recalled, "from my time pretending to be you. In my first encounter with him, he grabbed me by the collar and dragged me through Offal Court. He was a harsh man." Edward shared. "But I am still sad for you." Our eyes met as we solemnly sat. I was struck by Edward's sincerity.

"Thank you, my friend," I finally muttered.

***

Not long after, Edward left for the summer. When September and an invitation finally came, I was quite pleased. As I entered the palace delivery gate, one of the guards spoke to me.

"Visiting with His Majesty?" His question stopped me cold. My skin bristled at the confrontation even though my invitation was right in my pocket. I could have just as easily come through the main gate, but entering through this gate seemed simpler, and, well, more exciting.

"I don't understand, sir," I responded. I was not sure what sort of trouble I might be in.

The guard smiled. "Don't fret. Your secret is safe with me. I suppose even His Royal Majesty the King needs a friend." His countenance was reassuring, which eased my mind. "I was the guard at the gate who grabbed you on the day when you first encountered His Majesty; back when he was the Prince of Wales. As he invited you inside the courtyard, I noticed how much you resembled His Majesty. So, when you started coming to the delivery gate a while back, I recognized you immediately. I inquired about you, and His Majesty's head groom, Richard, told me that it was all right to let you pass."

I relaxed when I found I wasn't in trouble, but I was still unsettled. I had thought that my wanderings were unobserved, and now I find that this guard had noticed me all along. I resolved to be more careful in the future, and to strive to be even more silent and unseen as I moved about the palace grounds.

"Sir, what is your name?" I asked.

"Ah, my name is William. I am Captain of the Guard," he answered, becoming quite flustered. "I meant no disrespect."

"Do not worry, William," I tried to sound as reassuringly as possible.

Frederic Fahey

"My name is Tom Canty. There has been no disrespect in the slightest. I merely wanted to thank you for keeping my visits with His Majesty private. As you say, His Majesty can use a friend, and I don't want my actions to compromise that. If you please, I will find my way, but I will be more careful in the future."

William let out a long breath. "Certainly, Master Tom. Your secret is good with me. And if you need my help in any way, let me know. I see a lot of things in and around the palace." With that, William gave me a quick salute and I returned a nod before continuing on my way.

When I arrived at the king's chamber, I found Edward slumped in his chair with a pensive, faraway look upon his face. I expected his mood would turn to elation when he noticed me, as it usually did, but he simply glanced up and gave me a pleasant but subdued smile. Clearly something was bothering him.

"Good day, Edward," I said. "I want to hear all about your summer travels, where you went and what amazing sights you saw."

Edward beckoned for me to come nearer and took my hand in both of his. "I am so glad you are here."

"What's on your mind, my friend. Are you all right?"

"Thank you, Tom, for your concern. These past few weeks have been quite difficult for me."

Tears rolled down his cheek. "I know I'm supposed to be strong. I try to be a good king, but my heart is elsewhere. I have been looking forward to our visits since midsummer. However, you find me today in a somber mood. I considered making an excuse, and informing you that we could not meet, but I wanted to see you. I am very sad, Tom." I did not say a word; instead, I waited for him to speak when he was ready.

"We were all very happy when we learned last spring that my stepmother, Queen Kateryn, was with child. My father and she had tried to have children without success. A couple of weeks ago, the queen gave birth to a beautiful baby girl, my infant cousin Mary. But the queen fell ill soon after the birth, and, a few days later, she died. When the news reached me, I was frozen by the sadness. As you know, she was like a mother to me.

"How does a king mourn? On the counsel of my uncle, I chose to look strong, to say the right words of grieving for the queen and to carry on. I

The Scoundrel's Son

could not attend the funeral which was held last week. Jane acted as the chief mourner. I am so proud of her! But I was not there to mourn my sweet stepmother or to support Jane. And that makes me even sadder."

His words were interrupted by an explosion of tears. He had consoled me in the spring when my father had passed, and now I was sharing his sadness. I sat holding his hand while he wept. Somehow, even in my very young heart, I knew that was enough.

After a few minutes, he raised his tear-soaked face. "Thank you, Tom. I am very sorry."

"There is no need to apologize," I smiled at him. "On my next visit, we will celebrate our birthdays! And we will laugh, I promise."

That made him smile. "I shall enjoy that very much. And come with some good jokes, Tom. I command it."

"I shall be well prepared, Your Majesty. And I will bring a gift for you."

"A gift? I wonder what it could be?"

"You will just have to wait to see."

When our visit was over, I exited Edward's chamber and started down the hall. Richard called to me.

"Master Tom, thank you for your kindness toward His Majesty." I waved as I walked on.

I started home, but I was still shaken by my visit with Edward. I needed something to brighten my mood, and so I headed to my mother's cottage.

"Look who's here, why don't ya!" she said with a smile. Nan and Bet rose quickly from their chairs and joined in greeting me. "What brings you to our stately home, Tom?"

"It soothes my soul to look upon your three beautiful faces!"

"Beautiful faces you say!"

The four of us burst into laughter. My mother went to get some cider and bread.

"Made anything new at the shop, Tom?" Bet asked. I reached into my pocket and pulled out a rather clumsily made, oversized locket. I released the latch to reveal an image I had drawn.

"Wow! You made this? That's Mother, isn't it?" Nan asked.

"Yes. It's not perfect by any means. I'll get better."

Frederic Fahey

"I think it's wonderful!" Bet exclaimed.

My mother glanced over and saw the locket and the likeness of herself. For a moment, she was stunned, and then her face sparkled. She brought the cider and bread, and I quickly snapped the locket shut and placed it back in my pocket.

"I like having Mother in my pocket. She's always close by," I explained.

As I looked upon their faces, I appreciated how blessed I was. This was my family. We were not perfect, but we loved each other as best we could. I had been trying to make them smile with my comment about their beautiful faces. But it really was why I came.

Over the next few days, my thoughts returned to Edward's sadness at the loss of his stepmother. The thought of death brought to mind something that had haunted me for a while.

"How did Father Andrew die?" I asked Father Christian as we sat eating supper.

A grave look furrowed his brow. "I only know what I heard from folks in the parish as I was not here at the time. A man was treating a boy roughly and dragging him across the square. Father Andrew tried to intervene on the boy's behalf, and the man struck Father on his head with his cudgel. Unfortunately, Father Andrew succumbed to these injuries a few hours later." Father Christian paused at that point. "From all the accounts I've heard, the man didn't intend to kill Father Andrew." I was dumbfounded by this story. I had known that Father Andrew's death had been sudden, but not that he had met with a violent end.

"Do you know, Father, what became of the man and the boy?"

"This is the part of the story that confuses me." Father Christian gave me a look that was both serious and caring. "I heard that the man was your father, and you were the boy."

I was totally numbed by the revelation. How could this be so? My own father had killed Father Andrew? And I was there? My mind was spinning like leaves in a gusty autumn wind. I couldn't make sense of the story at all. But then, it occurred to me that this took place during the masquerade, and the boy was not me but most likely Edward. I remembered Edward's story of being dragged by my father through Offal Court. But I had not heard of the fatal encounter with Father Andrew. Edward certainly would not have known it was Father Andrew, or maybe even that it was a priest. He likely did not even know that the person had died because of the attack.

My father had died in the spring, and, just a few days previously, I had helped Edward handle the loss of Queen Kateryn, the only mother he had ever known. Now I learned the true nature of Father Andrew's death. And I was just shy of turning eleven. However, as fate would have it, death would not be a stranger to me in the years to come.

Chapter 7

A few weeks later, I returned to Whitehall. It was the middle of October, the week of our shared birthday. I packed my gift for Edward in my satchel and headed towards the palace. The crisp air kissed my cheeks as I made my way under the blue, autumn sky. It was a marvelous day to be outside and all of London appeared to be taking advantage of it. It was as if everyone knew that the dreary weather of early winter was just around the corner, and so it was best to enjoy these clear, apple-picking days while they lasted.

When I entered Edward's chamber, I was pleased to see Jane, as I had not seen her since the spring. She and Edward were deep in conversation. I imagined they were likely discussing our place in the universe or some other lofty notion. It was what they discussed much of the time in those days. Jane gave me a smile as I entered. Her freckled cheeks added sparkle to her eyes.

"Fantastic! Master Tom has arrived!" Edward said.

"The two of you look so serious!" I observed. "I assume you were discussing how wonderful I am!" I jested. I then turned more serious as I addressed Jane. "It is good to see you, Jane. I was quite sad to hear of the passing of Her Majesty the Queen. I know that must have been difficult for you."

She gave me a soft look and responded after a slight silence. "Thank you, Tom. You are very thoughtful. It was, indeed, a hard time, especially after such a joyous birth," Jane said with a tinge of sorrow. Then her face brightened. "But I know she is now in Heaven with our Lord." Jane's consideration of Heaven seemed to bring her solace.

"Are you back with your parents?" I asked.

"Yes, I am. Right now, we are staying at Norwich Place on the Strand.

The Scoundrel's Son

But I am concerned for Lord Sudeley. Since Her Majesty's death, it seems the Lord Admiral has lost his compass."

At that point, a servant brought in three glasses of cider and a fancy cake with sweetened fruits and nuts. He also brought marzipan, a sweet mixture of sugar, honey, and nut meal.

"Oh, Tom," Jane said as she handed me a folded piece of cloth. "I have been working on my sewing, and I thought your mother might like this." I unfolded the cloth to find a delightful, embroidered sampler of fruits, birds, and flowers.

"This is beautiful! Thank you. How thoughtful of you to think of my mother!"

"You are quite welcome. I remember you describing how your mother kept a simple yet pleasant kitchen, and I thought it would be the perfect place for this piece." Words were beyond me as I marveled at both Jane's embroidery skill and her kindness.

Edward then announced, "To our eleventh birthday!"

"To our birthday!"

"Hear! Hear!" Jane added as we all raised our cups of cider. While many friends might exchange gifts on New Years Day, Edward and I decided to celebrate our shared birthday in this fashion.

Edward lifted a book from his side table.

"This is for you, Tom. Happy birthday."

I had never seen such a wonderful looking book. It was covered in fine leather with an exquisitely embossed design. When I opened it, I realized it was a book of the fantastic tales of King Arthur. I don't believe that Edward and I had ever discussed the legendary king, but I had always been fascinated by the stories of him and his knights.

"Thank you so much, Edward! This is the most marvelous gift I have ever received."

"I am glad it pleases you. I particularly like one of the stories that features a strange visitor from a far-off land to the king's court," Edward added.

"And here's a gift for my twin." I reached into my satchel and brought out a small felt bag and handed it to him.

"What could it be?" he beamed. He opened the bag and extracted what looked like a good-sized gold locket with a chain. It was rare that

Frederic Fahey

Robert would allow me to work in gold, but, for the king, he made an exception. The locket was about the size of the palm of Edward's hand. I had decorated the outside to the best of my abilities with the close watch of Robert, of course.

"It makes a sound!" Jane noted the ticking. Edward and Jane looked at each other, not really sure what to make of the gift.

"Push the release in the front." Edward did as I said. The lid popped open. On its inside, I had carefully painted a likeness of his father King Henry. He gently touched the image and gave me a tender look. Then he turned his attention to what the locket contained.

"Oh my goodness!" Edward exclaimed as his eyes shot open wide. Jane's hand went to her cheek as she looked on with amazement. "It's a small clock! A watch!" Edward realized as he looked at me with great surprise. "Did you make this?"

"I made the case. With a bit of Mr. Nobson's help. I rendered the image of His Royal Majesty, your father. But Mr. Nobson made the watch. We thought you might enjoy it."

He compared the time of the watch to the large clock standing in the corner of the room.

"It is only slightly off, just a few minutes," Edward noted.

"Knowing Mr. Nobson," I added. "That means the big clock needs to be adjusted!" We all laughed! "Hand it to me and I can show you how it works." I showed Edward how you needed to wind the watch each day to keep it running and how you could adjust the time if need be.

"You know, Tom. I receive many gifts from people far and wide, from people of great means. And yet this is one of the most wonderful gifts I have ever received! Thank you so much! And please thank Mr. Nobson for me."

"I certainly will."

"It is really amazing!" Jane noted. She then turned to me and added, "I play with my little frog all the time!" That last remark made me smile.

A week or so after our birthday celebration, Edward and I were playing a game of chess. I really enjoyed playing with him, and I could see that my game was improving. Edward still won practically all the time, but the games were taking longer, and I could see him deeply pondering his moves.

The Scoundrel's Son

"I would like you to take my place again," he announced. "There is a meeting of my Council today. I have noticed some friction between my uncles. Maybe if you witness this firsthand, you can give me your sense of this." The fact that he wanted me to now attend a Council meeting not only surprised me but made me a bit nervous. To this point, I had only participated in audiences with subjects in the great hall. I was becoming more comfortable in that role. I had even intervened in some cases.

There had been a case the previous spring involving a very young woman from Pudding Lane, a parish very close to Offal Court. Her clothes were threadbare, and her face covered with a thin layer of dirt. Her tears made rivulets through the mud as they ran down her cheeks. She did her best to perform a proper curtsy before me.

"Your Royal Majesty, I come to plead for my husband. He stole some food, I admit. It's not right, he knows it. But our wee ones are so weak. It breaks his heart, it does."

One of the royal attendants informed me that this was her husband's second such offense and the recommended punishment from the magistrate was to either remove his hand or brand a "T" for thief on his forehead. His wife had come to appeal the decision.

"What is your name?" I asked.

"Anne, Your Majesty," she said as she curtsied again.

"Mistress Anne, how many children do you and your husband have?"

"Two, Your Majesty. John's three and Margaret not quite a year."

"How old are you and your husband?"

"Jacob is twenty, Your Majesty, and I but eighteen. I plead for your mercy. Jacob, he's a good father, he is. But he aches for the sake of our children." She paused as her tears gushed. "If they ... ," she couldn't bring herself to name the possible punishments. "How could he find work? I beg you, Your Majesty." She looked at me through welled eyes.

I pondered the case. I knew of so many young parents in my parish barely able to provide for their children. Anne was indeed correct. If her husband was marked by either a lost hand or a brand, no one would pay him or even provide him food for his labors.

Lord Somerset was just about to intervene when I made a statement.

"Mistress Anne, thievery is a very serious crime. Other ways must be found to provide for your family. I will grant leniency just this once. If your husband comes before a magistrate again, his punishment will be even more severe. Do you hear me?"

"Yes, Your Majesty. God bless you!" she let out as she collapsed to the floor.

"Have Master Jacob seek out Father Christian of Offal Court. He will provide you with food for young John and Margaret, and he might be able to help him find work. Be on your way," I announced.

"Well done, Your Majesty," Somerset commented at the end of the session.

But now Edward was asking me to participate in a session with the Council. There would be more opportunities for me to misspeak and consequences for such errors would be high. On the other hand, a part of me was intrigued to witness the inner workings of the court. I would be walking on thin ice, precarious and exhilarating at the same time.

"All right, I will keep my ears open." We exchanged clothes as we had previously. However, this time I was not led to the great hall but to the small chamber where Edward's Council met in closed meetings.

Somerset presided over the meeting, directing the discussions to his liking. I soon realized that no one was expecting me to say anything, and so there would be less of a chance for a misstep. I nodded then and again and offered an affirmation when it seemed appropriate. The discussions involved the status of the treasury and the ongoing conflicts in the north with the Scots. It was all a bit confusing and complicated for me to follow. However, I listened most closely to the exchanges between Sudeley and Somerset. Sudeley's concerns tended to be a bit vague and not well stated as far as I could tell. He always seemed to return to the notion that Somerset had too much on his plate and perhaps it would be better if he concentrated on the foreign encounters like those with Scotland.

"I could be more involved with the guidance of His Majesty," Sudeley added, pointing to me from across the room. Somerset merely shook his head.

"I think His Majesty is maturing quite nicely," commented John Dudley, Earl of Warwick. "I look forward to the day when he will rule in his own right and that day will be here before we know it." He smiled at me before returning to the topic of the state of the realm. "But I am also concerned by the state of the treasury. We are in the midst of the harvest,

The Scoundrel's Son

and the collection of taxes should be considerable." And so, the discussion continued. However, at least on this day, Somerset appeared to have answers for all the concerns raised with the prediction of better days ahead. The meeting ended on an optimistic if not a high note. At its conclusion, Somerset asked if he could walk with me, and I agreed.

As we walked, Somerset returned to many of the issues raised in the meeting. He seemed to be trying to state the issues in a manner that he thought I would understand while trying to convince me that things would be all right.

"Certainly, the campaigns in Scotland have gone on longer and have cost more than anticipated, but I am confident that they soon will be resolved in an acceptable fashion." It occurred to me that he was just restating the challenges while not being specific regarding the solutions beyond the notion that things would turn out well. He was merely placating the king rather than having a true discussion.

"Yes, Uncle, I understand," was my simple response. What else could I say?

Somerset then proceeded to a different topic. "I do have some concerns regarding Sudeley. He appears to be a bit unsteady since the loss of his wife, Her Majesty the Queen. We must be mindful of any erratic behavior on his part."

"Yes, Uncle,"

"Sudeley tells me that you've been spending time with that boy, Tom Canty." I was startled by the turn in the conversation. I tried to maintain a calm expression while my heart raced. "I am not sure I am comfortable with you seeing him. He might be a bit of a troublemaker. He caused all that commotion a while back. I ask you to be careful, Your Majesty." This exchange really bothered me. I was striving to comfort and assist Edward in any way I could, not to cause him any "trouble."

When we reached Edward's chambers, I thanked Somerset and told him I certainly would be careful.

"How did the meeting go?" Edward inquired as we quickly changed clothes.

"I think it went well. There are many topics of which I am not very informed."

"It hardly matters," Edward smirked as he dressed. "My opinion is not really sought as of yet. I hope that will change someday soon."

"From what I could follow, Somerset wants to control the Council. He really did not encourage any discussion. Instead, he spent his time defending his own actions with the promise that all will be well."

Edward reflected on my last comment. Then he asked, "How did my uncles get along?"

"Well, they certainly don't agree on a number of items...mostly about you. Sudeley wants more say with regards to how you are being educated and groomed to be king."

"My Uncle Thomas, has always wanted to be more involved with me while my Uncle Edward has been opposed to this, even more so since the passing of my stepmother."

"Somerset is concerned about unsteady behavior of his brother," I added. "To be honest, I did not witness anything inappropriate during the meeting." I paused as I recalled Somerset's comments about me being a troublemaker.

"You seem deep in thought. Was there anything else?" Edward asked.

I hesitated. "No, not really."

A knock on the door came as Doctor Cheke had arrived, and it was time for Edward to join his classmates for his lessons. We said our good-byes.

Before I left, I asked Edward one last question.

"During our masquerade, do you remember my father ever striking a priest with his cudgel?"

"Well," Edward pondered. "I do remember him striking a man as he was dragging me along that one time. But I don't recall that it was a priest. Why do you ask?"

"Never mind. I just heard a story," I said with a shrug. "I hope to see you soon," I added as I walked out the door.

Chapter 8

The frigid wind of December had come to call which meant the Christmas season would soon arrive, so Robert and I were busy as could be at the shop. Robert's usual customers had requests for trinkets and special gifts for loved ones to exchange on New Years Day. He also set a goal for how many new items he wanted to have in the window for sale. Of course, he would have the typical items such as rings, brooches, pins, and silver bowls. But every year, he would imagine a new toy that might bring delight to some small child or even an adult who retained that child-like spirit.

It was a good time for me to practice my skills. With Robert so busy, he relied on me to get the routine repairs and tasks about the shop accomplished. He gave me the liberty to choose a creative project as well. That year I was attempting to design and make my first fancy tankard for ale. I had already shared a sketch with Robert. He reviewed it closely and asked a few pointed questions that showed he understood exactly what I was trying to do, even if I couldn't explain it so well.

"Not bad. Not bad," he proclaimed. "Room for improvement, for sure, but not bad." Coming from Robert, this was high praise. Sometimes he would observe me from across the room while I was working, and then say something like "You know, Young Sprout, what you might consider is this." And proceed to describe a real improvement to my project. As time passed, I came to relish those "You know, Young Sprout" moments.

I was pleased when I received the invitation to visit Edward a couple of weeks before Christmas. As I approached his chambers, Lord Sudeley was just leaving. He caught a glimpse of me.

"Master Tom, I am glad I saw you. I wanted to wish a happy Christmas to you and your family," he said as he handed me a fist full of coins.

"Thank you, my lord," I responded, a bit shocked by the gesture.

"His Majesty is in a fine holiday spirit! I think it is a splendid time for me to make my move."

"I beg your pardon?" I was not sure of what he was speaking.

"I have a plan of how I can best serve the realm but I need His Majesty's consent. It might be better if I can find a way to separate him from the entanglements of Whitehall, at least for a short time." Now he had me really baffled. "If you could suggest to him how much I care for him as well as his sister, Lady Elizabeth, I think it would be of great benefit." I did not know how I should respond since I wasn't even sure what he might be suggesting. I tried to act as if I understood.

"By the way, I see that you are wandering about the palace without escort. You seem to know your way. What gate might you suggest would be the best to leave the palace unseen?"

"I suppose the gate towards the river. It tends to be less guarded than those facing either Westminster or the Strand." This was a detail I had considered, and I blurted the answer before I had weighed the impact of the information.

"Hmm. I hadn't thought of that but what you say does make sense. Thank you Tom, and Happy Christmas!" With that, the Lord Admiral smiled and hurried down the corridor.

As I entered Edward's chamber, I was still holding the coins in my hand with a puzzled look on my face.

"What do you have there?" Edward asked.

"I just encountered your uncle, Lord Sudeley," I said as I showed him the coins.

"So, I see!" Edward answered with a smile. "He came to me with the strangest notion. He told me he was very fond of my sister, Elizabeth, and he might consider her for marriage. He wondered if I would be in favor of it." Edward shook his head slightly. Now some of what the Lord Admiral had just asked of me made some sense.

"I must admit I think it is a bit of a wild idea. My stepmother, the queen, left to meet the Lord but a few months ago. On top of that, Elizabeth's hand in marriage is something to be considered with due seriousness. As a result, I stammered more than I answered." After a brief silence, he continued, "I am not sure what to make of my uncle these days."

"He is a bit of a puzzle. I do agree," I said carefully. "He certainly would like to have more say over you and your upbringing. But Lady Elizabeth? Does he think his request to marry her would be granted?"

"I don't know," Edward pondered. "I think he is a bit desperate these days."

"Maybe so," was all I could think to say. Now I understood Sudeley's mention of Lady Elizabeth, but what of his comment regarding removing Edward from Whitehall and his question of the palace gates. I still couldn't make much sense of this. "Perhaps you should take some caution over the holidays."

"Enough about my uncle. How about some Christmas treats?" Edward waved to Richard and a servant brought a tray of sweetened fruits, nuts, and gingerbread with warm cider. We smiled at each other and reached for our favorite treat. I was partial to the gingerbread and sweet cream. It may have been more food than two eleven-year-old boys could handle, but we would do our best!

"Happy Christmas, Tom," Edward mumbled, his mouth stuffed with fruit and nuts. I answered in kind, my face covered in sweet cream.

The air had turned blustery as I left Whitehall. I bundled as tightly as I could and scurried with the wintry wind at my back. I couldn't get the Lord Admiral's words out of my mind. What was he thinking? Would his plan put Edward and Lady Elizabeth in danger? Had I inadvertently aided him in this endeavor? Perhaps I was fretting over nothing.

***

Although most folks truly enjoy the happy season, I knew firsthand that there were some for whom these times would not be so joyous. In Offal Court, there were folks who tended to be more miserable during times of celebration. My own father was one such person. My early memories of Christmas were tainted by his sadness and anger. Ale may help others to celebrate, but, for my father, it just further fueled his resentments.

I suppose this is why I came to enjoy the visits over the twelve days to people's homes with Father Christian. He knew just the right tone to set.

Frederic Fahey

When he should stay by the door, offer food and some goodies, and leave, and when it was right to stay a while and celebrate. There were a few quick prayers and a "God bless you" sprinkled in here and there, but this was a time to touch folks with affection who needed to be touched. He could preach the other three hundred and fifty days of the year.

After one of these visits, I told Father Christian I had something I had to do and excused myself. I took a turn towards the Brown home. I knew that Aly, Izzy, and their mother would do their best to celebrate the season, but I had packed some toys from the shop for her little brothers. I had salvaged these from the rubbish. Mostly they were the results of some of Robert's projects that did not turn out just as he intended. The Brown boys would enjoy them nonetheless. I put them in a bag and tied it with a ribbon. I quietly approached their home, placed the bag on the stairs, gave the door a good rap, and smoothly slinked into a neighbor's darkened doorway. Izzy came to the door and took the bag. Once she had gone back inside, I moved closer to listen for the boys' reaction. When I heard the squeals of delight, a bird fluttered in my heart. After I was safely out of sight down the lane, I noticed their door open one last time as Aly peeked out to see if she could spot the secret gift giver. In that instant, I was faster than she was.

***

"Lord Sudeley has been arrested?" I exclaimed in disbelief. "But he is your uncle!" Not long after the celebrations of Twelfth Night, I had received an invitation to come to the palace. I thought this might be a pleasant visit just after the holidays, but I soon realized Edward had other thoughts. Upon my arrival at Edward's chambers, I noticed that there were extra guards at the door who questioned me thoroughly. Richard interceded and escorted me to see Edward.

"I had just fallen asleep, one night a week or so ago, when I was awoken by the frantic barking of my dog. Perhaps for the additional warmth in winter or maybe it was your words of caution, but I had invited my pet to sleep on the edge my bed. Suddenly there was a noise and the dog started to growl. 'What is it, boy?' I asked. Then I noticed a figure in the dark. It was my uncle trying to sneak into my chamber in the middle

The Scoundrel's Son

of the night! He had his sword drawn! My dog attacked, and he then proceeded to kill my dog with his sword!" From the look on his face, Edward was trying to make sense of the incident. "By this time, the guards had rushed to my aid, and my uncle was quickly subdued."

"Where is Sudeley now?" I asked.

"He is being held at the Tower."

The Tower of London serves many purposes. It has special quarters for the royal family and distinguished guests, it houses the royal jewels, and it is an armory within the city. It also serves as a jail for select prisoners. It is the most secure fortress in the city, perhaps in the entire kingdom.

"Tom, I don't understand! My Uncle Thomas has always been kind to me. He would greet me with a smile and perhaps a few coins. He was good to my stepmother, the queen, my cousin Jane, and my sister." At the mention of Elizabeth, his brow creased.

Now the words spoken on my visit before Christmas came rushing back to me. Clearly, Sudeley had something in mind for Edward and likely Lady Elizabeth, but I still wasn't sure what it was. Maybe I should have shared my concerns regarding the Lord Admiral at the time, but I never perceived that he meant Edward any sort of harm.

I had to remind myself that Edward was not just a boy in fancy dress. He was the King of England, and there might be those who would attempt to take advantage of his good nature. And now I realized that may include close relatives. From that moment on, I was on the lookout for my dear friend. I would do all that I could, as meager as that might be, to protect him.

"What will become of Lord Sudeley?" I asked.

"I don't know. Tom, you need to take my place at the Council meeting." He did not ask this time; it was a command. "I have been listening to these discussions these past few days, and it has all stopped making sense to me. Listen and report back to me what you hear." I really did not feel as if I had a choice, so I simply nodded in assent. Although I was apprehensive to impersonate Edward at such a critical time, I did want to see for myself what the Council's thoughts were regarding Lord Sudeley. We made our exchange of clothes, and I was led by Richard and several guards to the meeting room.

I entered the room amidst the usual barrage of "Your Majesty" salutations. I nodded politely to all, including Somerset. Once I was settled, all eyes fell upon me. "Let us proceed," I proclaimed. Somerset directed the discussion and tried to maintain order, but there were several conversations occurring at the same time. From what I could tell, there were two factions. One group was inclined to take into account the state of Sudeley's mind since the passing of the queen, noting how devastating it must have been to lose such a lovely wife after the blessed birth of the infant Mary. By his account, Sudeley was only trying to assure that the security about the king was adequate. Evidently, it was not. They surmised that the Lord Admiral may have unsheathed his sword only to ward off the attacking dog, and that he meant no harm to His Majesty. They were inclined to imprison Lord Sudeley for his dangerous behavior but to spare him the sentence of death.

The other faction saw the Lord's actions as reckless if not treasonous. Warwick pointed out that Sudeley seemed to have been fortifying his castle at Holt with both arms and supplies. He felt his intent may have been to abduct both Edward and maybe Lady Elizabeth. In any case, he had put His Majesty in harm's way, and that such action could not be tolerated. As was often stated since his birth, His Majesty was the most precious jewel of the realm, and his wellbeing had to be protected at all costs. Other members noted that Sudeley had tried to gain their support for a larger role in the education of the king or for a potential marriage to Lady Elizabeth, and many had assumed it was just more of the Lord Admiral's rants. But now this reckless act brought a different light to these efforts. Sudeley needed to be beheaded for his behavior.

"Lord Sudeley must be brought to trial and, if found guilty, suffer the consequences," Somerset stated succinctly. With this statement, I knew exactly where Somerset sat with the matter. The results of such a trial were a foregone conclusion: Somerset was calling for the execution of his own brother. Being only a few years apart in age, as small children they had likely played games in the yard or sat with their sister, Edward's dear mother, and listened to stories. And yet now, he was not showing his younger brother one ounce of mercy.

When the meeting adjourned, Somerset walked with me to the king's chambers.

"These discussions must be difficult for Your Majesty," he started. "I

The Scoundrel's Son

know you were fond of Thomas."

"Yes," I replied, "they are quite difficult."

"I have feared for a while that he did not have Your Majesty's best interest at heart," he continued. "But I did not believe he would resort to such a treasonous act. I do all I can to protect Your Majesty from those who not only look to diminish your ability to reign but might also seek to bring you harm. "

"I am grateful for your protection."

"Your Majesty is young, and your heart is good—perhaps too good—to see the treachery. But I see it on your behalf, and it is my duty to protect Your Majesty." He stopped for a moment and looked at me directly. "Unfortunately, Thomas was trying to do you ill. I am afraid that these ill wishes do not end with Thomas. There are others of whom we must be most cautious, even within your Council. Others may not come to your bedchamber brandishing a sword, but they mean you no less harm. It was the dying wish of my sweet sister that I protect Your Majesty, and I intend to do so with all my heart."

We had circled back to Edward's chambers, and Somerset bid his goodbyes. "I am glad we had the opportunity for this difficult but necessary conversation. Your Majesty," he concluded with a bow.

"How was the meeting?" Edward asked anxiously when I entered.

"I do not think it looks very good for your Uncle Thomas. Most of your Council appears to be in favor of trying him for treason. I would think the result of such a trial would not go in his favor."

"My goodness!" Edward exclaimed. "I didn't realize the situation was quite so dire."

"And Somerset is clearly leaning this way. He is concerned," I continued, "that there are those who have their own interests at heart rather than yours or what is good for the realm."

"He might be right in this regard," Edward added.

I paused for a moment and looked my twin in the eye as I considered what I might say next.

"What is it, Tom?" Edward noticed my hesitation as he was pulling up his hose.

"I was thinking…Do you think you should be cautious of Lord Somerset as well?"

Edward was surprised by my warning.

"Maybe it is nothing." I continued. "But I wonder if a time may come when what is best for you and the realm differs from what is best for Somerset."

Edward considered this for just a few moments.

"Thank you, Tom. It is useful to have eyes and ears that are so innocent reporting to me. But my uncle has only my best interest at heart. He would never harm me in any way."

"I hope what you say is true."

As I walked back to Offal Court, I wondered if I was correct to share my thoughts regarding Somerset. Edward dismissed the possibility of Somerset not always considering his best interests, but would he not have said the same of Sudeley just a month ago?

Later that spring, as I expected, Lord Sudeley was found guilty of treason. The charges were presented to Edward who signed them and sent them on to Parliament. The case was vigorously discussed within the House of Commons, but, in the end, his execution was ordered. Soon after, he was beheaded upon Tower Hill. My suspicions of Somerset continued to bother me deeply. He was cunning where Sudeley was haphazard. I couldn't quite put my concern into words, but I sensed that some real danger might be lurking right around the corner. I vowed that I would stay alert and to do whatever I could to protect my friend even if we did not always see things in the same light.

Chapter 9

It was the first week of February when Robert asked me to come to the shop early. Usually, I was the first one there as I would have everything in good shape before Robert arrived from upstairs, but on this morning, he was already waiting for me. I was not late, but there he was raring to go.

"Finally, here, Young Sprout!" he greeted me. "Please tidy up. Our guests will be here in less than an hour."

I didn't know who these guests were, but they must be special for Robert to be so anxious. I gave everything a very good wipe and swept the floor with a bit more care than usual. Since it seemed likely that these guests would be entering the shop, I wanted to do an extra fine job in the area just inside the door. Within three quarters of an hour, all looked good in the front. I then got to work behind the workbench.

I heard the door open, and three men entered the shop and greeted Robert. One was doing all the talking while the other two seemed to be there for support. I did not recognize the man speaking, but his dress and manner told me that he was a lord of some kind. He was tall with a muscular build. His erect posture and the way about him indicated he had significant military experience. He had short, thinning hair, a well-trimmed graying beard, and clear, piercing eyes. I judged him to be about forty years old. He presented Robert with a crude design on a piece of paper.

"These weapons have been making their way on to the battlefield for a while now. Of course, cannons are very useful in siege warfare. These are similar as they rely on explosive powder, but they are smaller such that they can be handheld by a single soldier. The sword and the lance could become things of the past since armor is of little protection with these weapons. But, so far, they take a bit of effort to use and have not been shown to be too reliable. Sometimes they work and sometimes they do not.

This lack of reliability makes them practically useless in battle, particularly in close fighting.

"However," the lord looked Robert square in the eye. "If one could make a more reliable version, one that almost always was sure to work and easier to use, that could change everything."

I approached from the back. The drawing showed a tube that flared like a bell at one end with a wide handle at the other.

"Who is this?!?" the lord asked when he noticed me.

"This is Tom, my apprentice. I trust him wholeheartedly. He knows how to keep things private."

"If you say so," the lord said. "This project has to be kept secret!"

"Just to make sure I have this correct," Robert said, "a soldier would carry one of these weapons, like he might a longbow today. So, it cannot be too heavy. Some sort of explosive powder is placed at the base of the tube and a small metal ball on top of that. The powder in the tube is lit, setting off an explosion that makes the ball fly out of the tube. Is this right?"

"Yes. As I said, it is like a small cannon," the lord answered.

"What keeps the soldier safe from the explosion?"

"The tube, or barrel as it is called, must be strong enough to withstand the explosion. It is closed at the end nearest the soldier, which is why the powder and the ball are loaded from the other end."

"How is the powder lit? It would seem cumbersome to have to light a wick before using the weapon."

"That is true. Current versions bring a slow, continuously burning match in contact with the powder when these muskets are to be fired."

"Muskets?"

"Yes, they're also called hand gonnes or arquebuses. But now the term 'musket' is coming into favor. I have heard that some are looking into using flint to light them, but I don't understand how that would work."

"Hmm." Robert thought for a moment. "I could see how flint might be used. Let me think about this and see what I can do."

"Very good! I knew that when it came to metal work, you were the best."

"This will go beyond metal work. It will involve other materials and mechanics as well. And I will need a place to work. I cannot experiment with explosives in my shop."

The Scoundrel's Son

"I own some property not far from the city, perhaps an hour's wagon ride away. There is an old barn. It is not in use right now, but it is in good shape. It might serve you well."

Robert peered over his spectacles at the lord, and I knew what was coming next. "And there will be expenses."

"Think nothing of it! I will provide all you need!" the lord responded, with a wave of his hand. "And then some! I might be gone, off and on, over the next few months. There are some troubles in the western counties regarding the new book of prayer His Eminence, the Archbishop, and His Majesty the King have introduced. Frankly, I am a great supporter of these reforms. I think it is about time our worshiping focused on Our Lord and not on the dictates from the Bishop of Rome. But it seems that not everyone is as enlightened as I am and that includes His Majesty's own sister, Lady Mary." He placed his hand upon the shoulder of one of the men who accompanied him.

"Geoffrey, here, will speak for me while I am gone. He can show you to the barn next week and arrange for anything you require. Thank you again, Robert, for helping me with this very important project."

After the guests left, I asked, "Who were they?"

Robert shook his head and murmured, "It is best you do not know. This is a secret project. No one can know. Is that clear?" I nodded. "I have known the Earl for quite a long time, and I am indebted to him for helping me in a time of trouble." He paused as he pondered. "Let's just call him 'the Earl' for now." In time, his identity did become known to me. I apologize, my lady, but since he and his family are still alive and what I might reveal could be considered dangerous, I will continue to keep his name private.

"The weapon, or 'musket' as he called it, must be light if a soldier is to carry one into battle. So, all parts that do not need to be made of metal should be wooden." Robert shook his head. "I'm not too good with wood. Steel or iron I can handle. They are different than gold, silver or even tin for sure. I am not a blacksmith, but I can deal with it. But wood? I don't know."

At that, I perked up, "I know how to whittle and craft wood! I have been whittling since I could walk. I have not done much woodwork recently, but I think I can help!"

Frederic Fahey

"I do remember those toys you brought me on your first day," Robert responded. "You certainly have some skill with wood. Very well then!"

The following week, Geoffrey, the Earl's man, took us on a wagon ride out to an old yet sturdy barn. Robert surveyed the barn, making sure all the doors were secure and that the roof looked sound enough to protect our work from the elements. Geoffrey noted that, indeed, the roof did not leak, and there were no neighbors for several miles. We had also noticed that the barn was down a path and could not be seen from the road. Adjacent to the barn, there was a small cabin, probably the former quarters of the stable master. It had one room with a table, a few chairs, and a working fireplace. Robert finally nodded and proclaimed, "Not perfect but this should do."

Robert informed me that we would move all our work on this project to the barn. The drawings and sketches would be stored in the cabin. The shop would be closed on Mondays, which is when we would work on the musket. Each Monday, I was to meet him at the square at dawn, and we would head to the barn in his wagon. Within a few weeks, we had assembled quite a workshop. We each had our own bench, his for the metal work and mine for woodworking. He noted that besides my work on the portions of the musket that were to be wooden, he may also ask me to carve models for metal pieces that were to be cast. Robert had also constructed a forge. It turned out that Robert was excellent at making tools. He was able to fashion every woodworking tool that came to my mind. We were now prepared to get to work on the project, but Robert did have a concern.

"I have thought about this project for these past few weeks. I have some ideas, but I am not sure I am on the right path. I don't fully understand how a soldier might operate such a weapon in battle. How would he carry it? How would he put the explosives in the barrel? How would he hold the musket when it was to be fired?"

I had been wondering many of the same things. I was considering how to best fashion the handle of the musket, but it was the guess of an eleven-year-old boy who had only heard stories of war. Neither of us really understood the pressures and constraints of such a weapon being used in a true battle. Suddenly, I had a thought.

"Mr. Nobson," I announced. "I think I know the right person to help us!"

The Scoundrel's Son

The following Monday, we were back at the barn, this time with a guest.

"Amazing!" Lord Miles exclaimed, after Robert swore him to secrecy, explained the project, and described the musket at least as we understood it. "And you think this could really work?"

"So we are told," Robert replied.

Lord Miles scrutinized the drawings of the weapon very carefully.

"You are right. Weight will be an issue, so the more wood the better. The loading and firing approach that you describe is very close to that of a cannon. However, some batting may have to be placed after the explosive powder and the ball to hold them in place. A rod or some other object will need to be available to forcefully ram the powder, the ball, and the batting down the barrel."

Robert nodded as he made notes. "How would a soldier hold the musket when it is being fired?"

"I am not certain." Lord Miles grabbed a nearby broom. "Perhaps, like a crossbow." He lifted the broom to his eye and peered down the handle like he was aiming it.

"I would shape the wooden back end to fit either against the chest or the shoulder. This will make it more steady during firing. It might fit snuggly against the shoulder." He then held the broom with the straw against his right shoulder, his right hand close to where the firing section might be, and his left hand farther down the barrel. He cocked his right elbow against his chest for more stability.

He suggested we extend the wooded section under the barrel so the soldier could get a better grip.

"The more stable, the better the aim. Just as with a bow," he explained. "Also, I think the weapon should be made as long as practical. The longer the barrel, the more accurate the firing of the ball. Perhaps as with bows, there may be different designs for different purposes, longer barrels for shooting from a distance and shorter ones for closer in. Shoulder height might be a good place to start."

Robert frantically jotted down every word. Practically everything Lord Miles said, much of which Robert and I had not even considered, made good sense.

"I am still not sure how the musket, as you call it, is fired," Miles added. "With a cannon, it is aimed ahead of time, and, once the wick is set afire, all that is left to do is to cover one's ears. But how is that done with the musket?"

"I have thought a bit about this," Robert announced. "The Earl described a mechanism with a slow burning match that, when engaged, would light the powder. But he also mentioned an approach using flint." He pulled a drawing from the bottom of his pile. "Here we have a piece of flint attached to a spring mechanism." He then turned to me. "Tom, I'll need you to whittle these pieces for casting." He pointed to each part in the drawing. "When released by the soldier, the flint would swing and strike this piece of iron. A spark would result that would light the wick. This would eliminate the need for a burning match, but the trick will be to get this to work consistently." Robert then looked at Lord Miles.

"Well, you have certainly given us much to consider. Young Sprout was right. It was a splendid idea to invite you here today." Robert turned to Lord Miles while the three of us walked outside.

"Thank you. I know you are busy and taking a man away from his beautiful family even for a morning is a lot to ask. We are really grateful."

"It is my pleasure, Mr. Nobson," Lord Miles responded as he mounted his horse. "You have helped me on several occasions." He then said to me. "Tom, if you see my little friend, give him my greeting." I waved as he rode down the path.

Chapter 10

Spring arrived early in London that year with all its splendid glory. Birds noisily greeted the morning sun, flowers exploded into color, and the trees were blessed with new leaves in every imaginable shade of green. I was strolling through Offal Court one afternoon when I heard my name called from above.

"Tom Canty! Up here!"

Aly was perched on a high window ledge on the side of a church bordering the square. She beckoned me to join her, and I accepted the challenge. There wasn't much space for a foothold between the large gray stones of the church wall but plenty for the likes of Aly and me. I looked to see if anyone was watching and then scooted up the side of the building to join her. The window ledge provided a marvelous view down the river toward the Tower of London and beyond. We chatted about our families and other things. I then shifted my seat and gazed up the river toward Westminster.

"Where are you, Tom? You seem to be in a far-off land," she commented.

"I don't know. There is a friend I haven't seen in a while that I have been missing." Jane had returned to her parents' home after the queen's death, and it had been months since I had last seen her at the palace.

"Is it a girl?" Aly guessed with a sly smile.

"Why, yes, it is," I confessed. "But just a friend."

"I understand," she answered as she continued to smile. "Why don't ya go visit her? Maybe she'd like to see you as well." Aly made a good point. Why didn't I visit her?

"Maybe I should," I responded.

Aly leaned back against the window. "Definitely should." But, of course, it was more complicated than she could imagine. It would not have occurred to her in her wildest thoughts that the girl was a member of the royal family.

"And bring her a gift," Aly added.

Jane had told me that her family spent a good amount of time at Norwich Place along the Strand when her father, the Marquess of Dorset, was doing business in the city. The house had been owned by her grandfather and was one in a row of houses of the nobility on the north bank of the river. Jane's family also owned a large estate in Bradgate, Leicestershire where her parents went for the summer months, but Jane had told me she preferred Norwich with its libraries and closeness to the city.

Soon after my conversation with Aly, I decided to take a walk along the Strand one fine spring day on the chance that her family had returned to town. I found Norwich Place without any problem. It was near Somerset's splendid home and just around the turn in the river from Whitehall Palace.

It was early in the day when I arrived. I peered through the gate at a very attractive house of stone with a small but stunning garden on one side. The daffodils were in full bloom, adorning the fresh green of spring with vivid yellows. I could easily imagine Jane sitting on a bench amidst the flowers and trees with one of her books, contemplating the mysteries of the heavens. I could also tell that indeed the Marquess and his family were here. I had no invitation or any reason to visit. I am not sure why, but I was reluctant to ask Edward for his assistance. So, what was I to do?

It was the next Monday, and we were taking a break outside the barn after one of our discussions concerning the musket.

"What a wonderful spring day!" Lord Miles proclaimed. Just then, I had a thought.

"Are you acquainted with the Marquess of Dorset and the Lady Frances?" I asked him.

Lord Miles was surprised and intrigued by my question. "I have met the Lord and Lady on several occasions. They have invited me to go hunting a few times although the timing was never good. Why do you ask?"

By the smile on Lord Miles's face, I must have blushed considerably at his question. I could feel the blood rushing to my scalp and tingling

The Scoundrel's Son

every single one of my hairs.

"I have met their daughter, Lady Jane, on several of my visits with His Majesty. However, I have not seen her since autumn."

"I see," he responded while raising his eyebrow. His mind seemed to be turning like a windmill.

A week or so later, Lord Miles came by the shop.

"Tom! Tom! Are you busy next Tuesday afternoon?"

"Working in the shop. Why do you ask?"

"I have arranged a visit with the Marquess of Dorset at Norwich Place to discuss a business proposition. Do you care to join me?" he said with a wink. I was not sure of his meaning at first. "Perhaps Lady Jane will be there as well."

"Absolutely!" I gushed, finally understanding. "I would love to join you!"

"Wonderful! I will meet you at the shop at noon. I suggest you dress nicely but not formally."

I spoke to Robert about taking leave on Tuesday afternoon. "I think I can get by without you for a few hours," he said slyly, peering over his spectacles. "If I overheard correctly, there might be a young lady involved." Of course, this made me blush yet again. I simply nodded and went back to my work.

Tuesday finally arrived! I had two outfits that seemed appropriate for visiting Edward, which I alternated between. I chose the blue one since it had a slight design to the fabric that I thought looked good. I had purchased a book of stories from a nearby shop that I thought she might like. Robert helped me bind it nicely using some leather he had. Lord Miles arrived a little before noon, at which time I went into the back room, changed my clothes, and we walked to the Strand.

"I can make the introduction to the Marquess and the Lady," Lord Miles noted. "But the rest is up to you, my young friend." When we arrived at Norwich Place, we were met at the gate and directed to the foyer. We waited a brief while for a servant to greet us and bring us to a small sitting room. We were told that the Marquess and the Lady would be with us shortly. As we were waiting, Jane briskly walked by the door, stopped abruptly, and peered in.

"Tom?" she said. "Is that you?"

Frederic Fahey

"Good afternoon, Your Highness," I responded. "May I introduce to you Lord Miles Hendon. Lord Miles, this is Lady Jane Grey."

"I am very pleased to meet you," Lord Miles said with a proper bow.

"A pleasure to meet you as well," Jane responded. She turned to me. "Tom, what are you doing here?"

Just at that moment, Jane's parents entered the room, and a whole new set of greetings began. The Marquess had a pleasant look with a ruggedness consistent with his love of the outdoors. Lady Frances carried herself with a manner that demanded attention. She was the niece of King Henry and behaved accordingly. She noticed me immediately.

"Lord Hendon, who is this young man? It is striking how much he resembles my cousin, His Majesty."

Lord Miles introduced me as Master Thomas Canty, Ward of His Royal Majesty the King. He obviously had prepared for the introduction. Jane added that she had been previously introduced to me by His Majesty.

"Master Thomas and I have business in the city today," Lord Miles explained. "So, I asked him to accompany me here while Lord Dorset and I meet. I hope this does not present an inconvenience."

"None whatsoever," Lady Frances proclaimed. "Jane, could you show Master Thomas around the garden while your father and Lord Hendon do business?"

"Yes, Mother," Jane answered and started to lead me from the room.

"My goodness, Master Thomas!" Lady Frances exclaimed. "When I first entered the room, I really thought you were His Majesty."

"Yes, my lady," I said. "I have heard people in the court say we look similar, but I do not see the likeness myself."

"Come, Tom. Let me show you our wonderful little garden," Jane said. I bowed before the Marquess and the Lady, and Jane curtsied to Lord Miles as we left the room. Once we were outside and away from the adults, she faced me and smiled.

" 'I don't see the likeness myself.' Is that what you said?" Jane laughed. I sheepishly smiled.

"I was just trying to make pleasant conversation. Your mother is very nice."

"Certainly...when in the company of others," she said.

"I brought you something," I reached into my satchel and took out the

The Scoundrel's Son

book. "It is a book of stories. I thought it might offer a nice break from your serious reading." Jane accepted the gift with a genuine smile as she quickly flipped through the pages.

"Oh, Tom! This is so thoughtful," she said. "I should enjoy it very much!"

I was quite pleased that she seemed to truly like the gift. I smiled, trying not to blush. We strode around the garden amidst the amazing beauty of this tiny paradise in the city.

As we were walking about, two young girls entered the garden. It seemed they were curious of the strange boy being entertained by Lady Jane.

"Tom, these are my sisters," Jane said, "Lady Katherine and Lady Mary. Katherine and Mary, this is Master Thomas Canty, Ward of His Royal Majesty the King." I bowed to each of them individually and they nodded in return. Katherine appeared to be about three years younger than Jane and every bit as pretty as I had heard. Her delicate features were crowned with the fiery Tudor red hair. She shared the same wonderful smile as her sister. Jane had told me that her sister Mary was quite small for her age of four years old. This was indeed the case. She immediately peppered me with a flurry of questions.

"My name is Mary, and I am four years old. Are you friends with my sister? Do you live in a palace? What is your favorite color? Do you own a horse? Can I call you Tom?"

"Yes, my lady. You may certainly call me Tom."

"I love the flowers of spring!" Lady Katherine proclaimed, interrupting the interrogation, thankfully. "I think these are my favorites, but I love these as well!" Jane then proceeded to announce the name in Latin of each type of flower that Lady Katherine identified.

"Dear sister, you are amazing!" Lady Katherine exclaimed. "But is everything a school lesson with you?" At that point, a servant announced that Ladies Katherine and Mary's schooling was about to start, and the sisters said their farewells.

Jane and I sat down at a small table in the corner of the garden and chatted about Edward and the Royal Court, Robert's shop, my ongoing projects, and Jane's studies. Jane asked how my mother was doing. Even with all her sophistication, our conversation flowed easily. Finally, a servant arrived to inform us that Lord Miles was preparing to leave.

"Tom," Jane said, "thank you so much for coming."

"It was my pleasure. Could I visit you again?"

She gave me an awkward look. "I am not sure. We will see," she said. "We should return to the house." As we arrived at the foyer, Lord Miles was finalizing his goodbyes.

"Master Thomas, it was a pleasure to meet you," Lady Frances said to me. "Please tell His Majesty when you see him that I intend to visit before I leave the city for Bradgate. We would also love for him to visit us there during his travels this summer."

"Your Highness, I will certainly pass along your message," I said with a bow.

"I still say the resemblance is striking!" she noted to her husband as they exited the foyer.

As we made our way back towards Offal Court, Lord Miles simply asked, "Well?"

"Thank you so much, Lord Miles," I said with a slight blush. He smiled broadly and clapped me on the back as we ambled down the lane by the river.

Chapter 11

On a Monday in mid-April, we met with Lord Miles at the barn to test a working version of the musket. Lord Miles looked it over carefully. When he stood it upright, it reached slightly above his shoulders. Its design involved a lot more wood than we had previously planned. I used pine in this version as it was available and easy to fashion, but I figured I eventually would use oak given its hardness and strength.

"You have made good progress!" Lord Miles announced. "It is a little heavy, but I think a soldier could handle this all right." He lifted the musket, placed the back end against his shoulder and peered down the barrel. "The barrel looks straight and true." He turned the musket to examine the firing section. A wick was placed in a small hole in the side of the barrel towards the back end.

"Have you tried to fire it?" he asked.

"Not yet," Robert answered. "I thought today might be the day if the design met your approval. I have enough explosive powder for such a test."

Lord Miles examined the barrel very closely.

"If a cannon is not constructed close to perfect," he explained, "the firing can lead to the explosion not only ruining the weapon, but also severely injuring and sometimes killing the soldiers nearby. The integrity of the barrel is of utmost importance." He then turned to Robert. "I am very familiar with the quality of your work, Mr. Nobson, but we still need to be very cautious. But I say we give it a fire."

"All right! Tom, go fetch the stand," Robert directed.

"Yes, sir." I went back into the barn and came back with a stand that Robert had constructed to hold the musket while it was being tested. The stand was about shoulder height with two brackets, one that went under the musket's back end and another for farther down the barrel. Robert and I secured the musket to the stand. When it was in place, one could still access the wick easily from the side.

Robert and I had also constructed a target much like that used in archery training and competition, except it was a bit bigger as we were not so confident in the musket's accuracy. We placed the target about thirty paces away from the stand. Lord Miles took one of the balls and inspected it closely. Robert decided to make the balls of lead due to their weight and the ability to easily mold them.

"All right," Lord Miles said. "Let's give it a try."

Lord Miles took a cup of the powder and a funnel and poured it down the barrel. He stopped at one point and considered the amount. "I am not sure how much to use but let's try a little more rather than a little less for now." He continued to pour.

Robert handed him the ramming rod and Lord Miles plunged the powder down the barrel. He then placed the ball and, lastly, the batting to hold everything in place, and plunged it all down. We put the musket back on the stand, and Robert bracketed it in place. Lord Miles lit a candle and handed it to Robert.

"You should have the honor," Lord Miles proclaimed. "But once you light the wick, move away as quickly and as far as you can."

Lord Miles and I moved to what we assumed would be a safe distance as Robert stood with the candle by the side of the musket stand. He gave us one last look, lit the wick, and hurried towards us. After a few seconds, the powder within the musket ignited and exploded with a loud bang, a bright flash, and a cloud of black smoke. Robert fell to the ground, and the musket went flying backwards from the stand, flipped into the air, and landed on the ground. Lord Miles and I ran to Robert and helped him to his feet. The three of us were stunned by what we had just witnessed. No one spoke for what seemed a long time.

"Gentlemen," Lord Miles finally declared. "I think it worked!" We hurried to the target, and, yes, the ball had struck and lodged itself deep into the target. It was nowhere near the center, but the fact that it hit the target at all was a major success. We then walked to where the musket lay on the ground. Lord Miles turned it over gingerly, perhaps concerned that it might still be hot to the touch. Although we could see a bit of blackness

The Scoundrel's Son

around the hole where the wick entered the barrel, evidence of the firing, the barrel itself was still intact.

"I forgot about the backwards force of a cannon when it is fired," Lord Miles commented. "Obviously, the musket experiences the same force. We will need to secure it in the stand more firmly next time."

"At least, the test was not a total disaster," Robert stated.

"Not at all!" Lord Miles seemed surprised by the remark. I was not surprised in the least, as I had heard Robert comment on a number of wonderful projects he had designed in a similarly guarded manner. Lord Miles continued, "The musket fired and survived. We hit the target...basically. We learned some things. I'd say it was a marvelous success!" I knew exactly how Robert would respond.

"I suppose. But there is still much to learn! Much to learn!"

Over the next few weeks, we redesigned the firing stand to handle the backwards force including securing two large stones to its base. We then tested the musket several more times. Even after the fourth or fifth firing, the barrel was still in one piece, which even Robert considered a success.

Lord Miles and I were sitting on a log in the barnyard while Robert was busy tinkering away on a new mechanism he wanted to show us.

"How is my little friend doing?" Lord Miles asked. "I have not seen him since before Christmas."

"He is doing well," I stated but I then decided I would confide in him that I had been impersonating Edward and what I had witnessed in the royal court. I asked him if he had heard about the incident with Lord Sudeley and his execution. He noted that he had.

"I had always assumed," I shared, "that the royalty and the nobility acted in a more dignified and maybe even a more moral manner than we commoners. In Offal Court, we are merely trying to survive, provide a roof and a meal. In such desperate situations, some resort to trickery, thievery, and, at times, violence. The rest of us try to avoid these characters, often without success. However, I felt if one had enough money and resources, life would not only be easier but more genteel. If your bed was warm and belly full, what would be the need for thievery and bloodthirst? But now I see that the rich are just as vicious as the rest of us. Their quest is not for a roof and a meal, but for a nicer roof and a better meal. And power, it appears, is more seductive than gold. No one is spared in this quest, not even family members."

"I have witnessed what you say firsthand," Lord Miles shared. "When I returned to Kent and Hendon Hall after my time away, my own brother denied me. He had taken everything, even my beloved Edith. Only through His Majesty's good grace were things put right."

"Since the night Sudeley came to his chambers and was arrested," I continued, "Edward has become more wary of those around him. I have suggested he also be cautious of Lord Somerset. But he does not hear me."

"His Majesty needs to realize," Lord Miles began, "that everyone is looking for something from him. And this includes Somerset. He is an eleven-year-old boy. They presume they can do as they choose, and he will not object, at least not in a forceful enough manner. They will say that their actions are in his best interest, or even that which they propose was his idea. Perhaps he should ask himself before they even start talking 'What does this person want from me?' Then he might stay one step ahead." This was solid advice from Lord Miles that I planned to share with Edward.

"Lord Miles, please come," Robert called from the barn door. "I have something to show you." He led us to his workbench, where a piece of cloth covered his new project. I knew he had been working on something, but I wasn't sure what it might be. He removed the cloth to reveal a mechanical structure, perhaps a half foot long and half that high. I recognized several of the pieces that I had helped him cast.

"This is the new firing mechanism I have designed. It will attach to the musket near the back end of the barrel." On one side of the mechanism, a piece of flint was attached like a small hammer while on the other was a piece of iron. The flint hammer was drawn back against a spring until it was caught with a tiny latch.

"Keep your eye on the iron," he told us. He pushed a lever releasing the flint hammer which struck the iron causing a good-sized spark. It was much like starting a fire by striking flint against iron. He set the hammer several times and demonstrated that the device produced a spark practically every time.

"I've tried to make the firing mechanism as small and light as possible. The soldier would load the musket, aim it, set the hammer, and fire it by merely releasing it with no need to light a wick or a slow burning match," Robert explained.

The Scoundrel's Son

"That would be amazing!" Lord Miles announced, and Robert agreed. However, Robert indicated that there were still some issues that had to be addressed. He needed to work on the release mechanism so that it did not fire prematurely. He noted that the flint assembly sparked practically every time, which was good, but he had to find a way for it to reliably light the powder within the barrel. Currently, it only lit the wick sometimes.

"If I am able to come up with solutions for these issues," Robert inquired," do you think we are at a point where we could give a demonstration to the Earl?"

"Without a doubt," Lord Miles responded, and I agreed. Robert noted that the Earl's identity had to be kept secret so he could not involve Lord Miles in the demonstration. I figured that meant that I would be firing the musket for the Earl as I couldn't imagine Robert doing it. He could barely handle lighting the wick that first time.

To my surprise, Robert offered his hand to Lord Miles. "Thank you, Lord Miles. Your assistance has been invaluable."

"It has been a pleasure," Lord Miles answered. He then looked at me. "Tom, good to work with you as well. I must be going if I am to make it to Kent by sundown." He exited the barn, mounted his horse, and rode off.

Robert turned to me. "Young Sprout, thank you as well. We would not have come this far without your fine woodwork. You are blessed with many talents. And, in turn, I am blessed." He offered me his hand. In the more than two years I had worked with Robert, we had never shaken hands.

"It's an honor to work with you, Mr. Nobson," I managed to say as I grasped his hand.

"Well then," Robert said as he quickly pulled his hand back after a brief shake. "Back to the shop! Much to do, much to do."

Chapter 12

The following week, I received an invitation from Edward. It had been almost a month since our last visit. I examined the chess board as it was my move, but I didn't see too many options. Edward had captured my rook and my queen was under attack. His fingers continued their constant drumming as his eyes darted about the board.

"Relax, Edward, this is supposed to be fun!" He barely cracked a smile in response as I moved my bishop to at least feign an attack. At this point, the outcome was inevitable. I looked up from the chess board as a thought came to my head.

"It is the first of May next week. They have a May Day Festival in Westminster, don't they?"

"I am not sure," Edward said.

"You have never been to the May Day Festival?" I asked, surprised.

"Can you imagine the king wandering about the square during a festival?" Edward responded with a sad smile. "I would have so many guards around me I would not be able to see anything anyway."

"That is too bad. I just love the festival! The square decorated in flowers and banners of every color. People in the street and vendors selling their goods. Children as happy as can be. All celebrating spring. I think you would enjoy seeing all the excitement."

"I know I would!" He moved his knight, strengthening his attack on my queen.

"I understand we can't walk through the festival but maybe we could still be part of it," I said as an idea started to dawn.

As luck would have it, Edward's schedule allowed for me to visit on a day during the festival. I brought with me an extra set of my clothing

The Scoundrel's Son

including a cloak with a hood. After I was there for only a short time, Edward summoned Richard.

"I am not feeling well. After Master Tom leaves, I shall retire to my bedchamber for some rest. Please do not disturb me until it is time to prepare for supper."

"Yes, Your Majesty," Richard responded.

Edward quickly donned my extra set of clothing. Wearing my cloak, he left his quarters and headed to our arranged meeting place. I positioned several pillows under the bed covers so it looked as if Edward was sleeping. One thing that Edward's chamber did not lack was pillows. I put on a second cloak, checked that the hall was empty, and started on my way.

"Did you forget something, Master Tom?" Richard asked as I was closing the door.

"Yes, I forgot a book that His Majesty had lent to me," I whispered as I pulled a book from my satchel. "Shh! His Majesty is already asleep! I didn't want to disturb him!"

I met Edward in a small room around the corner, and we proceeded to the palace courtyard without being seen. It was challenging to keep our movements clandestine in the midafternoon sun, but we were able to reach a door to a stairway in the palace wall facing west that I knew was not well guarded. I had secretly explored this wall back during the masquerade. At just the right moment, we quietly ran to the stairway gate, slipped through, and scampered up the stairs to the top of the wall. We went to a spot that I knew to be well hidden but afforded a splendid view of the square in Westminster where the festival was being held. Of course, Edward could request to go anywhere within the palace grounds including the top of this wall, but then we would have been accompanied by at least two guards and four servants. Instead, here sat just my twin and I.

Edward's face shined as he peered down on the celebration. There was music mixed with laughter and colorful banners blowing in the wind. Young girls wore flowers in their hair and small boys galloped on broomstick horses, chasing each other through the crowds. Barkers lured customers to their games of chance that were most likely rigged but no one seemed to mind. In the middle of the square, young folks grabbed hold of the long ribbons and danced around the May pole.

"Your Majesty," I proclaimed with a broad grin. "Welcome to the May

Frederic Fahey

Day Festival."
Edward watched it all with the wonder of an eleven-year-old child.

***

However, the good times were not to last. A few days later, Edward summoned me again.

"Tom, I need you to take my place again." Usually, our meetings started with some pleasant conversation, but this time Edward asked for my help right up front. Naturally, I agreed, but his mood made me uneasy.

"The tenor of the Council meetings is changing," Edward spouted, his words spewing forth. "There is increasing tension between Somerset and other members of the Council." He kept rubbing an open sore on the back of his hand. I noticed his fingernails had been gnawed to the quick. "There are clearly those that are actively confronting my uncle. I need your help in understanding who is behind this dissension." We exchanged clothes, and I was led to the meeting room. As I took my seat, my left leg wouldn't stop twitching.

The issues of discussion of the Council hadn't changed. They were still centered on finances and the endless skirmishes with Scotland. There were also troubles in the western counties regarding some reluctance to accept the new Book of Common Prayer. But Edward's assessment was correct. Something was different. What had changed over the last few months was the intensity of the disagreements with Somerset's handling of the matters. The members didn't nod with assent, as I had seen earlier. Now the questions and criticism were more focused and aimed squarely at Somerset.

"We need to spend more time putting gold in the coffers and less time extracting it," one Council member noted.

"It was easier when King Henry was with us. The lords just paid their tributes with less question and delay. His Majesty is still young and does not demand the same level of loyalty. That is to be expected," another added, nodding to me briefly in an effort to reduce the slight. "As a result, Lord Somerset, as Lord Protector, should act forcefully on His Majesty's behalf to demand timely payment or there should be consequences!"

"With the Scots," a third noted, "we cannot outright win, and we do

The Scoundrel's Son

not lose. We just keep fighting and spending money. We have proposed direct engagements to end these hostilities, both military and diplomatic. But Lord Somerset chooses neither and so we wallow in the murk of his indecision."

"Gentlemen, we need to continue to show strength in Scotland or it will unravel into outright war," Somerset responded.

"Then show some strength for goodness' sakes!" a member hollered.

"I take your point, Lord Somerset," Warwick calmly noted. "I have fought as part of your forces these past few years. But I am afraid, in recent months, your lack of direction has left us in a muddle. We need to commit to a plan regarding the Scots that will be effective and won't drain our treasury." Warwick's criticism of Somerset was more sharply directed than before. In the past, his comments were more general and not so targeted. I struggled to get a bearing on Warwick. On one hand, his tone gave the impression of being supportive of Somerset while continuing with his stinging criticism.

I offered little to the discussion, responding occasionally with a nod or such royal proclamations as "I see" or "Interesting." But I listened intently and tried to observe every nuance. As was typical, the meeting ended with no real resolution, merely the opportunity to continue the discourse another day. As I expected, Somerset wanted to walk with me after the meeting. He was clearly agitated by how things had gone.

"Your Majesty can see that they do not appreciate all I have done to protect the realm," he started. "Ever since Sudeley's death, the attention has been directed toward me. Warwick is particularly cunning in his attacks. He has been as much a part of our endeavors in Scotland as anyone, and yet he places all the shortcomings at my feet." We stopped walking again as he grabbed my arm.

"We must do all we can to protect ourselves. They are all against us. They will try to take us down!"

"Yes, Uncle," was my only response.

Back in the king's quarters, Edward was eager to hear my impressions. I reviewed with him my observations. I told him that I concurred with his assessment of the intensity of the Council's criticism.

"What do you think of Lord Warwick?" I asked.

Edward's eyes narrowed. "Warwick has always been a close ally of my uncle, but now I don't know what to make of him, to be honest."

"Neither do I," I responded truthfully.

"We need to be cautious moving forward. There may be members of the Council that are not to be trusted," Edward added.

As was often the case, when the king said "we," it was not clear to whom he was referring. Did he mean himself? Everyone? He and I? He and Somerset?

"I still say you need to keep an eye on Somerset as well."

"I am not concerned about Somerset," Edward shot back. "He knows how to handle the Council and has my best interest at heart. I have already told you this!"

"But even you have noted the growing contention within the Council. And Somerset is not handling it well. My concern is where this might lead." Edward's hand shot up.

"Enough about Somerset!" Edward had never snapped at me before. Although he had asked me for my sense of things, he was not pleased with what I had said regarding Somerset. He was not accustomed to others disagreeing with him. He reminded me of a house fly in the way he was rubbing his hands. His response was to declare the visit over.

***

A couple of days later, we were back at the barn. Robert was inside refining the firing mechanism. As we sat on the log, Lord Miles reflected on what I had just shared with him regarding the recent discussions of the Council.

"I can understand your confusion with Warwick. He is very skilled in the art of persuasion. He will lead you to believe he is in your camp while all the while plotting against you. Somerset might be right to be concerned." Then he asked a question which surprised me.

"Right now, which members of the Council would Somerset consider to be his allies?" I thought about that for a moment.

"Honestly, I can't see he has any," I answered.

"Hmm," Lord Miles shook his head slightly. "In my experience, a man without allies is a desperate man. And desperate men often make bad decisions."

Chapter 13

Summer had begun to show its sunny face. The air was warmer, and the days longer. I was working later at the shop those days as the extended daylight provided me an opportunity to work on my own projects once the shop had closed and not have to walk home in the dark. On this day, I decided to walk through the square, as I liked seeing all the people having a good time. Soon the summer's heat would make being outside in the evening almost a necessity, but on this evening, the air was still pleasant, and neighbors were enjoying the opportunity to visit with each other.

"Tom!" I looked to see who had called. There was Jem Riley along with Willy and Ben standing under the huge oak tree in the center of the square.

I strolled over to the group. "Hi. What is goin' on?"

"We're goin' on a little adventure. Care to join us?"

"What sort of adventure?"

"Let's go for a little walk."

We walked together, not saying much, for almost a mile until we found ourselves outside a large house. The owner was clearly well off, not nobility, but it was a very nice house.

"I walked by this house a couple of times this week," Jem said. "No one's home. The family's gone to the country before it gets too hot. That's what I'm thinking."

"I wish I could go to the country!" Willy announced.

"Shh!" Jem pleaded for silence. "Listen to me! We're goin' inside. We don't take anything. We are not thieves! We'll just move things around a bit. It'll give the family a bit of a spook when they come home. Tom, do you think you can find a way in? I remember when we was small, you were good at squeezin' into places."

Frederic Fahey

I gave the house a quick look. It had a lot of windows. I figured that not all of them were as secure as they should be.

"Probably," I responded.

"Wonderful! Once inside, find your way to the door in the back and let us in." Jem had not even questioned whether I would choose to be involved. This adventure did not seem quite right to me, but it also seemed harmless enough. We would only be moving a few objects around, mostly for the thrill of being where we shouldn't be. Over the past few months, I had been spending a lot of time working in the shop and going to the palace. I thought it might be fun to be with some other boys of the parish as well as exciting to engage in some harmless mischief.

"All right," I said. "Meet me at the backdoor in five minutes."

I started to slink to the dark side of the house. By this time, dusk had started to set in, so there were plenty of shadowy places to conceal myself. I went around to the backdoor. I might as well check the easiest route first, but it was locked and secure. Next, I checked the first-floor windows. I did not want to climb if it wasn't necessary. The third window I checked had a loose latch. I did a little jiggling, and it slid open. Looking around, I found a stick that could hold the window open as I slipped through. Even though the curtains were closed on most of the windows, there was still enough light outside to see my way around.

I went to the back door and unlocked it. By that time, Jem and the boys were waiting for me. I cracked the door and beckoned them. They came quickly, and I let them into the house. I closed the door quietly behind them.

"Good job, Tom!" Jem said, patting me on the shoulder. "We're just here to take a look and to move some things around."

"Let's be quick about it," I suggested. "I seen some lamps lit in nearby houses, so let's get out before someone notices we're here."

Jem agreed. "Quarter of an hour and we're done." The four of us scattered about the house.

I went to what seemed to be the bedroom of the master and mistress of the house. I moved some things from the top of a chest of drawers to a small table beside the bed. On the table was a hairpin with an arrangement of jewels in the form of a star. I had seen several such pins while working in the shop, and this one was quite splendid. I moved it from the table to a

The Scoundrel's Son

mantle above the fireplace. As instructed, I then went to the backdoor where Ben was already waiting.

"Where's everybody?" he tried to say but his breath caught in his throat.

Jem quickly followed, but Willy did not seem to have as good a sense of time as the rest of us.

"Willy! Willy!" Jem let out a loud whisper. Finally, we heard the clip clop of Willy's oversized shoes.

"Sorry!" he apologized. "I got a bit lost." Jem shook his head.

"Go," I said. "I'll lock the door and meet you back at the oak tree in the square."

"Very good!" Jem seemed to be impressed with my approach and attention to detail. I let everyone out, and they quickly scooted across to a dark corner behind the house next door. I locked the door and snuck out the same window I had entered, removing the stick once I was outside. I slowly and quietly closed the window. It would still be unlatched but maybe no one would notice. As I headed back to the square, I felt a sense of exhilaration. It had been fun to partake in a bit of boyish naughtiness, and I liked feeling like one of a gang of chums. By the time I arrived at the oak tree, darkness had fallen.

***

That spring and early summer, I called on Jane at Norwich Place several times before she headed to Bradgate. At first, it was under the pretense of delivering messages to the Marquess from Lord Miles. Once my face was familiar to the staff at Norwich Place, I sometimes came unannounced. By then, no one questioned my presence. Our visits were always pleasant but brief. To an outside observer's eyes, Lady Jane was expressing proper gratitude to a messenger who was a ward of His Majesty. But to me, our time together was much more. I tried to not come so often that it would be considered improper, but I counted the days until I would again be blessed with Jane's sweet smile.

Jane seemed to also enjoy these visits. Once, she said, "I love studying and corresponding, as you know. However, our times together are a welcomed break." Her face lit as she regarded me. "Thank you, Tom, for your

Frederic Fahey

friendship."

Edward invited me to the palace for a last visit before leaving London for the country. I looked over the chess board and spotted an opportunity for a rare victory.

"Check!" I announced as I proudly moved my bishop into position. I could tell immediately from Edward's giddy chuckle that I had missed something.

"Say goodbye to His Eminence!" he responded as he took my bishop with his knight, leaving me with no further means of attack. I conceded.

"I was sure I had you this time! I can't believe you were able to protect your king with merely a knight and a pawn!"

"Sometimes, that is all it takes," Edward responded with a satisfied smile.

"My cousin tells me how much she enjoys your visits to Norwich Place," Edward said.

I froze a bit as his statement surprised me. I had not told Edward of my visits. "I'm pleased to hear that she finds them enjoyable. She is certainly quite pleasant company." I was not sure where this conversation was heading.

"How did these get togethers come about?"

I let my breath out slowly. It had not been my intention to keep our visits a secret from Edward. I just did not want to bother him with the matter. Or at least, that is what I had been telling myself. But then I followed this up with a slight untruth that I did not, at least at that time, characterize as a lie. I told him the same tale that Lord Miles had told the Marquess and the Lady, that he and I had other business, and Lord Miles asked if I would mind if we stopped by Norwich Place on the way. I didn't feel that Edward was as easily fooled. He asked how often I had been to Norwich Place, and I responded truthfully only on a handful of occasions.

"What is the intent of your visits?" he asked.

I wanted to ask him the intent of his question, but I chose to answer innocently. "To spend time with a good friend."

"You realize that you are a commoner, and that Lady Jane is of the royal family, correct?"

His question stunned me. Of course, I realized this, but did that limit with whom I could be friends? With whom I could visit? Wasn't I a friend

The Scoundrel's Son

of His Majesty the King of England for goodness' sake? Hadn't I spent many pleasant times with Jane in this very chamber?

"Tom, it is one thing for you and Jane to visit with me, here at the palace," he started to explain. "But it is quite another thing when a boy and a girl meet in the garden of her parents' house, don't you think?"

Did Edward think my intent was to court Lady Jane? Was that, in fact, my intent? Now my head was swimming.

"The hand of a young lady of the royal family is of considerable value. Some have even suggested that Jane and I should be betrothed."

I knew that in the royal court marriage was often arranged for political advantage. For instance, it had been suggested that Edward be engaged to his other cousin, Mary of Scotland, only six years old at the time, to avoid the possibility of her betrothal to the Dauphin of France. Still, the notion of Jane's hand in marriage as a commodity bothered me.

"Edward, I certainly meant Jane no disrespect. When I first visited Norwich Place, I had the sense that she was quite lonely. And so, I thought an occasional visit would brighten her spirit. I consider Jane a good friend, and, as such, I care about her wellbeing."

"You are my closest friend, Tom. I love you like a brother. I know you care for my cousin. But there are things that you still do not understand regarding the lives of the royal family. In some ways, things are even more complicated for the young ladies such as Jane and my sisters than they are for me as king.

"I forgive you for your innocence. But I forbid you to see Jane at any time outside of my presence."

"I understand," I said. I didn't apologize. As crazy as it sounds, I had come to consider Edward as an equal even if he was King of England. He had never spoken to me like I was a child before. I knew I did not understand many aspects of his and Jane's lives. I hardly understood my own life. My relationships were based on the people with whom I wanted to spend time and whose presence in my life made me feel good, not on political expedience or what advantage they could afford me. At that age and even today, that is how I feel.

Our goodbyes that day were a bit reserved, and since I would not see Edward again until September, it put a damper over the entire summer. I did decide to stop seeing Jane at Norwich Place, more out of my concern

Frederic Fahey

for her than to follow Edward's command. I did not want to cause her any trouble or show her disrespect. I also gave some thought to what my feelings towards Jane truly were. At not quite twelve years old, I was not sure I understood what love was, but I knew my feelings for Jane were different. I thought of her often and could barely wait to see her again. That much I knew.

Chapter 14

The time finally came that summer for someone to fire the musket while holding it in their hands. Until this time, it had only been fired while on the stand using a wick. Lord Miles had solved the lighting issue by suggesting that a small trail of explosive powder be laid along a groove leading from where the flint struck the iron to a small hole in the barrel. It was much easier to light the powder trail consistently than the wick. In tests, the powder trail lit more than nine times out of ten.

Robert and I stood and watched from a fair distance while Lord Miles loaded the musket, poured powder along the groove, and set the flint in its firing position. He placed the back end against his shoulder and aimed the musket at the target. He counted out loud to three and then engaged the flint assembly with a small lever. The flint struck the iron, a spark lit the powder trail, and the musket fired. Success!

"Amazing!" Lord Miles proclaimed as Robert and I rushed to join him. "As with the crossbow, there is a kick against the shoulder upon firing. However, if one is prepared for it, I believe it is manageable." He then smiled and said, "Robert, I think we have a new kind of weapon! Things may never be the same."

As the time to demonstrate the musket for the Earl approached, Lord Miles instructed me on how to load, aim and fire the musket. On my first firing, I ended on the ground on my back.

"I warned you about the kick!" Lord Miles laughed. After several firings, my method improved, and, on rare occasions, the ball even struck the target.

Finally, the time for the demonstration came. The Earl and several of his men arrived at the barn bright and early. Fortunately, it was a sunny day so we would not have to worry about the powder getting wet. I had set up the target and stepped off the distance beforehand. I made it long enough to seem reasonable in battle but not so long that I would have no chance of hitting the target. At this distance, I thought I could hit it at least half the time. I placed a table near the firing spot with the musket, the rammer, and the firing materials.

Robert handed the musket to the Earl, who moved it from hand to hand to assess its weight and the ease with which it could be handled. Robert described the design, how the flint assembly avoided the necessity of lighting a match, and the way it had to be set before firing. The Earl handed me the musket.

"Are we ready?" I asked Robert. He nodded and asked our visitors to stand back. I loaded the musket and aimed carefully as I set the flint. It seemed that I could hear everyone holding their breath. I counted to three, took a deep breath myself, and pulled the lever. The musket fired and I controlled the kick. The Earl and his company just stood for a moment, seemingly in awe. We all hurried to the target. On this fortunate day, the ball had struck the target. God was smiling on me!

"Incredible!" the Earl proclaimed with a burst of anxious laughter. He took the musket from my hands and examined it. There was a little blackness around the powder hole, but, other than that, the musket was unscathed. "I only have three questions. Can you train my men to fire the weapon?"

"Certainly," I responded.

"How many can you make? And how soon?" Those questions sent Robert's hand running through his bushy, white hair.

Robert agreed to provide the Earl with thirty muskets by the spring. If the Earl was pleased with the results, an additional thirty would be delivered by the following autumn. The next week, Robert and I met with a talented bladesmith who had constructed many a sword for the Earl. Robert described the metal components of the musket to him. The bladesmith indicated that he could certainly help in their construction, but that Robert would need to assemble and test the mechanics. This was agreeable to Robert. It would be up to me to fashion the wooden components. One day I pondered as I held one of the finished muskets in my hands.

"Robert, are you concerned with how these weapons may be used?" I

The Scoundrel's Son

asked. Robert stopped what he was doing, pushed his spectacles up his nose and gave me a good look.

"I am not. Over the years, I have been asked on many occasions to make weapons. My choice is those jobs I accept and those that I do not. I wholeheartedly trust the Earl, and so I do the work. It is then up to him to use the weapons wisely."

A few weeks later, I brought Robert a drawing of an idea I had.

"What do we have here?" He closely examined my drawing.

"I was thinking of a smaller version of the musket, what I refer to as a 'hand musket,' one that could be carried more easily and fired with one hand." The drawing showed that the hand musket was about a foot long with a back end designed to fit the hand rather than to brace against the shoulder. Otherwise, the design was very similar to the larger musket. The only other modification was a small guard about the lever to avoid it from being pulled accidentally.

"I see this as more of a personal item rather than one used by a soldier," I added.

"How would it be held during firing?"

"Like this." I extended my arm and pointed my finger at an imaginary target across the room. Robert pondered for an instant as he further examined my drawing.

"It could work. It definitely could work," he finally announced. Then he looked at me very seriously. "However, I fear it would be very dangerous if every man carried such a weapon."

***

As summer was coming to an end, Jem and the boys convinced me to partake in one last adventure. Soon families would be returning to the city from the country. Jem had found a house not too far from Offal Court. This would be my fourth adventure of the summer. We now had the plan worked out quite well. As usual, I would find a way to enter, and then let the others in by a door that was reasonably well hidden. We would go to different parts of the house and move things around. After about a quarter of an hour, we would meet at a prearranged spot and leave the house as secretly as we had entered.

Frederic Fahey

In midsummer, not only was the chosen house empty but the neighboring houses were as well. But as summer was coming to an end, I could tell that some folks had returned by the lamps lit in their houses. We had only been in the house for a few minutes when I noticed a neighbor was approaching the front door.

"We have visitors!" I tried to speak in my loudest whisper.

"Don't panic!" Jem instructed. "Quietly make your way to the meeting spot." Everyone followed Jem's command. We had discussed on several occasions what to do if such an interruption might occur.

"Hello?" There was a knock on the door. "Anyone in there?"

I peered out the back door and saw no one in the back alley. I quietly opened the door and the others left quickly. I locked the door behind them.

"Samantha? Clement? Are you here?" The neighbor had entered the house. Perhaps he had a key of his own. I held my breath as he practically walked right past me hiding in a corner.

I waited anxiously for my opportunity to tip toe to the window I had entered by. I then stood by until the neighbor had moved deeper into the house and quietly climbed through the window and dropped to the alley below.

Dusk was just falling, so I easily made my way back to the square. My heart was just starting to quiet when I got there. I arrived at the oak tree not only to see the boys, but Margy and Aly had joined them. Some young men were just starting to build a fire. The crackle of the dry firewood and the smell of burning leaves filled the brisk, late summer air.

"Well, that was close!" Jem proclaimed.

"Closer than you think!" I added. "The neighbor, he entered the house before I could leave. But I got out just fine."

"Tom," Aly perked up. "We never raced like we talked about."

"What race?" Jem asked.

"Tom thinks he's faster than me, he does."

"Nah, Aly's always been the fastest," Margy chimed in. "And still is!"

"I don't know," Ben commented. "I seen Tom move. Fast as a frightened hare, he is. I think he'd win!"

"Well, only one way to find out!" Jem announced. He pointed across the square. "Down to the horse trough and back. First one back and touches the tree is the fastest." This section of the square was not too full of people, so we could probably run the route without bumping into anyone.

"What ya say, Tom?" Aly asked with a wide grin. "You ready to be beat?"

"All right! Let's run!"

We each prepared for the big race in our own way. I moved around a little, trying to loosen my limbs, while Aly jumped about like a skittish fawn. She removed something from her hair and handed it to Margy.

"When I count three, the race begins," Jem stated. "One...Two...Thr..."

Jem hadn't even finished saying "Three" and Aly was running, so I was a bit behind right from the start. Aly had the long legs of a spry filly while I was a bit clumsier in my gait. As we reached the trough, others in the square had noticed the race. Everyone loves a friendly competition. My legs were perhaps a little stronger, and so, by the time we made the turn, we were close to even.

Now folks in the square were starting to cheer. "Run, Aly!" I heard Margy scream.

I had a small lead as we approached the tree. I was starting to feel confident when Aly gave out a slight grunt and gained some speed in the last instant. It was as if she had given that filly inside her an extra kick in the ribs. We were now all but even as Aly dove for the tree, touching it a fraction of a second ahead of me.

Cheers and hooting engulfed the square, particularly among all the women and young girls. On the other hand, the boys, including Willy and Ben, looked stunned. Jem was giving Aly a huge hug, lifting her off the ground. Amidst the celebration, he gave me a subtle wink as if to say that he knew I had let Aly win, which was not the case at all. I had every intention of winning.

"Wonderful race, Tom!" Aly said. "Closest I ever had."

"Here, Aly," Margy said as she handed something to her. Aly thanked her and placed the pin in her hair. I recognized it immediately. It was the hairpin with the jewels shaped like a star that I had moved from the table to the mantle on my first adventure with Jem and the boys.

I quickly said goodbye and left. I ate quietly and retired to my bed to ponder the evening's events. Father Christian could tell that something was wrong and asked if I was all right. I indicated that I was only tired after several long working days.

I figured that Jem must have stolen the pin and given it to Aly. Thoughts of what I should do, what I didn't do, and what I did do were bouncing around my head. How could I have been so foolish to accept Jem's adventures as innocent fun? Why did I not see that he was a thief all along? Were Ben and Willy stealing things as well? Did Aly know the pin was stolen? Was I blinded to the thievery by my own desire to have friends in my own parish, to be one of the boys? Of all the times I had warned Edward to be careful, it hurt that I had been so reckless in my own life.

My father had used me to lie and beg for him when I was young. I strove these past few years to leave that behind me. However, after all I had done to set things right in my life, it seemed I still was the scoundrel's son. I was helping Jem get into other people's houses so that he could rob them. Was I a troublemaker as Somerset had said? This was not what I wanted for myself, and I certainly was going to let Jem know it. This was my life, and I was not going to throw it away because I was afraid of Jem Riley. And what would I say to Aly?

A few evenings later, I saw Jem and the boys standing by the oak tree in the square. I decided now was the time.

"Jem, Can we talk?"

"Of course. Talk."

"Just you and me."

He looked at Ben and Willy and shook his head. "Right here's fine. What's on your mind, Tom?"

I paused for a moment and thought of how to begin.

"You lied to me, Jem," I started. "You were stealing from those houses all along. You're a thief and a liar."

Jem let out a smirk. "And what of it?"

"I'm not a thief. I don't steal from folks. I won't be part of your games anymore." Ben and Willy avoided looking at me as they stood without even an utterance. I could not tell if they were also part of the thievery, or if they were just in fear of Jem.

"You are a part of it, Tom," Jem said as he stomped forward. I stood my ground. I was a good inch or two shorter than Jem, but I was determined to make my stand.

"No, I'm not!" At this point, Jem was right in my face. I did not step

The Scoundrel's Son

back. I gritted my teeth and prepared for whatever Jem might have for me. He gave me a shove, which I met with a punch right in his belly. He swung wildly, just missing my head, but I did not miss punching him right in the face. Jem fell to the ground, blood gushing from his nose.

"No, I'm not!" I repeated. Jem lay on the ground holding his bleeding nose. I looked directly at Ben and Willy, who were stunned by what they had just witnessed. They did not come to Jem's aid. They did not want any part of me. I continued on my way.

"This is not over, Tom!" Jem yelled as I walked away.

"It is for me!" I proclaimed. I may not have said it loudly enough for Jem and the boys to hear, but the statement was mostly meant for myself.

Early the next morning before heading to the shop, I went to Aly's home. I knocked on the door and Izzy answered. I asked if I could speak to Aly.

"She's feeding the boys. Come in! Come in!" And so, I entered. Aly was bouncing from boy to boy, trying to settle them down and get them to eat their porridge.

"Hi, Tom! What brings you by?" Aly said as she had one of the boys by the scruff of the shirt.

"Can we talk? Perhaps go for a walk?"

Izzy could tell by my demeanor that I was serious about something. She nodded to Aly. "Go. I can handle these rascals!" She turned to the boys. "Can't I?" The boys all laughed and nodded in response. "Just don't be too long."

Aly wiped her hands on a rag and met me at the door. We went outside and started to walk down the lane.

"This about Jem? I heard you two had a bit of a tussle."

"It is," I answered. "Do you know about our adventures? How we have been going into people's houses just to move things around and give the people a bit of a scare?"

"I heard about it, yah," she nodded. "Sounds a little exciting!"

"That's what I thought." Then I changed the subject. "That pin in your hair the other night, the one with the star. Where did you get it?"

"Jem gave it to me. Why?"

"Jem stole it from one of the houses we entered, he did."

Aly stopped walking and looked at me in disbelief. She reached into her pocket and brought out the pin.

"This one?" she asked.

"Yes. I'm not a thief, Aly. I will not be part of Jem's misdeeds."

Aly gazed upon the pin. "It's the most beautiful thing I ever had. Jem told me it belonged to his aunt. She gave it to him before she died this summer. That's what he said, anyway." She turned to me with a sincere look that told me what she said was indeed the truth. She looked upon the pin again and ran her fingertips over it. The morning sun caught the jewels, and they sparkled upon her face.

"I'm not a thief either. I hope you believe me."

"I do believe you."

She handed me the pin.

"Do you think you can return it?" she asked.

"I'll find a way."

"Good," she said as we turned and headed back to her place. When we reached her door, she gave me a small kiss on the cheek. "Thank you, Tom. You are a good friend," she said as she ran inside.

As I walked to Robert's shop, I reviewed the last few days in my head. I felt I had done the right thing. I had made a silly mistake. But I faced the situation as best I could.

That night after work, I returned to the house of the first adventure. I could tell there were people home. I had placed the hair pin in one of the small cloth bags that Robert had in the shop along with a note that simply said, "I am sorry." I walked quietly to the door, placed the bag on the side of the doorstep, and gave the door a solid rap. I scampered to the shadows of the corner of the neighbor's house. The door opened and a woman looked out. "Hello?" she called. She then noticed the bag and picked it up. She gave one last look and went back inside.

Chapter 15

Summer came to an end, and Edward returned to the city. I was very pleased when his invitation arrived. I was still thinking of our last visit before the summer when he had confronted me regarding seeing Jane at Norwich Place. I wanted to make sure that my actions had not fractured our friendship.

As I entered Edward's chamber, I was thrilled to see that Jane was also there.

"Hi, Tom," she said with a smile. "How was your summer?"

"Very busy!" It certainly had been!

Edward spoke of his travels around the realm. I was fascinated since I had never been outside London. The thought of flowing fields of grain or forests so dense that you could not see through them was beyond belief. But I was mostly intrigued by his descriptions of the sea.

"So, you cannot see land on the other side?" I said in astonishment.

"No, of course not," Edward responded. He and Jane both were amazed that I had never been to the sea.

Jane spoke of her days at Bradgate, spending time with her sisters, and all the books she had read. She also spoke of a splendid concert she had attended. "I wish that I could play music."

I shared some funny stories. Edward told a fabulous tale of King Arthur. And, of course, there were the fruits and sweets. I must admit that I had dreamed on several occasions of the gingerbread served with a sweet cream topping.

"I have so missed seeing the two of you!" Edward declared. "Tom, can you come next week? I have a favor to ask of you." In the flutter of an eye lid, the corners of his mouth hardened. I knew exactly what he wanted of me.

"Surely," I answered.

"Boys and their secrets!" Jane grinned. "It is probably of worldly importance."

"Jane," Edward popped as his look lightened. "I have two sisters. Girls have their secrets too!"

"I have sisters as well, and Edward is right!" I acknowledged.

"I suppose we do, I must admit," Jane confessed, and we all laughed.

Of course, when I returned the following week, Edward wanted me to take his place again. The Council was already meeting regularly and, according to Edward, the skirmishes in the western counties had been harder to quell than expected. I remembered the Earl mentioning that his services might be needed in the west. I figured that this along with the usual concerns of the dwindling treasury and the never-ending troubles with Scotland had led to further division within the Council. As I changed into Edward's clothes, my heart started to quicken. Would the added tension sharpen the Council's focus on me? Would they look to Edward for his opinion and thereby shine the light on me?

When I arrived, the Council was already assembled. The greetings and pleasantries were curtailed, and the expressions of frustration erupted right at the start without the typical opening discussion of softer issues. My breath quickened as tempers in the room started to immediately rise. I was not wrong in my assessment. Nothing had been resolved since the spring. However, I needed not to be concerned that eyes would be focused on me. Practically all the anger was aimed directly at Somerset.

"We cannot continue to drain the treasury at this pace. Now we have uprisings in the west as well as the north! Something must be done," protested one lord. Others chimed in agreement.

"Gentlemen!" Lord Warwick seemed to be trying to calm the assembly. "Let's hear what Lord Somerset has to say. Sir, please present to us your path forward." As little as I knew of these things, I realized that there was probably no simple path forward. It may appear that Warwick was providing Somerset an opportunity for explanation, but, in fact, he was merely stirring the pot of discontent.

"I assure all of you," answered Somerset, "we are on the right path. This shortfall just before the harvest is to be expected."

The Scoundrel's Son

"We have heard these words from Somerset before, and, yet here we find ourselves with the treasury at its lowest point in many years," Warwick countered.

"You have heard these words before," Somerset countered, "because they are true. Let me remind the Council that I do not make these decisions alone. They are made with the consent of His Majesty and you, his Council."

"We have been part of these decisions, only as much as you felt is required, Lord Somerset." Warwick responded with a snicker. Many of the Council nodded in agreement.

I had witnessed many card games in Offal Court, and, as I have related to you, I have even participated in some. In the game of the royal court, Lord Warwick played his hand smoothly. He would act as if he was asking for calm while, at the same time, continuing to sow dissatisfaction within the Council. He was also a patient man. He assumed his time would come.

"Your Majesty can see what they are doing," Lord Somerset steamed as we strolled back to Edward's quarters. "They are attacking us from every direction. And Warwick is the worst of them. He thinks Your Majesty and I are weak, and our minds are soft, but he will soon see that this is not the case! Your Majesty's safety is my utmost responsibility! We are not without options. They will soon see and might even be surprised by what we can do."

For a while, I had known that Somerset saw enemies around many corners. Now it appeared that his fears were not unfounded. But this did not lead to an enhancement of his resolve and strength, but only to heighten his despair. His efforts were not focused on what actions may improve the hardships facing the kingdom but on his own survival. He seemed to have something in mind perhaps even something drastic, but what it entailed I was not sure.

"Your Majesty, you understand that your wellbeing is my greatest concern, do you not?"

"Yes, Uncle. I am very grateful," I paused to think and then inquired. "What shall we do in response?"

"When the time comes, we will be ready," was all he offered.

After returning, I recounted my impressions to Edward. "The Council is not content, and Warwick is stoking the fire. As hard as Somerset tries to appease them, they don't see things his way. His despair is on the rise. He is a cornered badger; the more desperate, the more ferocious he becomes. I'm concerned he might be planning something drastic. He won't say, but I believe he will do anything to survive.

"Edward, listen to me. As I said before, the line between your uncle's wellbeing and yours are blurred in his mind. He sees them as one. But they are not. I truly believe that there may come a time when Somerset's actions could put you in danger." I took a deep breath before continuing. "He understands how precious your life is to the kingdom. He will use this to his own advantage, not yours. You need to be very careful in the days and weeks ahead."

A silence hung over the chamber. The only sound was the drumming of Edward's fingers as he pondered my remarks. He seemed to be taking my words more seriously than he had in the past. Finally, he sat straight and responded.

"I understand that things are difficult right now," He was now actively scratching the back of his hand. A new sore was beginning to form.

"But I continue to have faith in my uncle. He understands the politics of the royal court better than anyone. We have been through hard times before, and we will weather them together. After my father died and I returned to court, everything was in a muddle. My uncle was there to support my sisters and me. He stepped right in and took command. His strength calmed the concerns of my subjects, nobility and commoners alike. I have faith he can do it again."

"But this is different," I objected.

"It is not different I tell you. Tom, I know you want the best for me. But please believe me when I say that my uncle is most skilled in dealing with the Council. He is my mother's brother and my father's most trusted advisor. He will take care of me."

I was at a loss. Edward could not see what I saw. He could not feel the desperation as I felt it. He wanted me to point the finger at Warwick and others and confirm his own beliefs regarding Somerset's resolve and political skill. But I could not merely appease him in good faith. I needed to sincerely express my concerns for his safety, and I was truly more afraid of Somerset than I was of the others. However, I could not muster the words to convince him, try as I might. I was not able to make him see the

The Scoundrel's Son

danger that I feared might be right around the corner.

"Edward," I finally relented. "I certainly hope you are right. I pray for your safety."

***

A few days later, I saw Aly as I passed through the square. She ran right up to me and gave me a hug. I was very happy to see that our friendship had survived the incident with Jem.

"I heard you returned the pin," she commented. "Thank you!"

"Yes, I did. How'd you hear?" It was always surprising how things like that sometimes just became known. Perhaps a servant in the house spread the word in the parish.

"From Jem. And he's quite angry about it, I'd say!" she shared. "He feels you've put the finger on him by what he calls your foolishness."

"I'm beyond worrying about what Jem thinks," I stated.

"Sure. Me too. I told him to not bother me no more. He wasn't happy about that either, but he's angry at you, mostly. Be careful, Tom! He can be right mean sometimes."

On an evening of the following week, I had just locked up the shop and was starting to walk home when someone punched me in the back of the head and pushed me into the narrow alley beside the shop.

"You're a fool to cross me, Tom Canty!" Jem spouted as he slammed me against a wall. He had taken me by surprise and wrenched my arm behind me. "You think you're better'n me, but you're not! All high and righteous! I saw your eyes glint when we went into them houses. You're just like me and you know it!"

Chapter 16

Between my confrontations with Jem and the happenings at the royal court, I was finding it difficult to sleep. As I lay in bed trying to calm myself, my thoughts continued to race in every direction. Some nights when the weather was on the warmer side, I would go for a walk to try to quiet my mind. I did not follow any particular path. I just went where my feet took me.

On this night, I wandered along the river towards Westminster. I found myself just outside Whitehall a little before midnight. Suddenly, the palace gates burst open and several riders on horseback emerged and rushed by me, heading west. To my astonishment, Edward was one of the riders! Why would he be riding at this late hour? My brief glimpse of Edward's face as he rushed by told me that he was distressed. I also thought I saw Somerset on one of the horses, but I was not sure. They all rode by so quickly.

I peered inside the main gate to find the guards scurrying about in a frantic manner. Something clearly was not right. I ran to where William, the Captain of the Guard, would usually be, and, as luck would have it, there he was.

"Master Thomas, I cannot speak long or say too much." He quickly related that His Majesty had been aroused a short time ago by Somerset and that they had just ridden off on horseback. It was strange that William did not know the reason for the trip. It seemed to have occurred with very short notice. Typically, when Edward left the city, preparations commenced days, if not, weeks in advance.

"Did they say where they were heading?" I asked.

"I overheard the mention of Windsor Castle several times. I am sorry but I must go now." He scribbled a quick note and handed it to me.

The Scoundrel's Son

"If you somehow find your way to Windsor, look for a castle guard by the name of James Coleman and give him this note. We served in battle together, and he is a close friend. He can help you." William clapped me on the shoulder and went to meet with other senior members of the palace guard.

It was then past midnight. I stood stunned. What should I do next? I knew nothing about Windsor Castle beyond that it was known for its strength and that it was not within walking distance. I also knew I had to find my way there. I needed to be sure my twin was all right. I went to the shop and left a note for Robert that I had to attend to an emergency but that my family was fine. I said I would be gone for a few days. I then headed home and packed a few things in a satchel. Although it was very early in the morning, Father Christian rose from his bed when he heard me packing. I told him I needed to get to Windsor straight away. He could tell that the situation was serious and only asked that I explain it to him "in due time." I thanked Father Christian and promised to take care of myself. He arranged for a neighbor with a carriage to take me.

"Where to, Tom?" the neighbor asked. At that moment, I realized I needed help from someone with far more experience in ticklish situations than me.

"To Kent and Hendon Hall," I replied.

"It's a bit of a trip but all right." He shook his reins and we headed for London Bridge. I didn't know how far Kent was or even if Lord Miles would be home. However, I was sure that I wanted him by my side as I headed to Windsor. Dawn was just breaking as we reached Hendon Hall, and, fortunately, Lord Miles was there. I explained to him what little I knew of the situation.

"I agree," Lord Miles reflected. "Something is not right. I am not sure what impact we can have in Windsor, but we won't know unless we go."

Lord Miles informed Lady Edith that he and I were heading to Windsor, and we may not return for several days. We ate a quick breakfast and prepared to leave. One of the stable hands had prepared two horses for us.

"How are you on a horse?" Lord Miles asked. "Can you ride?"

Growing up in the city, I had only been on a horse once and that had been at the fair where the horse walked in a circle for fun. Lord Miles could tell from my stammering that this was new to me.

"This mare is Becky Thatcher. Now we call her Old Becky. She will follow my horse, so all you need to do is hang on. Don't fall off, all right?"

"I will try not to." Once upon the horse, I tried to sit straight in the saddle mimicking how Lord Miles sat on his horse. But once we started to ride, and Old Becky went into a gallop, I hunched over her neck, grabbed handfuls of her mane, and held on as best I could.

And so, our journey began.

It was midmorning when we finally were on the road. Lord Miles told me that we would reach Windsor around noon. He also confirmed my notion that the castle was well fortified. He noted that it may be under attack, and that we would need to be very careful as we approached. I said that we had to get inside and see for ourselves that Edward was all right. Lord Miles questioned how that could happen given that the guards would be most attentive under the circumstances.

"We must find a way," was my only response.

It was just past midday when we arrived at Windsor. Through the trees, we could see the profile of the imposing stone castle with its towers and turrets sitting on the hill. The grand round tower of the keep came into view as we approached the town. Indeed, we found many guards on high alert, but there was no evidence of an attack of any kind. As I looked back on our ride, we had not noticed any unusual activity anywhere along our route.

"Wait in town while I see if I can find James Coleman," I said.

"No," Lord Miles announced. "We go together!" We boarded our horses and asked the attendant to store our belongings until we returned. I again asked Lord Miles to wait while I approached the castle gate figuring that a boy not quite twelve would raise less suspicion than a full-grown man. This time he agreed.

As I neared the gate, the guards went into alert. Before I knew it, I was surrounded by men with lances pointed at me from every direction. I raised my arms and gestured to the note from William clutched in my hand. As much as I was trembling, I still managed to say that I was looking for James Coleman. I was really hoping that this guard could read. It appeared that he could, as he inspected the note and examined me from head to toe. He then pointed to the left and said that Coleman's post for the night was

The Scoundrel's Son

at the king's gate further along the moat. I thanked him and ran back to Lord Miles.

We moved quietly to the king's gate, and Lord Miles waited by a small house across the road. Again, I approached with my hands raised asking for James Coleman. When Coleman identified himself, I handed him my note. I explained I had a companion waiting. He asked me to summon Lord Miles. He searched the two of us very closely. Fortunately, Lord Miles had left his weapons back with the horses. Coleman read the note again as he pondered his next move. I realized that we were either going to be successful, or we were going to spend several days in a guardhouse. Coleman looked us over once more as he rubbed his whiskered chin.

"I know the handwriting. It's from William, sure as I'm standing here. He says you can be trusted. He don't use such words lightly. William and I been through a few scrapes together. He saved my skin more than once." He glanced at the note one last time, folded it and handed it back to me.

"If William trusts you, then me too."

He told us where Edward would likely be within the castle. Although the path he described had several turns, my mind tended to be well suited to handle such details. Once through the gate, the royal quarters were in the building across a large courtyard. The halls of Windsor were darker and felt colder than Whitehall. This place exuded a sense of strength while Whitehall emphasized royal splendor. The corridors were stark and foreboding while Whitehall's were adorned with portraits and drapery. On the other hand, Windsor provided many shadowed corners.

"It seems you have experience sneaking around castles," Lord Miles whispered appreciatively.

We arrived at the corner of two long halls down from the royal chamber that Coleman had described. As I peered down the hall, I was relieved to see Richard outside the chamber with several guards.

As Lord Miles and I started to walk towards the chamber door, we were seized with considerable force from behind by several guards. Richard looked our way when he heard the commotion. As you can imagine, he was quite surprised to see the two of us. He came to us directly and calmed the guards by explaining our close association with His Majesty.

"Is His Majesty all right?" I anxiously asked.

Richard did not answer my question but asked us to wait with several of the guards as he entered the royal chamber. After only a few moments, he reappeared.

"His Majesty will see you. He is very glad that the two of you are here."

Edward sat alone with his head down. When he saw the two of us, he tried to smile but it would not come.

"Tom! Miles! I cannot tell you how happy I am to see the two of you!" His eyes became misty as we hastened to him. I grabbed his hand and Lord Miles squeezed his shoulder.

"What has happened, my friend?" Lord Miles asked. "Are you all right?"

"I am fine, but I am afraid to say I don't really know what is happening," Edward was upset to the point of tears. "Close the door and take a seat, and I will tell you all about it. I need to tell someone." Without hesitation, we did exactly as Edward asked. Once we were settled, he began.

Chapter 17

Last night a little after ten of the clock, I was lying in my bed when I heard some commotion. I was about to call to see if everything was all right when my servant announced that Lord Somerset was at the door.

"At this hour?" I asked, surprised. Before the servant could say a word, my uncle burst into my bedchamber.

"Your Majesty, we need to leave immediately. I have asked your servants to prepare."

"What is happening? Where are we going?" I asked.

"To Windsor Castle, Your Majesty. We must leave right now! I will explain in detail once we arrive. All I will say at this point is that there are some within your Council that wish to take hold of the kingdom and do us harm. Most of the Council will meet us at Windsor, and we will determine how best to protect Your Majesty in the first place and to deal with the usurpers in the second." I was astounded by what I had just heard. Was there an armed rebellion originating from within my own Council underway as we spoke?

"We are in grave danger!" he added and left the room before I could ask a single question. I decided that pressing for answers was only slowing us down, and, if the situation was as dire as my uncle claimed, it would be best to set out for Windsor as soon as we could.

Once I was dressed, some of my belongings gathered, and my group of personal servants prepared and assembled, we went to the stables and mounted our horses. My uncle rode beside me as we headed west just after midnight. I have ridden horses all my life, and I am quite comfortable in the saddle. However, such a long, hard ride in the dark was still a challenge, and I had to pay close attention.

But my mind was in a twirl. Would we encounter danger on the way?

Frederic Fahey

Was it safe to travel on an open road? Did we have enough armed guards to protect us? Were my sisters, Mary and Elizabeth, safe? Was someone riding to warn their households? What would we do once we reached Windsor? Who was behind this rebellion? All these questions scurried inside my head like mice in the walls of an old manor. I was in the dark, both on the road to Windsor under a crescent moon as well as in my understanding of what was happening around me.

We finally arrived at Windsor Castle. Its stone walls appeared dark and cold under the faint moon light. I could understand why my uncle would choose Windsor if we were under attack. Besides the Tower of London, Windsor is the best fortified of all the royal castles. Even with my limited military training, I could see that its position on the hill and the high, stone walls provided solid protection against invaders. However, there was also a bit of sadness whenever I came to Windsor as this is the final resting place of my dear parents who are buried here at St. George's Chapel. I prayed that they would look over me during this dark time.

I expected that there would be many anticipating our arrival, as my uncle would have sent an advance party to prepare for us and to further man the castle. But it seemed the caretakers were surprised by our appearance. Several of them met our party with torches in the courtyard. After a brief conversation, during which one of the servants glanced in my direction and bowed, he hastened inside, and the castle burst into an explosion of activity. My attendants helped me dismount, and I was directed to the grand hall while my bedchamber was being prepared. I sat in my riding attire dusty from the road, waiting for my uncle to come and provide me with the promised further explanation. Finally, he arrived.

"Your Majesty, I must apologize for the abruptness of my actions and the necessity for the late-night ride. Warwick is leading a small contingent within the Council in a rebellion against Your Majesty and the realm, and the threat is imminent. I don't believe that they know how aware I am of their plans, and that is to our profound advantage. I decided it would be best to make our move under the cloak of darkness and to come to Windsor. This is truly the best place for our protection and to prepare to best handle the usurpers. I have alerted the loyal Council members to meet us here first thing tomorrow to discuss our next moves."

At that point, Richard, who had also traveled with us from Whitehall,

The Scoundrel's Son

came and indicated that my bedchamber was ready. My uncle thanked him.

"It is late, Your Majesty, and you have had a vigorous and, I am sure, exhausting ride. I suggest that you change into your sleeping gown and try to get some rest. When the Council arrives tomorrow, we will be quite busy."

My uncle rose, bowed to me, and left the room. My head was still swimming in the currents of so many unanswered questions that I barely knew where to start. By the time I had formulated a reasonable question, he was already gone. He had not waited for me to ask a single thing.

It was almost four of the clock in the early morning by the time I was settled in bed. There was little chance of me sleeping at all. I lay awake trying to make some sense of what was occurring around me. Had Warwick started a rebellion? Or was he planning to start one? Before the incident with my Uncle Thomas, Lord Sudeley, I never once thought any member of my Council would contemplate doing me harm. They all have sworn to God to protect me. But Sudeley had come to my bedchamber with his sword drawn, and he was my uncle! Since then, I have become distrustful of practically everyone. And so, I have come to rely on Somerset even more.

As young as I am, I am not so innocent to not know what anyone will do for power. During my lessons, I had read the stories of the disputes between the houses of York and Lancaster and the wars for the Crown. I had heard about the battle at Bosworth Field where my grandfather, old King Henry, had gloriously defeated King Richard. Richard, the hunchback king, who had the young King Edward, my namesake of about my age, and his younger brother, killed in the Tower so that he could be named king. The very thought of King Richard coming for me in the night kept me wide awake until dawn.

I watched through the window as the autumn sun rose. Finally, Richard and my servants came to prepare me for the day. As you know, my life is orchestrated to the minute, every activity meticulously planned. But on this day, I knew nothing of what was to come. I broke my fast of the night as best I could, but, frankly, all the uncertainty had made me a bit queasy.

I sat all morning and there was no meeting of the Council. I had not heard from my uncle since we had first arrived at Windsor. Now, I was becoming frustrated as well as confused. I am king, I told myself. I need to know if my realm is under attack.

Finally, a little over an hour ago, my uncle came to me.

"Good day, Your Majesty."

At that point, I was beyond the place where niceties of a royal greeting would suffice.

"Uncle, I have sat here all morning. I need to know what is happening. You told me when we left Whitehall that you would answer my questions when we arrived, and then in the morning. Now it is almost noon and here we are!"

"I apologize, Your Majesty. I am doing everything in my power…"

"When is the Council to meet?" I interrupted. He had a troubled look on his face.

"They have yet to arrive, Your Majesty. I am sure they are taking every precaution…"

"How many have arrived as of now?"

"None, Your Majesty. But I am sure they are on their way. These are extraordinary circumstances."

I was stunned. No members of my Council, besides my uncle, had yet arrived! I needed some answers! I chose my next words carefully and spoke sternly.

"Uncle, I am very grateful for your guidance and protection during my entire reign. But I am no longer a nine-year-old boy. I shall turn twelve in mere days. And no matter how young I am, I am still your king. I need to know what is happening and how we plan to address it. I have so many questions. I demand some answers."

"Yes, Your Majesty," my uncle responded in as contrite a tone as I have ever heard from him. He then proceeded to relate to me how he had come to the realization that a rebellion was about to occur. No, we were not currently under attack, at least not to his knowledge. However, he felt, for my safety, it was prudent to be cautious, and so the ride at midnight. He knew for certain that Lord Warwick was behind the rebellion, but, when I pushed him, he could not provide me with any details as to how he knew. He did not know the nature of the rebellion or when it might occur. He had informed other Council members and requested they convene at

The Scoundrel's Son

Windsor immediately. The households of my sisters as well as my cousin Frances, Jane's mother, had been warned.

"Your Majesty, there are details to which I must attend, so I will leave now. It is my honor to serve you," he said as he left my chambers.

Again, I found myself alone trying to process what I had just heard until you arrived a few moments ago. Here I sit befuddled and frustrated until the Council meets which, I suspect, will not happen until tomorrow at the earliest.

***

Lord Miles and I sat in astonished silence as Edward concluded his harrowing tale. His breath hitched making it difficult to understand his last few words. He was frantically scratching the back of his hand.

"Tom and I are relieved to find you safe and sound," Lord Miles started. "You have had a frightening and very exhausting day. We will take our leave as Your Majesty needs to rest. As impossible as it sounds, try to clear your mind in order to get some proper sleep. You will need all your wits for what lies ahead. We will return tomorrow to make sure all is good. Of course, we will be close by if you should need us."

"I cannot express how grateful I am for the two of you, my most cherished friends. I feel safer just knowing you are near. God bless you!"

We left the castle and took some lodgings at a nearby inn. We had not eaten since our breakfast at Hendon Hall and so we decided on an early supper. I asked Lord Miles if he thought Edward was safe.

"I believe he is safe for the evening. I have seen no evidence of an imminent attack, either on the road or around the castle. I can often feel it in the air when a battle is near," he said, taking a sip from his mug of ale. "As we were leaving, I told Coleman where we would stay and asked that he send word if there were a disturbance at the castle. Let's follow my advice for His Majesty and do our best to get some solid sleep so that we will be ready for tomorrow." After eating, we retired to the room that we were to share. It occurred to me that I had not slept in almost two days. My body might have still been in midair as I was falling into the bed when a deep slumber took a hold of me.

Chapter 18

When I awoke the next morning, the sun was already high in the sky. I looked around the room and did not see Lord Miles. I splashed water on my face and was starting to dress when he entered the room.

"Good morning, Tom. You were still fast asleep when I arose so I decided to take a quick ride around the area to see if I could find any sign of a rebellion. I found nothing. I spoke to several folks along the way to see if they had seen or heard anything. Nothing as far as I can tell." When I thought of it, I had not seen anything unusual either besides Edward's group riding out from Whitehall.

We visited Edward that afternoon as promised. He seemed to be in better spirits, having slept a bit and eaten a good meal by his own account, but still no members of the Council had arrived.

"I should return to London," Edward shared. "But how? Will my servants and guards travel with me without my uncle's consent? Probably not. I am a prisoner in my own castle," he said sadly.

However, there was news on the third day. Archbishop Cranmer arrived with a small group and requested a meeting with both Somerset and Edward. According to Edward, the archbishop had come as a messenger from the Council, who were very concerned with Somerset's actions, particularly with regards to Edward's safety. The Council wished that the situation be resolved without violence and that His Majesty be returned to London. Somerset was given twenty-four hours to submit. A rider would remain to bring his decision back to the Council.

"My uncle asked if these were the biddings of the Council or of the Earl of Warwick," Edward continued. "The archbishop is my godfather, as you know. He reported that these were the unanimous demands of the entire Council, and that no rebellion was imminent. This revelation was a

The Scoundrel's Son

total surprise to me! Even after all this, I was still inclined to take my uncle at his word."

As Edward related to us, when Somerset asked whether he would be brought to trial and who would determine his fate, the archbishop reported that the manner of how his case would be handled would be decided purely by His Majesty the King.

"I was astounded that my uncle's fate would be placed in my hands," Edward continued. "However, I could see that my uncle was greatly relieved by this response. My uncle answered that he was grateful that the Council had sent such a trustworthy messenger as the archbishop and that he would send his decision by noon of the following day. He told my godfather that he wanted the Council to know that his actions were guided solely by his commitment to my wellbeing and the protection of the realm.

"My godfather rode with his group back to London to report to the Council and await my uncle's decision. This is how things stand now."

As he concluded, Edward sat pensively with his head in his hands. I could tell that the day's news had left him still confused. I suspected that he was relieved to hear that a rebellion was not at hand. However, he was left with the notion that he had been deceived by his own uncle, who had essentially taken Edward hostage and used him as a pawn in the chess game of power. And, surprisingly, the Council had placed Somerset's fate in Edward's hands.

"I must say," Lord Miles started the conversation, "that was a lot for Your Majesty to chew."

"Honestly, Miles, I am still at a loss. I trust my godfather's word with all my heart. If he says there is no uprising, then I truly believe this is fact. I look forward to hearing from my uncle as to what his decision will be.

"Thank you again for being here in my time of need. The two of you are truly my good friends."

On our way back to the inn, Lord Miles wondered, "Will the Council really put the responsibility in His Majesty's hands? You have a better sense of the Council than I do"

After giving it some thought, I responded. "I think they will at least provide Edward with the appearance that he is making the decision. However, what the Council wants will be presented to him on a well-garnished plate."

Frederic Fahey

"Time will tell, I suppose," Lord Miles said as we reached the inn.

The next morning, Coleman sent word that Somerset had submitted to the Council's demands, and His Majesty was preparing to ride to Richmond, a royal estate outside of London. As a result, Lord Miles and I decided it was time to return home. In my haste to leave for Windsor, I had brought no money for lodgings and food, and so I apologized to Lord Miles.

"Don't be silly! It is my privilege to pay," Lord Miles responded. "Thank you, Tom, for alerting me to the situation. I would have been beside myself if ill had befallen my little friend, and I was not able to lend a hand." We rode back to London and said our goodbyes outside Father Christian's house. We agreed to go to Edward as soon as we were summoned, or if we heard that he might be in danger. We shook hands and Lord Miles rode back to Kent.

The next day, I went to Norwich Place. I had promised Edward not to visit Jane without his presence, but I hoped he would understand under the circumstances.

"I am so relieved!" Jane gushed as she brought her hand to her breast after I gave her a brief version of the happenings of the past few days. "My parents and I were beside ourselves with concern for His Majesty. Lord Somerset had alerted my parents that he and Edward had ridden to Windsor, but we had no further details. Thank you, Tom, for bringing such good news."

She reached out and took my hand. I smiled and tried to hide my blush.

"I have no doubt that he was pleased that you and Lord Hendon were there to support him."

A few days later, I received an invitation from Edward, and so Lord Miles and I rode to Richmond. At the castle gate, we showed our invitation and were escorted to Edward's chambers. He greeted us warmly and shared what had transpired since we last saw him at Windsor.

After their meeting with the archbishop, he and Somerset did not meet again while in Windsor. When the archbishop returned the following morning, Edward realized that Somerset had decided to submit to the Council's demands. The archbishop met with Edward in private at which time he presented him with a letter from the Council stating how happy

The Scoundrel's Son

they were that the situation had been resolved peacefully and that at no time did any member of the Council intend to initiate a rebellion against the Crown. The Council also requested that he come to Richmond to meet with them.

Edward rode to Richmond the next day, and once he was settled, he and the Council met with Lord Warwick speaking on their behalf. Warwick informed Edward that Somerset had been arrested and was being held in the Tower of London. He had been relieved of his responsibilities as Lord Protector and Governor of His Majesty's person.

"Has a new Lord Protector been named?" Edward asked.

"No, Your Majesty. The Council does not see the need for a Lord Protector. Your Majesty will be twelve years old in the next few days. It is our intention that the realm be ruled by the Council as a whole in full partnership with Your Majesty." If this were true, it would be in stark contrast to how Somerset had ruled, only looking to the Council for assent and never looking to Edward for anything.

"Your Majesty, I cannot begin to express my relief and happiness in the peaceful resolution of these events," Lord Miles said. "Your Majesty knows that I would have given my life for you."

"Yes, I know this is true," Edward said with a grateful look in his eye.

Edward turned to me and started to say something but then stopped in midsentence.

"Miles, would you mind if Tom and I had a few words in private?"

Lord Miles nodded, excused himself graciously, and left the chamber.

"Tom," Edward started, "I must apologize for not taking your warnings regarding my uncle more seriously. You saw something coming and tried to alert me. I should have been more on guard. I should…"

"No apologies are needed," I interrupted. "All that matters is that you are safe."

He then gave me a huge smile. "Oh, by the way, happy birthday to us!" The fact that this day happened to be our twelfth birthday had totally slipped my mind.

"Happy birthday to us indeed!" I responded. The two of us then exploded into a solid hearty laugh, one that was much needed. Edward was safe and we were together.

Over the next several weeks, I spent many long afternoons with

Edward as he kept me abreast of the proceedings of the Council. It was the Council's recommendation that Lord Somerset be charged with twelve counts including ambition, vainglory, entering into rash wars, enriching himself from the royal treasury, following his own opinion, and doing all by his own authority. After much discussion, Edward agreed to move forward with a trial but with the stipulation that his uncle's life be spared, given his years of service to both him and his father. In the end, his uncle confessed to all charges, and he was confined to the Tower indefinitely.

No Lord Protector was named. The Council conducted their meetings more openly and with broader discussions. Lord Warwick presided over these meetings but did not seem to overly direct the discussions, at least not early on. Edward's opinion was sought in all matters.

"I feel at last I am king, not just a student observing from the side," Edward told me.

It would be a while before he again would ask me to impersonate him. At first, I was relieved, but soon I realized that I enjoyed my unique view of the workings of the realm. However, I knew there would come a time when he would again ask me to take his place. I then would provide my twin with my counsel, protection, and all that I could do to soothe his spirit. I vowed that when that time came, I would be ready and able. I did not know at that time how difficult it would be to keep that vow.

Part II

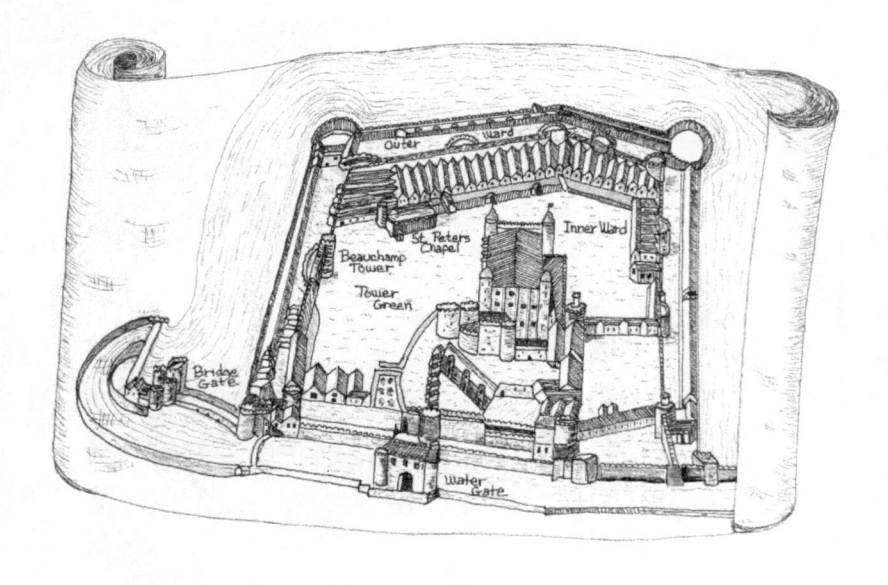

I rolled out a large piece of paper on which I had drawn
the interior of the Tower grounds.

Chapter 19

It was about three years hence, just after our fifteenth birthday, when things started to take a dark turn.

In the meantime, my life had continued without much incident besides the usual pains of growing. For a while, my bones were growing faster than my muscles could handle. As a result, I was about as gangly and awkward as a newborn colt. Fortunately, that stage had finally passed at least to some extent. I continued to live with Father Christian and work for Robert in the shop. In my estimation, my skills were improving in both metal and woodworking. Of course, Robert reminded me almost daily that there was still much to learn.

I recently had a wonderful visit with my mother.

"Always a blessing to see you, my boy. Your smile lights my heart, it does," she beamed with her usual exuberance. She let me know that my sisters were doing well. Nan had married a young man named Charles, the blacksmith of the parish. He was a good and hard-working man, and very well respected. Bet was keeping her options open but recently had been seeing the baker's son, John. Mother and I thought it was only a matter of time before he worked up the courage and asked her to marry him.

"Be good to have a baker in the family, wouldn't it?" Mother grinned.

The politics of the royal court had undergone considerable changes. Lord Warwick, who had been named the Duke of Northumberland, was now the Lord President of Edward's Council. Only occasionally, when Edward felt overwhelmed by his hectic schedule, would I impersonate him, and only when the topics being discussed were less controversial. I observed that there were fuller discussions and even some healthy disagreements as compared to the time of Somerset's control. Warwick, or Northumberland as I will now call him, at least gave the impression that he was merely presiding and not controlling the discourse as Somerset had. Speaking of Lord Somerset, he was released from the Tower after a few months, with Edward speaking on his behalf. However, he foolishly tried to undermine Northumberland and return the Council to his own control, which was viewed as a treasonous act. Even Edward's patience had waned at that point. Edward had never quite forgiven his uncle for his captivity at Windsor Castle, and so when the tide once again turned, Edward was not there to support him.

"Last week," Edward said in passing during one of our visits, "Lord Somerset was taken to Tower Hill and beheaded."

"What did you say?" I gasped, stunned by the statement.

"Somerset was beheaded," he repeated.

I was taken aback by the coldness with which he proclaimed the demise of his uncle.

"Are you not saddened by your uncle's death?"

"Certainly. I did all I could to protect him for the sake of my dear mother. But, in the end, we must deal with traitors in a resolute manner for the good of the realm." And that was the end of the conversation.

What was I saying, my lady? Oh yes, it was just after our fifteenth birthday. Edward was settling in after returning to Whitehall from his long summer's journey known as the king's progress. Thus, we were not able to visit on our birthday as we had in the past. The good side of the delay was that Jane joined us, which pleased me very much. Over the past three years, I had abided by Edward's command to not visit her on my own. So, I did not see her as often as I might like.

"I must say, I had a wonderful progress this summer," Edward reported. Early in his reign, Edward had not ventured very far in his summer travels, only visiting several of the castles and estates under royal control. But this past summer, his progress was much expanded.

"It sounds lovely, Edward," Jane said. "What impressed you most during your travels?"

"Hmm. That is an excellent question," Edward pondered for a moment. "I continue to be astounded by how beautiful our kingdom is. I witnessed people working in fields of wheat that seem to go on forever. We rode through lush, green forests filled with beautiful birds, many deer and other wildlife. I stood and gazed in awe as the sun set over the water on

The Scoundrel's Son

the western coast. God has truly blessed our people with the land's awesome splendor.

"Everywhere I went, my subjects showered me with their affection. Farmers and tradesmen, mothers and children, the elderly and the very young lined simple country roads or busy city streets for a chance to see me and express their love for me. I found this both humbling and inspiring at the same time."

"I don't know about other corners of the realm," I offered, "but in Offal Court, you are very loved. I keep my ears open, and all I hear is how big and strong you have grown. The older ones remark how much more you resemble the young King Henry with each passing day. You are an inspiration to your subjects. You give them a reason to work hard. They see your success as their success. They pray for your good health and wellbeing every day."

"You see, Jane," Edward said as he pointed at me. "This is why I keep Tom around!"

"I am so pleased that your progress was such a success!" Jane commented. "God has not only blessed us with the natural beauty of this good land, but also with your inspiring leadership towards the new and right ways to worship him."

With this remark, the tone of the discussion changed.

"We must remain vigilant regarding the Lord's work," Edward proclaimed. "During my travels, I saw many rejoicing in the new ways, which is wonderful. I am certain that the new Book of Common Prayer that the archbishop has just completed will inspire and enlighten the good people throughout the land. However, I also saw that many still cling to the old religion. With your help, sweet cousin, we must strive to show them the way."

"I will do everything in my power for the Lord," Jane responded. "As you know, I have been corresponding with Professor Bullinger in Geneva regarding your reforms. He confirms that you are on the right path. You are the new Josiah!"

"Jane, your confidence astounds me!" Edward remarked. "I would barely know where to begin a discussion with such a learned man!" Jane nodded in appreciation even as she seemed slightly embarrassed by the recognition.

Frederic Fahey

Over the years, I had listened to Edward and Jane discuss these reforms many times, but now religion was dominating almost every conversation. It was of the most importance to both of them. I was not totally clear as to the full significance of the reforms. To gain a deeper appreciation of my dear friends, I decided this would be the day I would seek further understanding.

"Suppose I am a loyal subject trying to better grasp the differences between the new doctrine and the old religion. What would you say to me?" I asked.

"We must focus our worshiping on the Lord and not be distracted by other idols and figures," Edward began. "It is wrong to worship saints and even worldly items as if they themselves were gods. So, all statues, stain-glass windows, crucifixes, and even candles that distract from the worship of God are being removed from houses of worship. When in church, you should only be thinking of your relationship with God." I had noticed the removal of these items when I recently attended church with Father Christian, but, until now, I did not understand the reasoning for the change.

"The new Book of Common Prayer," Jane continued, "is written in English rather than Latin. God's people should understand how to worship Him without having to know an ancient language. The Mass, many of the sacraments, and other services in the old religion are replete with superstitious practices that are held to be divine although they were developed by men, not by God. The eucharist is a symbol of the communion between Our Lord Jesus Christ and His followers at the supper before His death. We do not believe that He meant that the bread and wine are truly His body and blood. We see this as worshiping the bread and wine as an idol rather than focusing one's worshiping on our relationship with the Lord our God."

"We do not believe in papist divinity," Edward added. "The Bishop of Rome, or the pope, as he is called, is a man with no God-given divine powers. He cannot decide who can and cannot enter the Kingdom of Heaven. That awesome power sits with God alone.

"We have closed the monasteries. We have forbidden the saying of Mass, and now we have sanctioned our new book of prayer," Edward said, summarizing his recent actions of reform. "The advancement of these reforms will be the most important accomplishment of my earthly reign.

The Scoundrel's Son

All else pales in comparison. The Lord has made me the leader of His Church, and, through His grace, I intend to act in this regard."

"How do you intend to lead?" I asked.

"By providing a blessed example of faith. I was pronounced leader of the Church by the hand of God when I was crowned. By our faith, we enter the Kingdom of Heaven."

"Of course, the leader of the Church must also provide for his flock," Jane added. "What we do for the least fortunate of our brothers and sisters, we do for the Lord. If we lead in this way, others will follow."

Edward shot a look in Jane's direction. I sensed that they might not be aligned on this point.

Edward paused for a moment before taking the conversation in a different direction.

"My sister, Mary, is not making this easy for me. I admire her devotion but her obstinance regarding the old religion is very frustrating. I love my sister. I try to be patient. I look the other way as she continues to hold Mass at her residence in East Anglia, hoping she will eventually come to understand the blessings of the new way." Edward ended this statement with a forceful cough and took a drink.

"Are you all right, Edward?" Jane asked with some concern. "You seem to have quite a cough."

"I am fine, I am sure," Edward responded. "The air in these halls gets dry as winter approaches, and we start to use the fireplaces more."

I sat quietly and listened very closely. I understood a little better now, and a lot of what they said made sense to me. However, I still did not grasp why they saw these changes as so essential to the point of persecution and punishment. I also understood that there were political implications. At this point, Northumberland and much of the Council had embraced these reforms. But the strained relationship between Edward and his sister could lead to different factions among his subjects. One could argue that there were also financial motivations for the reforms. The closing of the monasteries and the absorption of their possessions had certainly improved the state of the realm's financial affairs. It was all very complicated. I let these things steep in my mind for several days.

Father Christian and I were sitting reading after dinner one night when I posed a question.

Frederic Fahey

"Father, what do you make of the new doctrine? Is Archbishop Cranmer right?" Over the years, our relationship had been based on respect rather than religion. Father understood that I was the ward of the king, and he knew where Edward stood regarding these matters. Since the beginning, Edward had been tolerant of Father Christian's guardianship as he saw it was the best thing for me. For this, I was very grateful. Thus, Father did not demand my attendance at Sunday services, although sometimes I did attend. As the celebration of Mass was banned, the open service was less structured, but Father Christian and other devout practitioners of the old religion continued to hold Mass secretly. I chose never to attend these services, nor did I discuss their existence with Edward.

Father Christian's kind eyes considered me. He placed his book on the table next to his chair and mulled over his answer for a little longer.

"Tom," he started, "I have been a priest for a very long time. I am truly devoted to my religion and all the good it does in the world. I see miracles of faith practically every day. I am amazed by the wonder of God's beauty and forgiveness.

"But we live in a parish where good people are challenged every day by their situation. I see the poor and the sick. I see children without food and the elderly who need care. I am but an old man. I cannot cure all that is wrong in the world. I would be a fool if I tried. But I strive every day to improve the lives of those around me through faith and charity. I listen to their prayers. I give them counsel when they are in a place to hear me. I comfort the sick and suffering and provide refuge to their tortured lives. I do not always succeed, and there are nights I question the value of my dedication. On those nights, I ask God to forgive my weakness of spirit. I wake the next morning with a refreshed outlook as I head back into the world.

"I don't have the answer to your question. I am a humble and imperfect servant. I know very little. I know I am merely a man, for instance. But I have faith in very much.

"There is much involved in running the Church. From the parish priest up to Pope Julius, these men hold the salvation of people's souls in their hands. Every day, our actions might make the difference between someone being saved or damned. I cannot fathom the weight that the world's salvation must place on the heart of Pope Julius. I have faith that his decisions

The Scoundrel's Son

are touched by the grace of God. However, we are but men. I know poor choices are sometimes made, in some cases very bad choices. I have made my share. I pray every night for forgiveness and the wondrous opportunity to do better tomorrow.

"I read what the reformers have written including the archbishop's Book of Common Prayer. For me, the spiritual work does not hinge on whether there are statues or candles in churches. It goes much deeper. In any earthly act of faith whether under these reforms or in the practices of the Church of my faith, there are tangible elements such as a book or a vestment. With respect to the miracle of the Eucharist, when we celebrate Mass, the Lord Jesus Christ is truly with us and in us. That is what I believe."

Father Christian paused and took a long drink from the cup of ale he always had by his chair when reading.

"I could perhaps use a drink a bit stronger tonight," he said with a smile. "Tom, I don't know if the archbishop is right. I can only tell you of my faith and what I see in the world. These are difficult times where people's beliefs will be challenged. Every man and woman, be they His Majesty the King, Lady Jane, Father Christian, or Tom Canty, must make a choice. I pray, Tom, that you make the right one."

As I lay awake that night, the words of Father Christian, Edward, and Jane caromed off the corners of my mind. What does it all mean? As I look back, I can see that Edward and Jane's perspectives were black-and-white with the certainty of youth of what is right and wrong, in contrast to being shaded with the grayness that comes with experience. However, as often as I have considered these solemn issues since then, the true way to the Lord is still not clear to me.

Chapter 20

As the year wore on, it seemed the pace of Edward's summer progress and the endless Council meetings upon his return had taken their toll. He looked completely exhausted and more often asked me to attend meetings with his subjects and minor social gatherings in his place. I wondered if his cough that had persisted since the autumn was making it difficult for him to get a good night's rest.

He then asked me, for the first time, to participate in a meeting with Northumberland. The lord had the solid frame and manner of a soldier with his well-trimmed beard and thinning, brown hair framing a handsome face. He could be very serious, like Somerset, but he was also charming with a quick smile, sincere eyes, and a friendly way about him. He did not dress as formally as Somerset did. Not only did he appear more comfortable in simpler dress, but he also wanted to avoid projecting any sort of imperial air. He wanted to make the point that he merely presided over Council meetings and was not the domineering Lord Protector that Somerset was.

"Good afternoon, Your Majesty. Did you enjoy your midday meal? I must say, you look refreshed."

"Yes, I did," I responded. "I guess I needed some good food. I must remember that the body needs nourishment as much as the soul. With our busy schedules, I sometimes forget to take care of myself."

"Indeed, Your Majesty."

I enjoyed this social banter with Northumberland. I don't recall Somerset ever engaging in such dialog about Edward's wellbeing in our private meetings.

"Archbishop Cranmer's new version of the Book of Common Prayer has been received quite well," he said. "There are some grumblings but no

The Scoundrel's Son

outbreaks as we saw with the distribution of the original version a few years back. I believe this is due in large part to Your Majesty's clear support of the book."

I thanked him for the compliment. For several minutes, we continued to discuss efforts regarding church reforms and how they were being received. This was an area that was of high interest for Edward, and Lord Northumberland encouraged it. I understood the importance that Edward placed on these efforts, but I sometimes wondered if this was a way to occupy Edward's attention while keeping him in the dark with respect to political and military matters. I decided to delve into some of these other arenas.

"What is happening in the rest of the kingdom and beyond?" I finally asked. "What is my cousin Mary up to in France? When might she return to Scotland? She is queen after all." Northumberland seemed surprised by my inquiry. I could not tell if he was pleased with "His Majesty's" interest in Scotland or merely annoyed. At any rate, he provided me with a rather simple summary of Mary's situation, her betrothal to the Dauphin, and the state of things in Scotland. At least for the time being, hostilities in the north seemed to have subsided.

"What is the current state of the treasury?" I then asked and, again, he seemed taken aback by my question. I knew the state of the treasury was always a concern. He answered that revenues from taxes were much higher than in previous years, for which he credited the successful progress of the previous summer.

"Your Majesty's subjects rejoice in seeing you, and they express their affection in prompt payment of their taxes."

The meeting continued for a bit longer, with me inquiring on a wide range of topics. In each case, I pushed Northumberland to be more specific. Although he appeared surprised by the depth of my inquiries, he answered without objection. Edward had often commented that he appreciated being more involved in governing the kingdom. Then how had he not asked these simple questions? Was he too focused on the state of the religious reforms?

"It pleases me to see Your Majesty taking such interest in issues facing the realm. Your reign will be one that will be remembered down through the ages as your youthful enthusiasm ripens with the wisdom of experience. You so remind me of your father when he was young, but the warmth of your mother's spirit also shines through in how kindly you respond to the plight of your less fortunate subjects." He noticed the time and stated that he had to return to his family as his wife had planned a social evening.

On my next visit, Edward remarked, "I do not know of what you and Northumberland spoke last time, but you…I mean I…really impressed him! He keeps commenting on how mature I am becoming. Thank you for portraying me so well!"

"It is my pleasure as always," I answered. "Perhaps my common charm impressed him."

"Do not overdo it with your charm of the streets," Edward joked. "I want him to still believe that it is me!"

"Yes, Your Majesty," I said as I bowed deeply. "I will try to remember not to spit on the floor during my next visit with Northumberland!" With that, we both had a wonderful chuckle. More seriously, I realized that Edward and I approached our encounters with Northumberland and the Council differently. Perhaps it had grown from my mechanical training, but I was more interested in how things worked rather than how they appeared on the outside. I was also not shy when it came to asking questions. As Edward tended to be more reserved, I hoped he would not be bothered by my more inquisitive nature.

***

Later that week, I was walking home from the shop when I encountered Aly on the street. I did not recognize her at first, as the winter's cold had her bundled in numerous shawls including one wrapped around her head. Between my work in the shop, my more frequent visits with Edward, and the dwindling daylight of winter, I had not seen Aly in a while. I commented that I thought she looked a little pale, and she noted that she had not eaten much that day. I suggested we stop at the bakery where I bought each of us a sweet roll and some cider. She proceeded to devour her roll in just a couple of bites. I asked about Izzy and the boys. She said that Izzy was planning to marry the tailor's son, Jacob. The boys, she said, were as rambunctious as ever, but that Jacob's presence and example were having a good effect on them.

The Scoundrel's Son

"Do you still see Jem and his chums?" I asked.

"Not much," she answered. "I try to stay clear a him. Me thinks he's headin' down the wrong path. I don't need them headaches in my life." Her face then brightened as she announced that she was now spending what little free time she had with a new group of friends. "You'd like them, Tom. They work hard and still have a bit of fun." She noted that a boy named George had shown interest in spending time with her.

"He's a good boy, he is. I'm sure you'd like him. He don't know what he wants to be yet. He talks of many things, maybe even soldiering. That scares me a wee bit. But right now, he's just talkin', so I let him ramble." I did not know George, but I told Aly I looked forward to meeting him.

"How about you, Tom? You're a bit busy these days. I stopped by Mr. Nobson's shop lookin' for ya. I ask Mr. Nobson of your whereabouts, and he just waves his hands and shakes his head sayin' you're meeting with someone or other."

"That sounds like a Mr. Nobson sort of explanation," I answered with a grin. "I'm workin' on a special job. I can't say too much." At that point, I had not spoken to Aly of Edward. She waved her hand indicating she didn't really need to know.

"Are you still seein' the mystery girl?" she asked.

At first, I wasn't sure of whom she was speaking, but then I realized she meant Jane.

"Once in a while but not too often. It's not easy for us to spend time together these days."

"Since you first talked of her, I figured she's from a bit nicer parish than Offal Court."

"Something like that." I smiled.

"Her family don't approve of you?"

"I might say that's true," I answered. Aly did not know the half of it!

"All I can say, Tom, is she'd be lucky to have you as a suitor!" Aly said resolutely.

I was getting nervous speaking about Jane and me, even in vague terms, so I changed the subject.

"How do you feel about His Majesty the King?"

Aly was surprised by my question. She thought for a moment before answering.

"Well, I don't think of him much at all. I'm busy worryin' about the boys and what George will do with his life. His Majesty's still very young. He's about our age, isn't he? I can't see any boys I know being up to rulin' the kingdom.

"But I feel His Majesty cares about us common folk. I know some who saw him last summer when he rode by the parish. They say he looked right at them and smiled. He even stopped and talked kindly to one small girl who couldn't walk. The next day a small wagon arrived for her. As much as the old ones speak of King Henry, I don't recall hearin' of any such kindness. The people love His Majesty and pray for his health every night."

I was pleased with what Aly shared. It confirmed what I thought regarding how the people felt about Edward.

Then she added, "Folks also talk of King Henry's daughters, Princess Mary and Princess Elizabeth. They remember them from their younger years. They don't come to the city too often now, and so folks wonder if they be all right." I was surprised she referred to them as the princesses. In the royal court, they were known as the Ladies Mary and Elizabeth.

"How old are they, do you reckon?" she asked.

"I think Lady, I mean Princess Mary is in her late thirties, a bit younger than our mothers. Princess Elizabeth is about the age of Izzy and my sisters, maybe slightly younger," I answered. "They are both well, me thinks."

"That's good to hear," she said and seemed to sincerely mean it. "I gotta go. It was so good to see ya, Tom," she said with a smile as she grabbed what remained of my roll and stuffed it in her mouth.

I purchased two bags of buns, one for my family and one for hers, before we left the bakery. She tried to refuse the gift, but I wouldn't hear of it. I was grateful for my friendship with Aly. She had become my best friend outside of the royal family.

Chapter 21

By February, it was clear that Edward was indeed ill, and it was not due to musty fireplaces or the usual winter's cough. Some days he would be fine while, on other days, he could barely stop coughing. I was now impersonating him regularly, and I was sometimes being summoned to court on a moment's notice. I tried to explain to Robert that His Majesty needed my skills for a special job, and that I might be gone more often. At first, he seemed exasperated.

"The Earl has asked for twenty-five more muskets in the middle of spring. I am going to need your help."

"Of course! When you need me I will be here!"

He gave me a worried look, but then just shrugged his shoulders and said, "I know you will. You are a good worker." He patted me on the shoulder. "We'll get by." Then he added, "By the way, I recently mentioned the notion of your hand musket to the Earl. He was very intrigued. Maybe we should fashion him one."

I was pleased that he thought my idea seemed to have some merit. I would go to the shop much earlier than before to try to complete my work before I was called to the royal court. I owed Robert all I could give him.

"You look very tired, Edward. Are you sleeping?" I asked.

"When I can. But this cough just won't seem to go away." On the small table next to his chair, there was a collection of jars and bottles. "I am told to take many of these cures and remedies," he said as he swiped his hand and knocked a number of the bottles to the floor, a few of them shattering. "None of them work." At the sound of breaking glass, several servants rushed into the room and swept up the scattered glass, liquids, and herbs.

"My mother," I noted, "says the only remedy that works is hot cider and honey with a bit of the drink mixed in. She would say it cures what ails you...particularly if you are heavy on the drink!"

"Maybe I should have your mother care for me," he smiled. "She sounds like a wise conjurer of cures."

"Or at least a good conjurer of strong drinks!" We both laughed and Edward started to cough again.

"I suppose this cough will just need to work its course," he said.

I practiced my ability to mimic Edward's cough to better impersonate him. I would sometimes act tired or disinterested, although I was always listening intently so I could report back to Edward, mainly on the issues that most interested him, typically those involving the religious reforms. In some instances, I would inquire about other topics such as our relationship with Spain or Ireland. It did not always sit well with Edward when he would hear of me taking a more active role in these discussions.

"Although the archbishop informs me that the reforms are well received," Northumberland began during a Council meeting, "there remain some who stubbornly hold to the old religion. Lady Mary continues to be a concern. We sent a messenger to East Anglia to speak with Her Highness about this. She says the right words and speaks kindly of His Majesty, but we still receive reports that she is attending Mass regularly at her estate. I fear that more people are rallying around her, which is impacting the acceptance of the reforms, despite what the archbishop says."

"Perhaps, I should invite my sister to come visit and have a conversation with her myself," I boldly suggested. All of the Council members, including Northumberland, turned to me in surprise, although many of them appeared to like the idea.

"Would Your Majesty also invite Lady Elizabeth?" one member asked.

"Certainly," I agreed. "But I would meet with Lady Mary alone during the visit. I believe I am the best person to convince her to support our reforms."

"I think it is a splendid idea," Northumberland responded although his manner appeared hesitant. "But perhaps we should wait until His Majesty is feeling better."

"On the contrary," I answered back. "I think the visit should be arranged as soon as possible. I welcome the opportunity for a pleasant visit and a heartfelt conversation with my sister." Much of the Council was again in agreement. Lord Suffolk, Jane's father who had recently been named to the Council, did not have much to offer. His style was to assent to the will of the majority without much contribution of his own. The discussion left Northumberland with little option but to concur. I wondered how Edward would respond to the news.

"You invited my sisters to visit?" Edward exclaimed. "Together? Tom, I am afraid you are speaking out of turn on my behalf. This makes me quite anxious."

"But the Council was in full agreement!" I told him.

"Even Northumberland?"

"Not at first, but he was finally convinced, I think."

"Or coerced, more likely!"

"Maybe. But, Edward, you need to convince Lady Mary of the importance of your reforms. She will not listen to the archbishop or anyone else, but she might listen to you. You cannot sit back and allow her to continue to worship as she will. Some of your subjects will see this as permission to follow her."

"My subjects will follow me, and I have the archbishop on my side. Mary is just a lady from East Anglia, not even a princess."

"That is not how your subjects see her. She is still the daughter of King Henry and heir to the throne."

"I am not sure my health will withstand such a confrontation." Edward rubbed his brow.

"I can handle the social events and the pleasantries during the visit while you concentrate on the more substantive discussions with Lady Mary," I offered.

"Let me think about it," Edward said as he sat back in his chair.

Ultimately, Edward agreed, and the visit was arranged for early March. As much as Edward had spoken to me of his sisters over the years, I thought it might be helpful to gather more information on the subject.

It had been over three years since my last visit to Norwich Place. I had followed Edward's order since returning from Windsor Castle that time, but now I needed Jane's insight regarding Mary and Elizabeth. I sent a message to Lord Miles in Kent asking him to provide a letter from him to Jane's father for me to deliver. I figured once inside Norwich Place, I could find a way to see Jane. I received such a letter from Lord Miles in just a few days' time. Upon my arrival, I was directed to the parlor and offered some hot cider, which I gladly accepted. I figured if I could sip it very slowly, I could extend my visit. I took a seat near the fire to warm my feet.

"Hello, Tom," Jane said as she entered the room. "This is a very nice surprise. My father is not here today. He will be disappointed he missed you." In the glow of the fire, I was struck by how she had blossomed from the little girl I had met six years ago to the young lady before me. She continued to have the slight build of her mother. She still retained her girlish face with delicate features bordered by her fine, red hair and highlighted by her shining, brown eyes that had a tint of red and sparkled when she smiled. I was pleased when she asked the servant to bring her a drink as well.

"How is my cousin doing? I hear he is still not well."

"I am afraid the reports are true. The cough from before Christmas has persisted. He doesn't seem to be able to shake it." I told her of the invitation to Edward's sisters. "He is planning a reception on their behalf. I wondered what his sisters were like. I don't expect to be invited but I don't want to embarrass myself if I am."

"My family has received an invitation," she acknowledged. "I imagine I will be attending along with my parents and sisters.

"Lady Mary is very formal and serious. I am told she has the reserve of her mother without her father's excitability. Her words are well chosen but will leave you guessing as to what is truly on her mind. My mother and Lady Mary were very close as young girls. My sister was named for Lady Mary, in fact. I saw much of her when I was small. However, since Edward has become king, she has spent most of her time in East Anglia, and I have only seen her on a few occasions. Because of our different views on religion, I am sure I am not her favorite cousin.

"Lady Elizabeth, I know quite well. You may remember that we both spent time at Sudeley Castle and Chelsea with Edward's Uncle Thomas and Queen Kateryn before her death. Lady Elizabeth is as smart as a whip but much more socially adept than her older sister. She is very engaging but also astute to the politics of the court. Do not be fooled by her easy charm and pretty smile. She is always thinking ahead to her next move. I was only nine years old when King Henry left us, but I believe Elizabeth

The Scoundrel's Son

is the most like him of his three children. She is not as devout as Mary, Edward, or I on religious matters. I have a sense she worships one way if she is with her sister and another when she is with Edward."

"This will be very helpful," which was true no matter whose clothes I might be wearing at the reception. I then asked her how she was doing these days.

"I am doing well. My father has been spending more time with Northumberland. I don't know what they are discussing. Unlike Elizabeth, I am less attuned to political matters. But whatever it is, it seems to have both my parents scurrying around."

My visit to Norwich was a success on several levels. I had gained some valuable insight regarding Edward's sisters. I also realized how much I had missed seeing Jane. I decided that this would not be my last visit to Norwich Place. I was not a fool. I knew, as Edward had noted years before, that Jane and I would never be together. But I still wanted to see her. I would be discreet, but I would make the most of my opportunities to visit her for as long as I could.

Chapter 22

Lady Mary and Lady Elizabeth arrived at Whitehall around noon on a Friday in early March. As I understood the schedule, there would be a small, intimate supper for the three siblings that evening. Of course, when various servants and attendants were included, it would be tens of people and hardly intimate. The next day would be comprised of a joint meeting with both sisters in the morning as well as separate meetings with each of them in the afternoon. The reception planned for Saturday evening would involve hundreds of invited guests. This would be the first social event in years attended by all three children of King Henry, so many of the nobility were eager to be present. Religious services would be held Sunday morning followed by a farewell luncheon. The ladies were scheduled to depart for their respective homes by midafternoon.

Edward asked me to be available at any time in case he felt too weak to attend any of the activities. Thus, I was present at the palace practically the entire time of the sisters' visit. He was particularly focused on participating in the private meeting with Lady Mary, which would also be attended by Northumberland. For much of the time, Edward was feeling quite well. He was able to attend Friday's evening meal and all the meetings on Saturday. Edward and I had a brief chat just before the reception was to begin. I asked him how things were going.

"Very well thus far," Edward shared.

"Even the meeting with Lady Mary?"

"Surprisingly so, it seemed to me. We spoke on many topics. Towards the end, I expressed the importance of the new reforms for our people and my grave concern of the consequences if we did not speak with one voice in this regard. By the end, I spoke quite forcefully, just short of demanding she conform. She spoke little but listened intently. I asked if she under-

The Scoundrel's Son

stood, and she indicated that she certainly did. I surely hope that is the case."

"I hope so too," I responded. I was not sure how to interpret Lady Mary's response to Edward's question. Was she saying she agreed with Edward's position? Or was she merely indicating that she understood the words Edward spoke?

I could see in Edward's eyes that he was very tired. Although he tended to have good days and bad days, recently one meeting was about all he could endure even on a good day.

"Are you going to be all right for the reception?" I asked.

"I believe so. I will try to keep as still as possible and do the best I can. But please be alert just in case."

At the reception, I wore a formal outfit provided to me by Richard. As the reception got underway, I was completely overwhelmed. I had never in my life, even during the masquerade, seen so many people in one room. A wedding in Offal Court may involve thirty or sometimes forty folks, and this was hundreds. I was possibly the only person in attendance by himself. Others attended as at least a couple if not an entire family. I was struck by the colorful array of clothing on display. They ranged from elegantly simple to those bordering on outrageous. One lady whom I was later told had spent time in France came with her face painted white with bejeweled beauty marks stuck to her face. Peacock feathers extruded every which way from her dress, one of which persisted in being squarely planted in her husband's face as they sauntered through the reception. At first I was nervous that folks would realize how much I resembled His Majesty, but as was true through practically all of my dealings in the royal court, very few gave any mind to a commoner, even if he was the ward of the king.

I finally spotted Jane and her family across the hall and made my way in that direction. Lord Suffolk and Lady Frances were busy greeting people as I approached. As members of the royal family, they seemed to have a line of well-wishers of their own. Their three daughters standing behind them were only occasionally introduced by their parents to various friends and acquaintances. I approached from the side to avoid the line. When Jane saw me, a smile burst upon her face. I bowed as I approached, and she nodded in response.

"Hello, Tom! I am very pleased you decided to attend. Do you remember my sisters?"

"I certainly do. Lady Katherine, it is good to see you again." Katherine was even more beautiful than I had remembered. Her face was fair and delicate and blessed with dimples on each cheek. She shared Jane's expressive brown eyes.

"Lady Mary, it is such a pleasure to see you again," I said as I took a deep bow. I was reminded as to why Jane referred to her as "Little Mary." Even for an eight-year-old, she was indeed very tiny in stature, closer to maybe the size of a four-year-old. However, just as I had remembered from our brief encounter at Norwich Place, her mind was bright and active.

"Are you still a ward of the king? Are you His Majesty's friend? How long have you known my sister? Do you live here in the palace? Are you an orphan?..."

Lady Frances noticed the activity behind her and turned toward us.

"Mother, do you remember Master Thomas Canty, Ward of His Majesty?" Jane asked. "He is also an associate of Lord Miles Hendon."

"Why, yes! How are you, Master Thomas?" Lady Frances asked. Before I could answer, a familiar voice boomed from the other direction.

"My lady and my lord, may I present my wife and my children," Northumberland announced. As Lady Frances turned to greet Northumberland, I decided this was a good time to move on. To the best of my knowledge, Northumberland did not know of me or my relationship with Edward. He was not as involved with the royal court six years previously when our masquerade was revealed.

"My ladies, it was a pleasure to see all of you this evening," I said with a bow.

"I very much enjoyed seeing you as well, Master Thomas," Lady Mary said with a curtsy. "I hope we meet again very soon."

"Lady Mary, I will look forward to it." Jane's smile conveyed how much she appreciated the special attention I had afforded her youngest sister.

From a distance, I watched Northumberland present one of his sons, perhaps about my age, to Jane. He was a tall boy with sandy colored hair and a handsome face. He and Jane spoke for a while.

Not long after, one of Edward's servants approached me and indicated that His Majesty needed my assistance. Edward and I had arranged that we

The Scoundrel's Son

would meet back at his chambers if necessary. When I entered the chamber, I was surprised to find Richard there as well.

"I have decided to let Richard into our confidence," Edward informed me. I thought this was a good move on Edward's behalf. Maintaining our secrecy while making the switch in the midst of such a reception required a bit of care. I had sometimes wondered if Richard knew of my impersonations long before this.

"I know we are still greeting people, and I have not introduced you to my sisters as of yet, but I really need your help." Edward said that he had suddenly become quite tired and was afraid he might start coughing or even faint if he did not rest.

"Of course," I responded. Richard presented me with an identical set of the royal clothing being worn by Edward that night. He helped me change quickly. Once Edward was comfortable in his bedchamber, Richard escorted me back to the dais without a word. I took Edward's seat between his two sisters.

"I just needed to splash some water on my face," I explained to the ladies.

"It looks as if it has done the trick, my dear brother," Lady Elizabeth said. "You look much refreshed. Earlier, I thought you looked a little pale."

I had not seen either lady since Edward's coronation, six years previous. Lady Elizabeth had grown from an overactive adolescent to a confident young woman. She had the easy smile that Jane had described. I then turned toward Lady Mary, who gave me a pleasant enough smile but seemed to be in deep thought. She was a harder book to read. I wondered if she was thinking about her earlier meeting with Edward.

For the next couple of hours, many of the nobility and their families came by the dais to pay their respects. All referred to the sisters as My Lady, Lady Mary, or Lady Elizabeth, until one lady introduced to me as being from West Suffolk clung to the notion that they were still princesses.

"Your Majesty, is it not wonderful to have Princess Mary and Princess Elizabeth with us this evening?" she asked. All eyes were on me to see how I might handle the indiscretion that some might consider disrespectful to the king.

"Yes indeed," I responded, taking the hands of Edward's sisters. "We are so blessed to have my dear sisters, Lady Mary and Lady Elizabeth, with us tonight." With this remark, all returned to normal.

What did strike me was the high regard that all in attendance still had for the royal ladies. Perhaps it was just that the two of them had not been at such a gathering at the royal court in quite a while, but they were receiving more attention than me in my role as "His Majesty." I had seen the admiration for the Ladies Mary and Elizabeth in Offal Court, but now I was witnessing that the same held true for the nobility.

In a lull in the festivities, Lady Mary turned to me.

"I was wondering, sweet brother," she asked softly, as if not to let anyone else hear, "if Father has ever come to you."

"I am sorry, my sister. What did you say?" I wasn't sure I had truly understood the statement. At that point, Lady Mary's father, King Henry, had been deceased for six years.

"Sometimes in the dark of night or the faint light of the early dawn, Father appears to me. His broad face shines and his eyes twinkle. He sometimes shares words of wisdom or guidance, or he asks if I am all right. He is only there for a few heartbeats and then he is gone. Has he ever come to you?"

I was not sure how I should respond. "I am sorry to say no, but I would welcome him dearly. You are truly blessed, my sweet sister."

At that point, our remarkable conversation was concluded as the reception line resumed. I reached over and patted her hand. She gave me an appreciative smile.

Northumberland and his family soon approached. He and his wife, Lady Jane Dudley, presented their children in attendance. The older ones were all boys. He introduced the tall boy who had spoken to Jane as Guildford. He was a bit shy and awkward, as he had yet to learn to manage his long limbs. I think I was right that he was about my age or maybe a little older. His older brother, Robert, seemed to be paying distinct attention to Lady Elizabeth and she to him in kind.

Soon another group was presented and then the next, and so it went for quite a while. I now understood why Edward needed my help. Even I, in good health, was becoming exhausted, and all I was doing was smiling and nodding. Lady Elizabeth was in her element, greeting each party with renewed enthusiasm that lent the impression that they alone were special in her mind. Lady Mary, on the other hand, had the same smile cemented

The Scoundrel's Son

to her face for the entire time. She barely said a word as she nodded at each party. And still, each and every party felt blessed by the attention given to them by the two ladies.

Towards the very end, the Grey family came by. It might be that as members of the royal family it was expected that they would be among the last. Lady Mary perked up as Lady Frances approached her. I remembered Jane saying that they had been close as children. Lady Mary grasped Lady Frances's hands and gave her a genuine smile. Lady Elizabeth and Jane also exchanged some kind words, perhaps reminiscing about their time together at Sudeley Castle.

Then Jane looked my way. She gave me a curtsy as she would His Majesty but then stopped and took another look. She looked deep into my eyes. She seemed frozen for a moment until her mother beckoned her to come say hello to Lady Mary. At that point, her trance melted. She smiled and silently mouthed the words, "Hi Tom."

The rest of the visit appeared to go very well. The three siblings attended church services on Sunday morning without incident and, by all accounts, the dinner was friendly and cordial. Edward asked me to take his place for any last goodbyes before the ladies headed home. Edward, dressed as me, was sitting with a book in a small meeting room nearby. I was in Edward's chamber feigning reading some books on religion that Edward had left on his side table when Lady Elizabeth entered.

"It was so nice to see you, Edward," she said. "Please take care of yourself. I imagine your duties as king can be quite daunting. You seem a little tired." I thanked her for her concern and bid her a safe journey home.

A while later, Lady Mary arrived. After some pleasantries and gratitude for arranging the visit were exchanged, she asked if she might have a word with me privately. I agreed and asked the servants to give us a few moments. I was a bit apprehensive as I wondered what this would be about. She looked me squarely in the eye and addressed me directly.

"My dear brother, I thought about our meeting yesterday late into the night and early this morning as I said my morning prayers. I fully understand what you are asking of me as I said yesterday." She took a breath and spoke with notable resolve.

"But I must tell you that I cannot abide by your request. My faith in God is much too dear for it to be foregone for political convenience. If I were to accept your new doctrine, as you call it, I would be rejecting Our Lord and, as a result, my soul would burn in Hell. You may be prepared to accept eternal damnation, but I am not. I pray that the Lord will shine His grace on you, sweet brother, and that you will see your way back to the true faith." At the end of her remarks, she curtsied.

"May God bless you, dear brother." She left the chambers and headed to her carriage without waiting for a response.

When I told Edward of the exchange, he remained silent for several moments.

"My sister's pride is her gravest sin. It blinds her to the riches of the new way. I was trying to save her soul, not condemn it! Why didn't she see that?"

There was nothing for me to say. I still believed that his meeting with her was the best chance for a reconciliation. If Edward could not convince Lady Mary of the virtues of the new ways, who could? But, alas, a simple way was not to be.

"I should never have expected the righteous path would be easy," Edward finally proclaimed. "But that does not make it any less blessed." He did not say another word. He and I sat in silence for quite a while before I finally rose, went to him, and put my arm around his shoulder to comfort him.

Chapter 23

As the stubborn bluster of March turned toward April, the arrival of spring did not heal Edward of his illness as was hoped. His condition continued to deteriorate. He was now coughing deeply on a regular basis. Edward's servants provided him with what seemed an endless supply of linen into which he would cough, soaking them in blood. Healers and physicians of great renown from across the kingdom and beyond were summoned in the hope of a cure, but none was found. Many of the treatments only seemed to worsen his situation.

Growing up in Offal Court, I was no stranger to sickness and dying. The poor witnessed such suffering every day, whether it was an elderly grandfather at the end of his life, a young mother after a troublesome birth, or a small child who had contracted the sweating sickness. In our cases, there were no cures or remedies. There were only the endless prayers that the Lord would see fit to let illness and death pass this house. In most cases, such miracles did not occur, and we were left with the tragic loss of another life.

For many in my parish, they considered this as a matter of not having enough, the curse of the poor. If only we had a cleaner house free from rats and other vermin. Or a warmer house. If only we had more food so the elderly and the young could be better nourished. If only the healer had come when called. Deep down, we knew the nobility and royalty also suffered. Hadn't King Henry's older brother, Arthur, died as a very young man of the sweating sickness? Hadn't Queen Kateryn and even Edward's own mother died soon after giving birth? But these realities did not stop the poor from bemoaning "If only."

It pained me deeply to watch my dearest friend suffer so. I sat, week after week, and watched Edward become sicker and sicker. Although I had

Frederic Fahey

certainly watched folks suffer from illness in my family and in the parish, it had yet to touch someone so close to me as Edward. I was now being asked on almost a daily basis to sit in for Edward, and I was more than happy to serve him in this way. So often, there is nothing one can do to relieve the suffering of a friend. I worked on my ability to portray Edward in his sickness. I learned to mimic his coughing and his moments of sheer exhaustion. I had several linens with the corners dipped in meat juice to mimic his bleeding. I had been given this unique opportunity to aid my best friend in his time of need, and I embraced it with all my heart.

After one Council meeting, Northumberland asked if he could meet with me privately. I informed him that I could but that I was tired and then would need to return to my chamber for some much-needed rest. As with Somerset, Northumberland and I may have a short dialogue right after the Council met, but it was unusual for us to then have a separate meeting. I wondered what might be on his mind.

"Your Majesty should consider the succession to the throne," he began. "I have noticed recent improvements in Your Majesty's health, and I am sure as I can be that Your Majesty will fully recover and soon will be as fit as a stallion. However, Your Majesty's recent illness has led me to think that we should develop a devise of succession so if the need should arise in the future, the very distant future for sure, that we are prepared."

"I must confess," I said, "that I have not given this any thought." I wondered if Edward had.

"Your father developed such a plan," Northumberland continued, "which was approved by his Privy Council and later by the Parliament. He declared that Your Majesty was his immediate heir, which, of course, no one questioned. However, he also declared that Your Majesty's sisters, first Lady Mary and then Lady Elizabeth, followed in succession, even though their births had been declared illegitimate. As you know, no woman has ever been crowned the ruling queen in the history of the kingdom of England.

"If we look at the royal family and the descendants of your grandfather, the old King Henry, we could consider your two sisters as we have discussed and the living descendants of your father's sisters: Queen Mary of Scotland, Lady Margaret Douglas, Lady Frances Grey along with her daughters, the Ladies Jane, Katherine, and Mary and her niece Lady

The Scoundrel's Son

Margaret Clifford. For the reasons we have discussed, I would suggest that Your Majesty remove your sisters and their heirs from the line of succession. It would also seem obvious not to consider Mary of Scotland, who is betrothed to the Dauphin of France, and also Lady Margaret Douglas. Thus, I would concentrate on the future male heirs of Lady Frances and her daughters followed by her niece Lady Margaret Clifford."

While I was being escorted back to Edward's chambers, I considered how best to disclose this conversation to him. It was reasonable, as Northumberland had stated, to consider a devise of succession. But it touched on Edward's mortality. Even if I wasn't convinced that Edward would get better, and I was starting to have my doubts, I had yet to deal with the thought that he might die in my own mind, let alone discuss it with Edward. When I returned to Edward, I briefly summarized the Council meeting. I took a deep breath before I continued.

"Edward, Northumberland spoke to me about developing a document that lays out your intentions regarding the succession to the throne."

I could see the fear in his eyes as I broached the subject.

"Of course, once summer arrives and you can walk in the sunshine, I am sure this cough will finally subside, but it seems reasonable to be prepared." I couched the discussion much as Northumberland had.

"I suppose it is good to be prepared," he finally responded once he had regained his composure.

"The archbishop and I have made great strides in promoting the new reforms in the Church. I fear that if the Lord should see fit to take me into his heavenly kingdom, that my sister, Mary, would return the realm to papist rule and the old religion. I must do everything in my power not to let that happen. If we exclude her on the grounds of the condition of her birth, then we likely need to exclude Elizabeth as well. Northumberland makes an excellent point regarding Mary of Scotland and Lady Margaret Douglas too. That leaves the male heirs of my cousin Lady Frances, her daughters and her niece of which, of course, there currently are none."

"Edward, I remind you that there is no need to consider the lack of male heirs today but for that day many years from now."

"Yes, of course," Edward responded but with a hint of sadness.

"Also, Edward, I must say that gaining acceptance of this document will likely require all of your considerable talents of persuasion. I fully understand your concern regarding Lady Mary. However, from what I have witnessed, your subjects, both common and noble, continue to show their affection for her. It will take a lot of convincing for them not to see her as the heir to the throne." Edward nodded as if he comprehended what I had said, but it was not clear he grasped its full meaning. I told myself that this was of little consequence, since Edward would have a very long and prosperous reign and that Lady Mary would merely continue to be a troublesome thorn in his side; perhaps, to convince myself that it was true.

***

It was time I should inform Jane of the seriousness of Edward's condition. It was a pleasant, spring afternoon, and so the servant brought me a cup of cider while I waited for Jane in the garden at Norwich Place. The sun tried to warm my skin while my concern for Edward chilled my insides. When she arrived, I rose and greeted her properly and she invited me to retake my seat. Although she seemed distracted, she still expressed concern regarding Edward's health.

"How is my sweet cousin? I pray each day for his recovery," Jane said. I informed her that, unfortunately, he did not seem to be improving, although I did not go into too much detail. For instance, I did not describe how, on some days, he was too weak to walk, or that he was now coughing up blood regularly. However, she seemed to grasp the severity of the situation. Jane then started to sob. Seeing her tears tore at my heart. I tried to relieve her fears of Edward's illness as I did with him by saying that I fully expected his good health to return, and...

"I am to be married," she interrupted.

"Someday, I realize."

"In a month or sooner," she continued, "and my sister Katherine as well." I was totally frozen by this revelation. Now Jane was openly crying. I had a clean hand linen in my pocket, which I offered to her.

"To whom?" was the only response I could muster.

"Guildford Dudley, the son of Lord Northumberland and Lady Jane Dudley."

"The tall boy from the reception?"

"Yes. Apparently, my parents, along with Lord Northumberland, feel that it is of the utmost importance for me or my sister to produce a male heir as soon as possible. Even Little Mary is to be betrothed, and she is only eight years old."

The hasty arrangement of these marriages was already underway before my discussion with Northumberland regarding succession. It was clear that this was all part of his scheme.

"How old is Lady Katherine?"

"Barely twelve," Jane responded.

I sat silently as Jane continued to weep.

"I don't want to get married," Jane said. "And surely not to Guildford Dudley."

"Did you let your parents know that?"

"Of course, I did. But I understand the value of my hand. I have understood it for practically my whole life. But to now be faced with that reality in such an immediate sense is yet another thing. With Edward's illness, the situation has become even more crucial."

I so much wanted to comfort her, to go to her side, to hold her hand, to even embrace her. My heart was also weeping. But, instead, I sat across from her, with my cup of cider and the proper manners that I had learned these last few years and watched my dear friend cry. It was dreadfully painful to feel so helpless.

"I must do what I can," Jane finally announced, "for my country and, more importantly, for my God. It is my duty as a member of the royal family."

When I left Norwich Place that day, I took a long walk by the river and tried to make some sense of all that was happening around me. My best friend, a boy of exactly my age, was most likely dying. I was watching his illness unfold each day. And now I learned that a girl who has touched my soul in a way that I could not totally comprehend was to be married, not out of love but out of patriotic and spiritual duty. Not even in my wildest imagination did I consider that Jane and I would spend our lives together. I knew the day when Jane was to be married would come. But to see her in such torment over her lot was so painful. I found a place to sit under a beautiful elm tree near a bed of marigolds freshly in bloom and gazed down the river. I put my face in my hands and cried for a long time.

Frederic Fahey

***

"It's always good to see you, Tom." Aly said as I reached into my satchel and withdrew the bread and cheese that I had purchased for the two of us. I also brought a jug of cider and two tin cups. "Hmm. This looks like quite a meal indeed!" She took a large bite of the bread and cheese.

"Aly, I really need a friend, I do," I started. "I want to share a secret. But I gotta ask you to swear on all you hold dear that you not tell a single soul, not even Izzy or George!"

"You're scarin' me, Tom," she said as her eyes narrowed.

"No need to be a scared. But it's best you keep what I tell you secret. All right?" Aly swallowed what was in her mouth and took a long drink.

"Tom, you can trust me. I swear to ya," she said with conviction. "Does it have to do with the mystery girl?"

"In part. I'll get to that. Just let me tell my story." And so, I proceeded. I went back to the masquerade and how I first met Edward, about my early visits with my best friend who happened to be His Majesty the King, and how I became acquainted with Lady Jane. I told her of my impersonations of Edward. Aly sat very still as I described my ride with Lord Miles to Windsor Castle. I concluded by describing Edward's illness and Jane's announcement, just yesterday, of her impending marriage. When I finished, Aly sat silently for a while.

"That's quite a story, Tom," she finally said. "I knew your life had some wrinkles in it, but I never thought it involved His Majesty. I really don't know what to say." Of course, I realized no one could possibly guess what was happening in my life. There were days I could barely believe it myself and I was living it.

"Aly, I don't need you to say anything. I just ask that you believe what I say is true and that you don't tell a soul," I responded.

"You can be sure that your secret is safe with me," Aly pledged. "I believe you with all my heart, I do!" She then added, "I don't know what I'd do if I were you. But I'd try—and this is easier to say than do—but I'd try to face each pinch you're in without thinking your friends are royal. What's there to do if my close friend is very ill? How do I treat the news that any girl I care for is to be wed? Me thinks this'll make things a bit simpler." She softly caressed my trembling hand. "I'm here if you need me, Tom."

The Scoundrel's Son

Later, I realized that her little piece of advice was very helpful. Anytime the situation with Edward or Jane seemed to be spinning out of control, I would try to return to what I referred to as "Aly's rule" and leave aside their royal positions. It helped me keep things in perspective. I knew it was good that I shared my story with Aly. I was blessed to have such a good friend with whom I could talk in these trying times.

Chapter 24

Jane's wedding was the most anticipated social event of the spring as there had not been a royal wedding since that of King Henry and Queen Kateryn a decade previously. Three weddings were to take place at the same time. Jane was to be married to young Lord Guildford Dudley. Jane's sister, Lady Katherine, would wed Henry Herbert, son of the Earl of Pembroke and Lady Anne Parr, the late queen's sister. Katherine Dudley, Guildford's sister, would marry Henry Hastings, son of the Earl of Huntingdon. Lastly, little Lady Mary was to be officially betrothed to Arthur Grey, a distant cousin. Lady Mary's wedding would not take place for some time due to her young age. Northumberland and Jane's parents were doing all they could to produce a male heir in the Grey family as soon as possible.

Edward would not be able to attend but ordered his royal Master of the Wardrobe to provide the dresses for the wedding. He also arranged for many of the jewels to be worn by the three young brides.

"I want it to be clear that I am very much in favor of these marriages," he told me.

Jane would wear purple, a color legally forbidden except for the immediate royal family. The two Katherines would wear gowns of silver and gold. The weddings were to be held at Durham Palace; the Dudley's city home located on the Strand just down the river from Norwich Place. It was much larger than Norwich Place and appeared even more splendid from the street. Hundreds or maybe even a thousand guests were to attend the celebration that would extend over several days.

"It is going to be quite an affair," Jane declared with a huff as we sat in the garden a week before the festivities. "I am not usually impressed by such things, and I feel a woman's dress, even on her wedding day, should

The Scoundrel's Son

be much simpler. But I must admit that the dress and jewels from Edward are magnificent."

"I have little doubt that you will be the most beautiful bride," I said.

"I would guess that title will be held by my sister, Katherine, but thank you, Tom, for the compliment." Jane stated that her sister seemed quite happy with her impending marriage although Jane felt that the pomp and splendor of the affair is what really excited her.

As the wedding day approached, I knew that I had to be there in some way. I contemplated asking Edward if I could attend as him, but the planning for His Majesty's appearance would take days, and it would draw much of the attention away from the celebration itself. I decided, instead, to attend as myself. I wore the outfit Edward had provided me for the reception for the Ladies Mary and Elizabeth. On the day of the weddings, I arrived at Durham Palace and walked in behind a reasonably large family party. The guards did not question me in the slightest. I had gotten quite good at looking like I belonged and going where I pleased. I followed the crowd down to the chapel where the weddings would take place. The chapel was tightly packed with many well-wishers, but I found a vantage point in the shadows where I could easily see the altar, but others could barely see me.

Finally, the time came and the three brides, led by Jane, processed down the aisle. Jane looked stunning in her splendid purple gown of silk brocade with an intricate floral pattern. The gown was fitted to the waist and about the shoulders with a bodice that had a square neckline. Her neck was adorned with a most fabulous necklace of diamonds and pearls with matching earrings. The gown bloomed below the waist like a glorious, inverted purple rose, and was adorned with a wealth of diamonds and pearls that sparkled as she gracefully strode to the altar. Her magnificent red hair was loose and flowing down well beyond her shoulders. Her face portrayed a graceful resolve. It was well accepted that Lady Katherine was the fair one of the sisters, but Jane's beauty, both physical and spiritual, pierced me to my soul. I let go with a slightly audible gasp as I finally took a breath. I could feel a tear roll down my cheek as Jane and the two Katherines took their places at the altar.

After the ceremony, as I followed the crowd to the great hall, the fact that Jane was now a married woman struck me like a club to the head. I hoped that she would find happiness and purpose. I could barely imagine this sweet girl as a mother, but I knew in my heart that she would embrace the role with strength and wisdom. She would be a marvelous mother.

Lord Guildford, on the other hand, appeared to be paying more attention to his mother, Lady Jane Dudley, than to his lovely wife. His mother seemed almost to be annoyed that the three brides were garnering more attention than she was as hostess. Conversely, young Lord Henry Herbert was showering Lady Katherine with attention, much to her delight. Lady Frances looked quite pleased with all that was happening around her.

I had told myself that I would only attend the ceremony and then I would leave, but I found myself milling about the crowd, looking for different and better views of Jane among the other newly married brides.

"Are you not Master Thomas, Ward of His Majesty?" a small voice asked from behind me. When I turned, I did not immediately locate the source of the inquiry until I glanced down to see little Lady Mary Grey's smiling face looking up at me. Her pretty blue dress and jewelry made her look a bit older than her eight years despite her small stature.

"Greetings, Lady Mary," I said with a smile as I bowed deeply before her diminutive frame. "How sweet of you to remember me. You look wonderful today. Your beauty is beyond words. And congratulations on your betrothal."

"Thank you, I suppose," she responded with a sigh. "Lord Arthur and I will make a splendid looking pair! I don't even come up to his waist!"

"Should you not be up on the dais with your sisters and Lady Katherine Dudley?"

"Does it look like they are missing me?" she laughed, and I had to smile as well.

I gazed back at Jane whose simple smile was less than convincing. Lady Mary had apparently noticed this as well.

"I thought brides were to be happy on their wedding day," she commented.

I departed the ceremony and returned home. I was very tired by the time I was in my bed, but I lay awake for some time with the vision of Jane's beauty dancing in my head.

About a week after the wedding, I learned that Jane had returned to Norwich Place, and so I arranged to deliver another letter from Lord Miles.

The Scoundrel's Son

She entered the garden and politely invited me to sit but her manner was quite serious.

"Tom, I am afraid we cannot continue to visit, just the two of us," she said directly and to the point. "It is not proper for a married woman. It was probably not proper before now but be that as it may. Very soon, I will be moving to the Dudley house, and so, going forward, we can only visit in the company of others. I must say, Tom, I will very much miss these visits."

"I will miss them as well," I replied. That simple phrase was possibly the most understated thing I had ever uttered. Truly, I would miss spending this precious time with Jane from the bottom of my heart. I had lived from one visit with dizzying anticipation to the next. I was not surprised by Jane's decision that we could no longer visit, but that did not make the reality hurt any less.

As I prepared to leave, I noticed a slight bruise on Jane's wrist that she was trying to cover by tugging at her sleeve. It was then that I also noticed a redness under her eye.

"What happened to your wrist?" I asked.

"Oh, it is nothing," she answered with a forced smile. "I have to work at being a better wife."

***

As I studied the chess board, I could not believe what I was seeing. I looked and looked again to make sure I was not missing one of Edward's traps. I finally made my move taking his rook with my queen.

"Checkmate!" I exclaimed proudly.

Edward gave the board a thorough review. "And so, it is!" he conceded. "Congratulations!" My victories were very few; I rejoiced with a good chortle. He then started to cough. With all that was happening around Jane's wedding, it had been a few weeks since I had last visited Edward. I could not believe my eyes when I saw how much his condition had worsened in a short time. His pallor was even more pronounced. He had lost considerable weight, and he was thin in the first place.

"I have written a devise for my succession as Northumberland has recommended," Edward announced as he took a piece of paper written in

Frederic Fahey

his own hand from his side table and passed it to me. Not surprisingly, it excluded Lady Mary and Lady Elizabeth on the grounds of their illegitimate births. Thus, the succession went to the male heirs of Lady Frances and then to those of her daughters, Jane, Katherine, and Mary. It then passed to the male heirs of Edward's cousin, Lady Margaret Clifford.

I looked the paper over several times. "It would seem that the most likely source of male heirs as we speak would be Jane or Katherine, given their recent marriages, or possibly Lady Margaret," I concluded.

"I suppose that is so," Edward agreed. I did not mention that there might not be any male heirs at the time of his passing although the thought crossed my mind.

"I heard from Jane that you attended the weddings," Edward said. "Did you receive an invitation?"

"Not an official one," I admitted sheepishly. "You know I have my ways of entry. The brides were unbelievably beautiful. You should be very proud of your Master of Wardrobe. He outdid himself this time."

"I do not approve of you sneaking around as you do!" Edward reprimanded me sternly. But then his words softened. "But I am glad to hear of the success of the ceremony. As you can imagine, all I hear from my observers are the good things they think I want to hear."

Edward started to cough, producing blood and other matter from his lungs. It hurt to see my friend so ill. When he finally caught his breath, he asked if I could present his devise to the Council. "I am just too weak today," he said. I looked at the clock and saw I had three hours until an engagement that I had previously arranged.

"Of course," I said. I was apprehensive that someone might notice that I was not as thin as Edward, given his recent loss of weight. However, the many layers in the royal garb and white linen he had come to wrap about his neck hid this fact quite well.

Once the Council was assembled, I handed Edward's paper to Northumberland. He read it to himself several times before reading it aloud to the group. I noticed many of the Council members expressing agreement while others seemed to be considering each individual word very deeply. Lord Suffolk smiled broadly at the announcement that the male heirs of his wife and three daughters were the first to be considered. He rearranged himself in his chair and took a deep breath, expanding his

The Scoundrel's Son

chest like that of a proud peacock.

"There are eight members of the royal family besides His Majesty," Northumberland observed, "and not a male in sight!" Of course, if there were a male heir, passing over the Ladies Mary and Elizabeth would be more straightforward.

"Is there a concern whether the subjects of the realm will accept the exclusion of Lady Mary and Lady Elizabeth?" one of the Council members inquired. I was wondering the same thing.

"They will accept what His Majesty, the Council and the Parliament tell them to accept," Northumberland responded forcefully.

Many members of the Council voiced their general agreement with the devise, although some had similar concerns regarding the exclusion of Edward's sisters. All did agree that once the devise was finalized and approved by the Council, they must seek approval from Parliament immediately.

"Of course," Northumberland added, "we are only discussing these issues so that they are in place in the distant future when the need should arise." He then turned to me. "We are all heartened to see His Majesty in such fine spirits this morning." The Council members noted their approval with applause and shouts. I returned to Edward to report on the support for his devise. I checked the clock as I entered his chamber. I still had time before my arranged meeting.

"I am so glad to hear this. Thank you, Tom, for presenting this on my behalf. I am very grateful." He had clearly been concerned with how the Council might react. This concern seemed to have left him even more drained and exhausted.

"I will leave you now, my friend, so you may rest. I promise I will return in the next day or so," I said with a bow.

I checked the clock on my way out of Edward's chamber and saw I still had almost a half an hour. I moved quickly to a small room down the hall that Edward sometimes used for smaller meetings. I entered the room without being noticed and opened the drapery to let in some sun. In the bottom of a cabinet, I had left my satchel with the royal outfit from the reception for the Ladies Mary and Elizabeth. At the end of the visit, I had stowed it away thinking it may someday come in handy. I changed quickly, opened the door just a crack, and took my place in the chair upon the dais.

Frederic Fahey

I had arranged the room so that I was not visible to those walking down the outside hall. Soon, there was a knock at the door.

"Your Majesty, Lord Guildford Dudley is here to see you," a servant announced.

I had taken one of the invitation letters I had received from Edward and altered it carefully to indicate that His Majesty had invited Lord Guildford for an audience.

"Please come in, Lord Guildford. You may close the door behind you." Guildford did as I directed and then approached hesitantly. He bowed deeply.

"Your Majesty," he greeted me.

I asked him to take a seat. "It was with much regret that I was not able to attend your marriage to my sweet cousin. I hear that it was a marvelous ceremony and celebration." We spoke regarding the wedding, its splendor, and who attended. I asked if Lady Jane had moved to the Dudley house. He said that she had, after spending several days with her mother at Norwich Place.

"Is she finally settled? I am quite concerned with her happiness and wellbeing," I said. He replied that she was now settled.

"Do you and she get along well? Are there any troubles between the two of you?" Guildford looked surprised by my question and started to stammer.

"We are new to each other and the situation of marriage. She understands her duties as a wife but is slow to embrace them." At that response, I sat forward and eyed him intently.

"Do you find that physical intimidation is successful in handling these situations?" I rose and started to walk slowly towards Guildford's chair. "My cousin is strong of mind and spirit, but, physically, she is as tender as a young fawn," I said, as calmly and clearly as I could. Guildford tried to rise quickly from his chair as I approached, but his gangly nature and nervousness hindered his efforts. I grabbed the scruff of his blouse in my left hand and pushed him back into his chair. As much as I strove these past few years to portray a gentle nature, my Offal Court jagged edges sometimes found their way to the surface.

"We men understand the intent and value of intimidation with each other. We sometimes find it necessary to make our point strongly with

The Scoundrel's Son

another gentleman. Don't you agree?" I was now within a hand's width of his face. I could practically smell what he had eaten for dinner.

"On the other hand, it is our duty to protect the women in our lives, not to intimidate them. They lighten the burdens that torture our souls. They are the future mothers of our children. We are bound to treat them with the utmost honor and respect. Don't you agree?"

"Y-Y-Yes, Your Majesty!" Guildford stuttered.

"I am pleased that we agree on this," I said as I released his blouse. He fell back in his chair, looking up at me with wide-eyed shock. I jabbed his chest with my finger.

"I want to hear that my dear cousin is being treated with the respect she deserves. Do you understand me?"

"Yes, Your Majesty," he answered meekly.

"I did not hear you!"

"Yes, Your Majesty," he said more loudly.

"I am glad to hear it. This conversation is to be held in confidence among gentlemen. This matter is between you and me."

"Yes, Your Majesty," he responded.

I returned to my chair.

"I am glad to see Your Majesty looking so well," Guildford said trying to ease the tension in the room. "I had heard Your Majesty had been ill."

"I appreciate your concern, Lord Guildford," I responded. "I am feeling much better today. Thank you. You are dismissed." Guildford rose and bowed to me before retreating as quickly as his long legs would carry him from the room.

Chapter 25

Lord Miles sipped his ale and considered my news about Edward's declining health.

"I will make it a point to visit my little friend very soon. But as summer has just begun, I have many things to attend to."

"You are not understanding me, Lord Miles," I interrupted. "There might not be much time left." Suddenly my eyes began to fill with tears. Although I had known for some time that Edward's death was a stark possibility, putting it into words made it even more real. I was but a boy of fifteen years. I only knew of death as something viewed from a distance. Until then, I had not at all comprehended the intimate and consuming nature of sharing a loved one's last days on earth.

Lord Miles finally heard me. He took a deep breath and placed his arm around my shoulder.

"All right, Tom. Find a time when we can visit."

Such a time was arranged a few days later. As we were led to Edward's bed chamber, I was reminded of the time during the masquerade that I had visited King Henry while he lay near death in this very room: the dim light with the drapes drawn, the smell of the flowers, and the profound silence that allowed us to hear each creaking floorboard as we approached Edward's bed. Edward was sitting, propped up on several pillows. His eyes were closed as we entered the room, but he quickly opened them, and a smile dawned upon his face as we drew closer.

"Tom and Miles!" he exclaimed. "My good friends! I am so pleased to see the two of you!"

Lord Miles stopped right where he was, and his face froze, stunned by Edward's frailty. I went to Edward's bedside quickly to give Lord Miles time to recover.

The Scoundrel's Son

"Good afternoon, Edward. How is my twin feeling today?"

"About the same I suppose. I am afraid we will have to postpone our tennis match." We both snickered, which caused him to cough for a few moments.

Lord Miles approached the other side of the bed. He spoke of Lady Edith and how their daughter had grown. I described a rather ornate bowl I had designed at the shop. We reminisced about the masquerade, and my amazement at how many servants it took to dress a prince. Lord Miles described one of their harrowing adventures that I had not heard before, this one regarding a crazy hermit. We made small talk attempting to avoid the profound situation before us. Edward seemed more than content to listen.

"I tried to warn you," I said, "that it would not be much fun being a pauper! You just would not hear it!"

"At one point I said to myself," Lord Miles added, "if this urchin tells me one more time that he is the King of England, I will throw him across my lap and give him a few smacks on the bottom!"

Lord Miles and I laughed. Edward sat quietly and smiled. I was thankful that, on this day, he was able to enjoy the merriment without falling into one of his dreadful coughing fits.

"This visit has raised my spirits!" Edward finally announced. "I have not enjoyed myself so much in quite a while! I want you two to visit me much more often once I feel better!" I felt my heart dip at Edward's words of improving health as his eyes told a different story.

"We will do just that!" Lord Miles responded. He and I took Edward's hands.

The three of us cherished the moment for a minute or two without a word. Edward then asked me if I would stay a while longer as he had something to show me privately. Lord Miles gave Edward's hand one last caress. Although the scars of Lord Miles's hands told of many difficult and rugged times, they cradled Edward's hand with a striking tenderness.

"I will be back very soon, my little friend," Lord Miles said as he bowed deeply and gracefully. "Your Majesty." He then turned and left the chamber.

"I've had a bit of a crazy notion these past few days," Edward shared. "I would like to hear what you think of it."

"Certainly. What is on your mind?"

"If something were to happen to me, could you pretend to be me and rule in my stead?"

His words struck me like a thunderbolt. "Your Majesty, please do not ask this of me! I beg you! I have done all that you have requested without hesitation. I have come to your aid when I feared for your life. I would do anything for you and the kingdom." I went to my knees.

"But I fear this deception would drain me of my soul. It would take from me all that I am. I beg that you do not lay this burden upon me. I would take your place in death if I could, but do not ask me to take your place in life."

"Please rise, Tom," Edward said. He seemed almost embarrassed. "As I said, it was just a crazy notion. My mind sometimes runs in strange directions these days."

"Bring me the paper on my desk." He pointed to his small writing desk across the room. The paper was the hand-written devise of succession that I had seen before. "Northumberland and I have discussed this, and I have made some minor alterations." As I read the paper, I saw the scratched and additional words in Edward's own hand. The sentence that had once said,

"To the L Frances heirs male, for lack of such issue to the L' Jane's heirs male," now read

"To the L Frances heirs male, if she has any such issue before my death, to L' Jane and her heirs male."

I read the words again; I could not believe what my eyes were seeing. By merely adding the two words "and her," he had potentially changed the course of English history.

"Am I reading this right?" I asked in disbelief. "You are naming Lady Jane as heir to the throne of England?"

"Yes, you are reading it correctly," Edward said.

I stood frozen by the notion. Lady Jane? The Queen of England? And not just queen, but queen regnant? No woman had ever been crowned as the ruling queen in the kingdom's history. Jane was a sixteen-year-old girl, of whom most of the realm's loyal subjects had never heard. On the other hand, they all knew Lady Mary, and hadn't the Parliament blessed King Henry's will declaring her heir to the throne despite her illegitimate birth?

The Scoundrel's Son

"My dear friend, I beg that you know my love for you as I say these words. You are my twin, the only brother I have ever known. We are bound by all things but blood." I looked Edward directly in the eye. "It is my fear," I stated as plainly as I could, "that this would be the gravest error of your reign."

Edward closed his eyes as his expression crumbled with disappointment with my response. He finally gestured with a wave for me to continue.

"The people see Lady Mary as the heir to the throne, quite and simple. She is the oldest child of your father, King Henry. Your subjects have known her since birth. They still speak of her mother, Queen Catherine, who went to war with the Scots while your father was fighting in France, even as she carried Mary in her womb with armor shaped to her delicate condition. They hold Lady Mary in great reverence without much regard to her religious beliefs or the situation of her birth.

"As for Lady Jane, those who know her appreciate her wonderful intelligence and her devotion to God. But the possibility that she would rule the kingdom has not entered their minds, not even for a brief instant. The common folk don't even know who Lady Jane Grey is. Her name is as foreign to them as the fourth cousin of the emperor of Russia. No one beyond Northumberland and a few Council members will accept Jane as queen regnant as long as Lady Mary is alive. When the dispute for the crown arises, I fear you will be placing Jane in grave danger."

Edward continued to sit still. At first, I wondered if he had fallen asleep, but then his eyes opened, and he looked straight into mine.

"Tom, you are mistaken. Besides, the Council voted unanimously to endorse this new version a few days ago. Northumberland has already aligned over a hundred judges and other experts to vouch for its validity. We will now move for endorsement by the Parliament. And if things do come to pass and my sister chooses to object, Northumberland is an outstanding general who could easily put down a rebellion."

"Edward, I am not questioning Northumberland's abilities as either a political or military leader. The fight will not be between Northumberland's thousands of soldiers and what meager force Lady Mary can muster in East Anglia, but between the notion of Lady Jane as queen regnant and the expectations of your subjects."

Frederic Fahey

After a bit more discussion, I finally conceded. "I sincerely hope that I am wrong, and you are right." I was at a loss for words as I held his hand. My mind was scrambling when Edward squeezed my hand with a strength that brought me back. His tear-filled eyes went wide, and he looked at me straight. His lower lip started to tremble.

"I am afraid, Tom!"

I sat down on the edge of his bed, leaned in, and wrapped my arms around him. Our tears mingled when my cheek caressed his. Our embrace without words lasted for quite some time.

Chapter 26

A few days later, I awoke upon a glorious summer's morning. The sun was shining as the city came to life. My spirits were high as I headed to the shop bright and early with a new but unfounded optimism. Perhaps Edward and his Council would reconsider, or, at least when the devise reached the Parliament, that smarter heads with less to gain or lose would prevail. Lastly, Edward would miraculously recover and none of this would come to pass. I stopped by the bakery and bought some of the hot buns that I knew Robert loved. I arrived at the shop and proceeded to tidy up. When Robert came down not long after, he was surprised to see me.

"Young Sprout, you look refreshed this sunny morning!" I gave him one of the still-warm buns. We broke our fast together before our day at the shop got underway. It was a good day at work, and I accomplished much. I tried to catch up on some of the work that had fallen behind since I had been spending so much time at Whitehall. By the time I was ready to leave for the day, it was past seven of the clock. But since it was just past the solstice, it was still light so I took the opportunity to head to Whitehall.

I arrived at the palace's service gate and entered in my usual way. If there was any change in mood at the gate, it went without my notice. However, as I approached Edward's chambers, I realized that something was wrong. Servants and healers were going in and out of the chamber with deep concern carved into their faces. Edward's condition must have taken a turn for the worse. I slipped into the shadows to watch. Finally, Richard exited the chamber, and I scooted across the hall into the light and got his attention. When I saw the expression on Richard's face and his deliberate step toward me, I knew.

"Master Tom," he spoke very slowly. "I am very sorry to have to tell you that His Majesty has gone to join the Lord." I stood still for a few moments as the blood seemed to rush from my body. I returned to my dark corner and slumped against the wall as my eyes filled with tears. I felt a hand on my shoulder and turned to see Richard's kind face.

"May God bless you, Tom," he said softly. "You were a good friend to His Majesty. He loved you dearly." He pulled me to his chest as I burst into tears. I let Richard try to console my sorrows in the shadows. In the six years I had known Richard, we had barely spoken beyond the hollow greetings and goodbyes of acquaintances. But we two knew Edward well, certainly better than most. Richard had attended to him every day of his reign.

"He was my dearest friend," I eventually managed to say. We wept together in the shadows for several moments.

I headed back home. It had been less than an hour since I entered the palace, but now the evening looked gray to me. As I noticed the normality of the people's activities, I understood that the news of Edward's death had not been announced. I was the only one outside of Whitehall with the profound knowledge that the king was dead. I sat on a nearby bench as the loneliness and grief swept over me.

When I finally reached the house, Father Christian was not home. I doused my face with water and curled up in my favorite chair. I had never experienced the loss of someone so close to me. I sat numb for a long time until the door flew open, and Father Christian burst into the house. He whistled as he made himself some supper. He came towards our little sitting area with his meal and was startled to see me huddled like a cat in my chair.

"Oh, Tom! I didn't see you there. Isn't this a marvelous summer's twilight?" It was then that he noticed that something was amiss. "Are you all right?" he asked as he pulled his chair closer to mine. I started to sob.

"Father, my dearest friend is gone." With those few words, my heart sank, and my eyes gushed. Father Christian pulled his chair even closer and grasped my hand. When I finally looked up, he embraced me.

"Tom, my dear boy," he repeated over and over as he patted my back and handed me a clean hand linen. I knew that Father Christian was no stranger to death and grieving. In his life as a priest, he had presided over countless funerals and consoled so many who had lost loved ones. I sup-

The Scoundrel's Son

pose he always had clean hand linen in his pocket, just in case.

"Tom, God loves you as I love you," he said soothingly. "Perhaps not today, but in time, I pray you will come to rejoice the fact that you had such a good friend as His Majesty. I don't mean because he was king, but that he moved something inside you. Not everyone has such friendships in their lives. I pray that your splendid memories of His Majesty, those that deeply touched your soul, will someday replace your sorrow, and that you will realize that you are a better man for having been blessed with such a person in your life."

I returned Father Christian's hug with all I had, body, heart, and soul. He went back to the kitchen and prepared for me some supper and a cup of ale. He placed it on the table next to my chair, probably knowing that I would not touch it. I did not move from that chair for at least an hour.

At some point, I moved to my bed. I remembered that first day when Edward rescued me outside the palace gate, when he and Lord Miles disrupted the coronation, and he revealed that my splendid nutcracker happened to be the Great Seal of England. I reminisced about the look on his face when I gave him the watch, and the relief when Lord Miles and I entered the room at Windsor to find that he was safe. I remembered the stories, the jokes and the outright laughter that shook our bellies.

And then my thoughts turned to the times Edward and I had spent with sweet Jane. I sat up straight as an arrow in bed, my heart racing like a charging steed. Jane! Oh, my goodness! My dear Jane!

Jane was going to be named Queen of England! Perhaps it had already occurred. Had she been informed of the details of Edward's devise before this? It had never occurred to me to ask this of Edward.

Where was she? Was she at Durham Palace? Or had she gone to the country for the summer? Where did the Dudleys go in the summer? Then I thought back to the masquerade. Where did they take me when King Henry died?

The Tower of London! Of course, Jane would be heading to the Tower of London! It had become a tradition that, after the passing of the previous king, the new king would reside in the luxurious royal quarters at the Tower until his coronation. But when would Jane be brought there? Probably in the next few days, at least by the time of the announcement of Edward's death. I was not sure when that might be. In the meantime, I was as pent up as a stallion waiting to race when all I could do was wait.

The announcement finally came two days later. I was in the square near the shop when the crier arrived. As luck would have it, I happened upon Aly.

"Hi Tom," she said when she saw me. "Do you know what is goin' on?"

I shrugged my shoulders feigning ignorance. Then the crier proclaimed the sad news. Aly looked at me through the wide eyes of shock and grasped my hand firmly.

"Oh, Tom, I am so sorry!" This affection from my good friend caused a tear to roll down my cheek. At that point, I thought I had wept all the tears to be had.

I heard many expressions of deep sadness that the blessed king had died so young, only fifteen years old. He was on the threshold of ruling the kingdom in his own right. His reign was so full of promise. He was the most treasured gem in the entire realm, and now he was gone.

"The king is dead!" the crier concluded. "Long live the queen!"

These words had never been pronounced in English history. As unique as they were, they did not surprise folks as being ruled by a woman was the only alternative at the time. But what did surprise everyone were the crier's next words. "Long live Queen Jane!"

"Queen Jane?" These words, spoken as a question, were on the lips, or at least in the minds, of practically everyone.

Aly gave me a puzzled look.

"I don't understand," she said. "Princess Mary is queen. Who's Jane?"

"His Majesty's cousin."

"But that's not right! King Henry said Princess Mary followed Prince Edward …"

"I know, but King Edward said Lady Jane."

"She's only a girl!"

"He was only a boy."

This exchange between Aly and me was being echoed by practically everyone in the square. I now knew that what I feared and what I had tried so hard to explain to Edward would come to pass.

As Aly and I left the square and found a place removed from the clamor to sit, it became personal, the loss of Edward, my concern for Jane, all

The Scoundrel's Son

of it. Aly could see I was devastated. She let me sit quietly while the rest of London erupted in a confused frenzy.

Aly needed to head home to look after her brothers. I suddenly felt the overwhelming yearning to see Jane, to speak to her, to be with her. Could I find a way to enter the Tower? Built almost five hundred years ago, it was the strongest and most secure castle in the land. If there was a way to enter, I needed to find it. There must be a way! But who would know?

***

William shook his head as the two of us stood in a shadowy corner of Whitehall's grand corridors. "You ask the impossible, Master Thomas. The kingdom is in a delicate state! The passing of the king has just been announced!" I pleaded with my eyes as he gave me a probing stare. He let out a gasp but beckoned me to follow him. He led me to a storeroom and handed me a guard's uniform. I started to thank him, but he quickly and forcibly clasped his hand over my mouth.

"Shhh! Listen carefully!" he whispered very clearly. "If you are questioned, do not mention my name!" After I agreed, he continued. "I imagine by now Her Majesty has been taken to the Tower. Go and observe the changing of the guard at the Bridge Gate and determine how best to fall in line as the relieved guard prepares to file inside. Enter with them. The king's... I mean the queen's residence is within the large tower on the wall of the inner ward facing the river. There is a small entrance that provides direct access to the royal residence on the left side where this tower meets the wall." He squeezed my shoulder. "Do not ask any more of me." I shook his hand and mouthed the words "Thank you." I stuffed the guard's uniform into my tunic and headed home.

The next day I found my way to Kent and Hendon Hall to share the sorrowful news with Lord Miles. He sat across from me resting his elbows on his knees as he slumped forward with his head bent.

"I will dearly miss my little friend," he shared softly. "During our adventures together, he was not the easiest boy with whom to deal, I can tell you that! Even in your ragged clothes, he still pranced around like the cock that ruled the roost!" He said with a smile, "I suppose it was because he did rule the roost! I was more inclined to think he was crazy than King of England, but something about the boy touched me. I could not just leave him. I needed to help him if I could." We shared an embrace and a few more stories before he brought me back to the city.

Chapter 27

I turned my attention to how I might gain entrance to The Tower of London. As you know, it is the most intimidating edifice on the river. I could see the top of the White Tower located within the Tower's inner ward from the street outside my home. The Tower is surrounded by a moat with two entrances, one across a well-guarded bridge and another to the river used, for example, for the arrival by barge of the royal family or other distinguished guests. Not surprisingly, these are referred to as the Bridge Gate and the Water Gate. Once inside the Tower's wall, one is merely in the outer ward, and must then pass through another wall to reach the inner ward. William had informed me that Jane would be residing in the royal quarters built into the wall of the inner ward. Penetrating these barriers would be a much more formidable challenge than finding my way about Whitehall or even Windsor Castle. I am not saying impossible, just formidable.

As William had recommended, I went to the Tower that evening to observe the changing of the guard. I found a dark corner for me to hide on the north side of the moat, farthest from the river. From here, I could see along the moat on the west side of the Tower down to the bridge. Suddenly the changing began. I could tell by the ringing of church bells in the distance that it was precisely six of the clock. Upon command, the relieved guard marched down the center of the bridge while the new guard marched to the outside on the right and left. The filing was very orderly but not well observed. The sergeant of the guard tended to keep right of the gate and so I would file from the left. Once the changing was complete, the new guard snapped to attention. I then waited patiently in my corner for the next changing.

Sitting in the shadows, I thought of Edward and our strange and wondrous friendship. What an unlikely couple of chums were we. In his last few days, Edward and I had our starkest disagreement and yet it was also our most intimate time together. Now he was gone, leaving an emptiness as if a chunk had been torn from my heart. I prayed that Father Christian was right and that someday I would feel blessed for having Edward in my life.

I heard the church bells ring nine as the amber twilight gave the Tower an ominous and foreboding glow. The sun soon set, and night slowly fell upon the city. Through this transition, I was surprised to find that my eyes could still see in the almost total darkness. However, with the night also came the haunting uncertainty of what lie ahead. What was in store for my sweet Jane? Was she up to the ominous task ahead of her? Who would be there to guide her in the early days of her reign? I presumed that Lady Mary had been informed of the passing of her brother. I remembered the night during the masquerade when King Henry died. Elizabeth was whisked to Whitehall in the middle of the night, and Somerset informed us of the king's passing. It was not until the following day that his death was broadly announced. What was on Mary's mind? How would she react to the news that Edward had died, and Jane had been named queen?

At midnight, the sergeant called his first order and the guard changed again, in exactly the same manner as the previous time. I surmised that the changing occurred every six hours. The midnight change would provide the most cover since it was midsummer, and there would be considerable daylight during the other changes. I decided I would attempt entry the next night at midnight.

Accordingly, I placed the guard's uniform in a satchel and headed to the Tower and my corner in the shadows from the night before. I changed into the uniform and hid my satchel with my street clothes under a loose rock where the dirt was relatively dry. Just before midnight, I slunk along the moat to a position close to the guard that was stationed the farthest to the left of the Bridge Gate. The clock in my head told me that the changing would begin quite soon. It turned out to be more than a quarter of an hour as my anticipation had led me to move more quickly than I had thought.

When the time arrived, the sergeant yelled the order, and the guard stood at attention. I did the same and slowly sidestepped my way closer to the left most guard. The sergeant yelled again, and the guard took two

The Scoundrel's Son

steps forward and then turned toward the gate, in my case to the left. On the third order, all began to march. As we started to march down the bridge, the sergeant had a perplexed look on his face. I wondered if he had noticed there was an extra guard on the left. I marched as straight and proper as I could so as not to call attention to myself. I could see him pointing to each guard as we entered and trying to count them, but since the new guard were obscuring our rank, and we were already on the move, it appeared he finally decided all was fine.

Once inside the wall of the outer ward, we marched toward the guard's quarters. As we turned a corner, I was able to separate myself from the rest and duck away since I was last in line. I then started to do some exploring. I moved quickly from shadow to shadow as I surveyed the outer ward, staying alert so as not to be seen. I found the tower William had described, circular, larger than the rest, and very close to the Water Gate. I then recalled when I arrived at the Tower in the royal barge following King Henry's death and was directly escorted to the royal quarters within. I found the entrance to the tower, the postern gate, that William had mentioned. It was still the very early morning, and I was able to nestle into a dark corner. There were two guards currently stationed there. I wondered if there might be more guards adding to the confusion as dawn approached. I bided my time.

The sun was just starting to show its face when I moved toward the postern gate. I noticed some shuffling of the guard, so I quickly moved to become part of the unorderly interchange. All things considered, it all had gone remarkably well, and I thought I had made it into the royal quarters when one of the guards spotted me.

"I don't remember you. What is your name?" he asked.

"Thomas Canty, sir," I announced as I sprang to attention. As soon as I had said it, I regretted that I had not used a false name.

"Thomas Canty? I don't remember a Thomas Canty among our ranks," the guard became very suspicious. "Who do you report to?"

Now I was in trouble! If I gave him a wrong name or even hesitated, he would know I was an imposter. I did not know what fate awaited me, but I knew it would not be good. Afterall, I was trying to sneak into Her Majesty's quarters.

"Thomas Canty is with Her Majesty's personal guard from the

Frederic Fahey

palace," a familiar voice announced from behind me. I continued to stand at attention, but, from the corner of my eye, I saw Richard, Edward's master groom, walking towards us. "He is under my watch."

"Yes, sir," the guard responded loudly as he nervously sprung to attention. I let out my breath slowly as my heartbeat tried to return to normal.

As we walked, Richard spoke to me under his breath. "I must admit, Master Tom, I am surprised to see you here."

"I was hoping that I might have a brief visit with Her Majesty." Without even looking at me, Richard smiled.

"You never cease to amaze me, Master Tom."

He guided me to a small meeting room. "Her Majesty has some time after she breaks her fast and before her first meeting with the Lords Northumberland and Suffolk. I will bring her by." He pointed to a cabinet in the corner of the room. "Until then, you can hide in here." I hid in the cabinet for only a short time before I heard the door open, and Richard speak.

"I thought Your Majesty might enjoy some quiet time before your first meeting. I know you have a busy day ahead. I will let Your Majesty know when the Lords Northumberland and Suffolk have arrived."

"Thank you, Richard," Jane said. As Richard prepared to leave, he instructed Jane's ladies to do the same. It was a bit of an unusual request but not totally uncommon. Once I heard the door close and was sure all had left, I slowly pushed the cabinet door open and gazed upon Her Majesty Queen Jane, looking as precious and fragile as I had ever seen her. Her royal dress of flowing silk was the golden color of the sun. It was fitted to the waist with a high bodice about her neck. Her sleeves bloomed as did her gown below her waist resembling the fresh flower of foxglove sparkling at dawn. On her head she wore a bonnet also gold in color adorned with many lustrous pearls. Amidst the royal splendor, her pale features appeared even more delicate, more breathtaking than a rose petal. Although she certainly looked the part of a young queen, I wondered if she truly felt like one.

"Good morning Your Majesty," I said softly, trying not to startle her.

"Oh!" Jane exclaimed, putting her hand to her breast. "It's you, Tom! What are you doing here?"

I knelt before her. "I came to see if Your Majesty was all right."

The Scoundrel's Son

"Oh Tom!" she said. "It has been an absolutely dreadful last few days!"

She proceeded to tell me how she had been taken to Syon House along the banks of the river just outside the city where she met with her father along with Northumberland, and several members of Edward's Council. To her surprise, her mother was also present.

"My parents informed me of Edward's passing. My heart shattered at the news. Of course, I knew he had been very ill, but I still prayed for his recovery."

Quickly, she realized she had not been summoned merely to inform her of Edward's death. Her father told her about Edward's devise of succession, and that his will, on his deathbed, was that she succeed him as ruler of the kingdom of England.

"My mind went blank even as Northumberland presented Edward's reasons. The weight of the sad news regarding my dear cousin as well as what was being lain before me overwhelmed me, and I sank to the floor in a cascade of tears. 'I cannot accept this burden,' I finally said out loud. 'This crown is not mine. Lady Mary is the rightful heir.'

"All in the meeting, including my mother, strove to convince me otherwise. As their words flew around me like a flock of frightened birds, I closed my eyes and prayed to God for the repose of the soul of my sweet cousin. I also asked for His divine guidance whether to accept this truly awesome burden. At last, I decided that God had placed this challenge before me, and I must accept the Crown. My reign would be in the Lord's service. I will accept whatever duties He deems fit for me. I pray for the strength and wisdom to carry them out.

"On the next day, the tenth day of the month, my reign officially began. I was then brought by barge to the Tower to await my coronation."

Tears started to run down Jane's face. As strong as her faith in God was, I feared that this was still too much to ask of her. Since there had never been a ruling queen, there were many things that I did not understand.

"Does this mean Lord Guildford is king?" I asked, thinking of Guildford's immaturity and violence towards Jane.

"Absolutely not! I am almost seventeen years old and close to the age of King Henry when his reign began. I am queen and ruler of the realm. I could name Guildford as a duke, and he will serve as my consort. But he will not be king! I expect the Council with Northumberland presiding to remain as it was under His Majesty until I come of age in a year."

"When will your coronation be?" Jane was already queen. The coronation would merely be a reason to celebrate and consecrate the start of her reign.

"It is yet to be scheduled, but I don't expect for at least a month."

Jane's look turned somber as she changed the subject. "A message arrived yesterday from Lady Mary to the Council stating that they should immediately pledge their allegiance to her as rightful queen." This did not surprise me in the least since I was quite sure that Lady Mary would not simply concede given that, like Jane, she was incredibly headstrong and driven by what she thought was morally right.

"Does this not concern you?" I asked.

"If I am the rightful queen, then God will protect me," was her simple response.

At that point, there was a knock on the door and Richard announced that the time for Her Majesty's meeting had arrived. I took her hand as she rose from her chair.

"Jane, if I can be of any service at all, I am here for you," I offered.

"Be my friend, Tom, and pray for me. That is all I ask," she said with a loving smile that melted my heart. I hid in the cabinet again and waited.

"Master Tom," Richard finally called to me when it was safe to come out of hiding. He handed to me a doublet and a piece of paper. "On your next visit," he instructed. "Wear this doublet, which will identify you as one of Her Majesty's servants and present this order that I have signed for you at the gate."

"Thank you, Master Richard," I said.

"I saw, firsthand, what your friendship meant to His Majesty over the years," he said. "Right now, Her Majesty needs someone like you."

I exited the Tower without incident and walked back home, thinking of Jane and the delicate situation in which she found herself. She was righteous but still a very sensitive young lady unaccustomed to the politics of the royal court. I, on the other hand, had witnessed firsthand the treachery that lay ahead. She would have to determine whom she could trust for advice. Also, Lady Mary was not going to give in easily or flee to Spain.

The Scoundrel's Son

Jane would need to learn quickly.

Later, as I lay in bed, I did as Jane had asked, and I prayed for her. I prayed that she would be given the time and space to grow into the most wonderful queen that I knew she could be. And that she would come to find happiness in her service to the realm and to God.

Chapter 28

A few days later, I left the shop to find Jem Riley standing across the street staring at me and smiling. I had seen him around, but I had not spoken to Jem since our brush a few years back. I did not like his look.

"Tom Canty!" he called out. "Just the one I wanna see."

"Hello, Jem," I replied and continued to walk toward home. From what I had heard from Aly and others, he had progressed from being a bit of a rascal to someone dabbling in more serious business. Rumor had it that he had arrangements with a number of cutpurses and burglars in Offal Court and Pudding Lane finding buyers for their stolen goods.

He approached me with a brisk step and talked as we walked along.

"You know, Tom, I can't sleep sometimes, particularly on these hot, summer nights. I find myself walkin' around the city at all hours."

"I don't have time to chat," I said, but he wasn't deterred.

"So, I'm wanderin' the other night, and I find myself near the Tower of London."

At the mention of the Tower, my ears perked up, but I continued to walk as if I was ignoring his chatter.

"I see someone up to something on the west side of the moat. I duck into a shadow just as you taught me when we was young. I see him change into a guard's uniform. 'What's he up to?' I ask meself. But then I see that it is you, Tom, as sure as I'm standing here."

"I don't know what you are talking about," I said, not slowing down.

"Oh, I'm sure you do know. I remember how good you was, sneaking into people's homes. You got a certain style, you do. I knew it was you straight up.

"I remember your little speech. So high and righteous! You're not a thief you said. But now here we are. You're up to somethin', Tom, and I

The Scoundrel's Son

want a piece of it." At that point, we had reached my house.

"Jem," I said as I turned to face him. "Just leave me be. For your sake as well as mine, just leave me be."

I entered the house as Jem continued to shout after me, "This isn't over. I'll be back, you can bet I want a piece of it!" I firmly closed the door. I probably should have paid more heed to this exchange, but, right then, I had other things on my mind besides Jem Riley.

***

I could tell from the talk on the street that Jane's early days as queen were not going to be easy. There were some willing to dismiss Lady Mary's claim due to her illegitimate birth, but most still saw her as King Henry's daughter and the obvious rightful heir to the throne. There was also growing distrust of Northumberland. The people blamed him for all the confusion and contention regarding the royal succession. His actions were viewed as greedy and power grabbing. There were even rumors that he had King Edward poisoned to gain power. Jane, whether a lady or a queen, barely entered the discussion at all. She was perceived as a young girl stuck in a struggle between the Princess and the Duke.

Maybe the tide would turn. Maybe Lady Mary's inability to mount any kind of army against Northumberland's considerable military might would lead folks to finally accept the reign of Queen Jane. Maybe Lady Mary would decide to flee to Spain or be captured and then her claim would be quelled. Maybe.

"Everything seems to be a muddle right now," Jane said to me a few days later. Since my first visit to the Tower, much had changed, but there was still much unresolved. Lady Mary had moved to her castle in Framlingham in East Anglia, which could be better defended if need be. Northumberland sent a naval brigade to dissuade Mary's cousin, Charles, King of Spain and the Holy Roman Emperor, from sending reinforcements or providing her with an escape by sea. Northumberland sent his son, Robert, with a small force to bide time until it was deemed necessary to send a more substantial army. The Council was debating who should lead that larger force.

"It was suggested my father should lead the force," Jane said, "but I pleaded with the Council that his rightful place was by my side. He really does not have much military experience. Instead, Lord Northumberland headed east this morning. He served admirably in Scotland and the Italian Wars, and successfully squelched the rebellion led by Robert Kett a while back."

"Then who is presiding over the Council?" I asked.

"My father," she answered. I tried to not let Jane see that this news concerned me deeply. In my time observing Edward's Council, Jane's father had not impressed me with his talent for persuasion. He was certainly not as gifted as Northumberland in this regard. If the situation in the east or even here in London did not resolve quickly, it would take much effort to hold the Council steadfast in their support of Queen Jane.

"I have written a number of proclamations expressing the need to stay united against the improper claim to the throne by Lady Mary, signing then as 'Jane the Queen.' I need to be seen as the ruling queen." That was certainly true, but, thus far, her actions did not seem to be perceived that way.

Still, there was reason for hope. Northumberland was marching towards East Anglia to confront Lady Mary. Although her forces appeared to be growing every day, her commanders may not have the wherewithal to successfully defend her position against Northumberland's substantial army. If Jane and her father could hold the Council together without defections to Mary's side for just a few days, things may very well start to turn in Jane's favor.

However, when I returned a couple of days later, on the eighth day of her reign, things, instead, had turned for the worse.

"I am at a loss, Tom. I don't know what to do!" Just from her physical appearance, anyone could see that the last few days had been very hard on her. Her face was even paler than usual and the darkness around her eyes bore witness to her lack of sleep. The royal gown that had been fit to her slender frame just a week ago was now hanging uncomfortably from her even slighter shoulders. She sat tight as a lute string clutching her prayer book.

Practically all, both in the east and within the Tower's walls, had gone horribly wrong. The hope that Northumberland would gain support and add to his army as he marched east was not realized, as the distrust for him evidently extended beyond London. Many lords had already pledged their

The Scoundrel's Son

allegiance to Lady Mary, and this trend was growing rapidly. Reinforcements expected to meet Northumberland's army in the east either arrived in much smaller numbers or never at all.

"We are receiving reports that Northumberland's own forces are starting to defect to Mary's side," Jane's hands were trembling, and her voice quivered as she shared this with me. The Council that had begged her to accept the Crown less than a fortnight ago was now turning against her. At one point, her father suggested they lock the gates to the Tower, not only to keep rebels from entering, but to keep Council members from leaving. However, many members still found a way to leave. I imagined if I could get in, then they could get out. It seemed, at this point, the only supporters solidly behind Jane's queenship were those with little choice, that being her parents, her husband, and Guildford's mother.

I could not think of a single thing to say at this point. She started to weep and shake miserably. I held her hands in mine. "My sweet Jane," I murmured softly.

"Tom, would you pray with me?"

"Of course," I replied without hesitation. Jane started to pray while I sat and listened, occasionally responding with an 'Amen' when it seemed proper. As she prayed, I could feel the calm rising in her being. I would have sat with her for the rest of time.

Chapter 29

I was working in the shop the following day when I heard some commotion coming from the square. The rumble of the crowd outside the door continued to rise, and so I decided to wander outside to see what might be happening. A man stood on a small platform preparing to make an announcement. I recognized him as a member of Edward's, now Jane's, Council. Finally, he began to speak.

"I now stand before you representing the Privy Council to proclaim the Lady Mary to possess the Crown as the right and just ruler of the realm. Long live Queen Mary."

The speaker may have made further pronouncements, but I did not hear another word. It may have been the gleeful shouting of the crowd and the chanting of "Long live Queen Mary!" as the men hurled their caps in the air, or it may have been that my mind just went numb. I stood stunned while jubilation and revelry exploded around me. I left the square and started to wander through the streets of Offal Court and Pudding Lane. The news was spreading like fire during the dry season. At the same time, my mind was also crackling with so many questions! How could the Council that had begged Jane to accept the Crown a mere nine days ago now turn their backs on her in favor of Lady Mary? Nine days! Was that the extent of their loyalty? Nine days?

Was Jane's father part of the discussion? Had anyone stood in support of the sixteen-year-old girl they had just placed on the throne? Had Northumberland been defeated in the east?

But, of course, the question of most concern to me was what would become of my sweet Jane. Was she all right? Where was she? Would she and others, including her father and Northumberland, be arrested? Lastly, where did the kingdom go from here? Likely, no one knew the answer to

The Scoundrel's Son

that question. There had not been this level of uncertainty regarding the Crown since the Battle of Bosworth Field between the old King Henry and King Richard. But my mind continued to circle back to Jane's welfare like a hawk on the prowl. What should I do to help her? What could I do?

As if on their own accord, my feet led me to the Tower. I assumed that Jane would still be there, but I was not sure. Perhaps she and her husband had been allowed to leave. But if she was still there, had she been moved to a prison cell? The guard at the Bridge Gate had been tripled from what it had been a few days before. I was quite sure my royal doublet would be of little use for entry at this point. What should I do next? I needed to see Jane, but how?

The very next day, a note arrived from Richard, asking me to meet him at a tavern near the Tower at a specified time that afternoon. I was excited to hear what Richard had to share but my heart was bouncing about in my chest as I arrived. What was he going to tell me? Was Jane in dire peril? Was she safe? When I arrived, I spotted Richard sitting in the corner with an ale in front of him.

"Master Richard, all I do these days is worry about Her Highness's whereabouts and wellbeing," I blurted before I had even sat down.

"I imagined so," Richard replied. "Lady Jane asked me to tell you that she is still at the Tower, and she is fine."

He told me that Jane was now a house guest of Mr. Partridge, the Gentleman Gaoler of the Tower, and his wife. They were good people, and they were treating her well. She was permitted three attending ladies, and Richard had been allowed to continue to act as her groom. She was free to wander the grounds including the gardens, the stables, and even the menagerie.

"She has been provided with some of her books, which makes her happy," he added. "She is dreadfully lonely and frightened, but, as you know, she is an extremely strong young lady."

"I know this indeed. Thank you so much, Master Richard. Your words have lifted a heavy load from my heart. Are her parents and Lord Guildford also being held?"

"Her mother and Lady Dudley have been allowed to leave the Tower. Lord Suffolk and Lord Guildford, on the other hand, continue to be held. Neither has seen Her Highness since the proclamation for Queen Mary."

Frederic Fahey

I then asked the question that had been on the tip of my tongue like a fledgling bird anxious to take flight.

"Is there any way I can see Her Highness?"

Richard looked about the tavern to make sure no one was within earshot. He rose from his seat.

"It is good to see you, Master Tom." As he bent to shake my hand, he whispered "Meet me tomorrow at noon at the Bridge Gate." He then briskly left the tavern.

I made a point of being early, but Richard was already there waiting for me when I arrived. He brought me across the bridge and into the inner ward. On the edge of the Tower Green, there was a small cottage for Richard's use. When I entered, Jane was sitting at a small desk reading her prayer book. She was in a simple brown dress with her hair pulled back and tied. She was concentrating on her book so intently that she did not notice when I entered. She turned expecting to see Richard and noticed me. She smiled with a level of serenity that I had not seen in her since before her marriage to Guildford. This peaceful look suited her well.

"Tom!" she said brightly. "Richard mentioned he had a surprise for me, but little did I guess that it would be you! Take a seat."

I did as she asked, and she proceeded to tell me of the night her reign ended.

"We were assembled for dinner in the royal quarters awaiting Father's arrival. Guildford and I were accompanied by our mothers when Father entered the room. I could tell immediately that something had gone dreadfully wrong. I asked him if he was all right. He looked at me through pained eyes. He glanced at the royal silk above the table, and, in a fit of anger, grabbed and yanked it down, tearing it in two.

" 'This is no longer your place, my dear,' he exclaimed as he held the tattered shreds of the silk in his fist. He announced that the Council had officially proclaimed Mary as queen. 'You must change from the royal dress and settle for a private life.'

"Of course, I was preparing for a private life before the Crown was thrust upon me. I explained to those at the table that I was more than willing to lay aside the royal garb. I only agreed to don them out of obedience to my parents. I then looked at my father and simply asked, 'Now, might I leave?' At that, he looked at me pitifully and left the room without a further

The Scoundrel's Son

word."

I did not doubt her sincerity regarding her willingness to relinquish the Crown. As brilliant and strong as she was, she was not prepared to handle what had been lain before her, certainly not without the guidance of competent advisors. Her father, and even Northumberland, had not been up to the challenge. I wondered if being confined to the Tower was not preferable for this sweet girl than being imprisoned upon the throne.

"I must admit that I am a bit relieved not to be the queen. I don't know what God has in store for me going forward. The Lord knows my faith and will protect me, and so I place my fate in His hands," she professed as she gripped her prayer book even more tightly.

"Do you know the whereabouts of Lord Northumberland?" I asked.

"Here," she said and pointed out the window to a tower rising from the wall on the inner ward. "I believe his sons are being held in the Beauchamp Tower, along with Guildford. I don't know which tower holds Northumberland. It appears the queen has decided to be lenient with all Council members except him.

"My father's fate is still uncertain. Mother is preparing to go to the queen when she arrives in London in a week or so. She plans to plead on his and my behalf. Maybe the good feelings from when they were children will work to our benefit.

"I am preparing a letter to the queen explaining my part in the whole affair. I understand we do not agree on religious matters, but I have always known her to be a thoughtful woman. I hope that she will realize that I never wanted the Crown for myself, and that it was forced upon me, most notably by Northumberland. How could she not see it this way?"

How indeed I asked myself.

Chapter 30

Several weeks later, Queen Mary triumphantly rode into London. As her cavalcade proceeded to the Tower, the streets rang with endless enthusiastic chants of "Long Live the Queen!" I arranged with Richard to visit with Jane soon after.

"I knew that the queen would lay much of the blame for the upheaval at the feet of Northumberland," I commented. "But I was surprised at how soon thereafter he was tried and beheaded."

"I am disgusted by Northumberland's shallow conversion," Jane angrily shared. In the few days leading up to his execution, he followed the lead of other Council members by openly renouncing the new ways and embracing the old religion. After he had convinced Jane to accept the Crown on religious grounds, it seemed he was content to turn his back on these beliefs in a feeble plea for the queen's mercy. "As young as I am, I question what good is a few more days on earth in exchange for the eternal damnation of one's soul." Jane added.

This statement frightened me deeply. I supposed that conversion might be necessary for the queen's good favor in her own case. It seemed with every passing day that Jane's commitment to her faith was becoming more resolute.

"Father is back at Bradgate," she informed me. "It seems that Mother was at least able to convince Her Majesty of this small mercy during their visit." On the other hand, Jane, Guildford and two of his brothers were still being held. "She told Mother that she is leaning towards our release but here we stay."

On the first of October, Mary was crowned as the first queen regnant in English history. In the ceremony, her unique circumstance was recognized by declaring that she would serve as both king and queen. Jane's

The Scoundrel's Son

very brief reign was all but forgotten. Again, the streets erupted in celebration with the city leaders providing wine, a rare treat for most Londoners. Bands played in the squares; fireworks exploded. Every man, woman, and child appeared to be rejoicing Mary's ascension to the throne.

The kingdom was returning to the old religion under her rule. The Mass was again being celebrated openly and many churches planned to revert to their earlier appearances. Queen Mary held a special Mass for the salvation of Edward's soul. It was hard to believe that it had been less than three months since Edward's death. The world had changed several times over since then.

Although Mr. and Mrs. Partridge were treating her well, and she was allowed to walk freely within the inner ward, I could tell during a visit in mid-October that Jane's captivity was starting to weigh on her.

"Sometimes, Mrs. Partridge and I walk along the top of the wall of the inner ward," she shared. "I can see the river and the land beyond. I see the leaves changing color, and I am reminded of how much I love the autumn. The gardens of the Tower Green are very nice, but I long to sit in the garden at Norwich. Do you remember, Tom, how nice it was for us to sit in our little paradise along the Strand?"

"I do remember."

"But even more so, I miss walking with my sisters among the trees at Bradgate. Oh, Tom, I wish you could have been there. There was such a variety of trees, each bursting into its own brilliant color of autumn. Reds and oranges of every hue! It was as if the forest was aflame. Mostly I remember the yellows like a golden thread delicately embroidered across the forest. Katherine and I, and later little Mary, would collect leaves of our favorite colors and arrange them in bouquets for Mother and Father.

"But now all I can do is gaze over these walls and dream of my days among the trees of Bradgate. I dream of sitting in the garden or curled up by the fire with one of my favorite books. I long to hear my sisters' laughter. I even miss Katherine parading around in her newest dress or little Mary's endless questions and giggles. I miss it all, Tom." Her eyes appeared even larger as they misted. "Will I ever leave this place?"

"I am sure of it," I said although I wasn't sure at all.

I pondered these things as I walked in the brusque, cool autumn air on my way back to Offal Court. Would Jane stay in the Tower forever? Even if she was moved to another location, would she ever be free? Suddenly, my thoughts were abruptly interrupted.

"Gotta few minutes for an old friend, Tom?" Jem had caught up with me as I hurried along.

"What's on your mind, Jem?" I said as I continued to walk. Jem kept pace.

"I got my eye on you, I do. You haven't lost your style, have ya. Seems you come and go at the Tower like you please. Me thinks you know someone inside. You're up to something, that's clear. But just what I don't know. But now I'm thinkin' that's all right. I got my own ideas. There's lots of pretty things inside the Tower that would suit me."

"I've no interest in what suits you," I said as I started to walk away.

"It would be a pity if Aly or your sisters had to be involved."

I turned on my heels and shoved Jem against the wall of a nearby building.

"Stay away from Aly and my family!" I shouted in his face. "If you so much as look at any of them, it will be with deep regret!"

"Calm yourself, Tom. I have no ill intentions. But you and I will speak again. Of that, you can be sure. We both could gain much from bein' partners."

My blood was still pumping when I finally reached home. I thought my time at Whitehall might move me beyond the likes of Jem but apparently not. And it was my prowling about the Tower that had attracted his attention. That night as I started to fall asleep, I could still hear Jem's voice saying "You are just like me" as my father's sneering face danced before my eyes. Try as I might, would I always be the scoundrel's son?

The next morning, I headed for my mother's cottage. She always seemed to have a way of lightening my load when I was feeling lost.

"Tom! You look like you just lost your best dog! Come on in. I got some good cider and I just cooked up some apple jam!" Just those few words made the sun start to shine in my chest.

As she went about warming up the cider and cutting a piece of bread for me, I gazed upon the embroidered sampler Jane had made and given to me for my mother years before. It was the only decorative piece on my mother's walls. And so, my thoughts returned to Jane's captivity. It all came back to Her Majesty Queen Mary. Although there were many

The Scoundrel's Son

rumors, I truly did not know what Her Majesty's intentions were regarding Jane. I had met Her Majesty briefly on just a few occasions during the masquerade, and, in recent years, my only interaction with her had been her visit along with Lady Elizabeth to Whitehall the previous spring. Something about that visit started to ring in my head.

I did not give it much thought at the time, but at the reception, she mentioned she was sometimes visited by the spirit of her father, long deceased. I wondered if the spirit of her sweet, recently departed brother might also come to her.

After sharing some fine cider, bread, and jam with my mother, I returned to Father Christian's house and went right to the chest where I kept my clothes. Towards the bottom, I found the royal garments I had worn the night of the reception. As I held them in my hands, a plot started to materialize. I changed my clothes, threw my satchel over my shoulder, donned my hooded cloak, and set out for Westminster.

It had been several months since I last visited Whitehall, but I knew the layout and its routines well. Deliveries were made to the palace in the very early hours, and so that's when I planned to arrive. As I had so many times over the past six years, I entered through the delivery gate without much notice. I could find my way to the royal chambers with my eyes closed by this point. However, entering the royal chamber might be another issue. There were two guards at the door to the anteroom where I had typically entered. I slipped in the shadows around the corner to the entrance to the queen's room where King Henry's wives would have entered his chamber. Since this entrance had not been used during Edward's reign, there was only one guard there, and he was nodding in and out of sleep. I swiftly skulked along the wall and entered the royal chamber. Underneath my cloak, I was wearing most of my royal garb. From my satchel, I extracted the last few items, the jacket and the hat, and completed my outfit.

I entered Her Majesty's bedchamber. It was still predawn, and the curtains were pulled making it almost totally dark. As I started to feel my way around the lightless room, I realized that the furniture was just as it was when Edward slept here, and so I easily moved about the chamber. I sat in a chair across from Her Majesty's bed. Slowly my sight improved even in the near blackness. As I waited patiently for her to stir, I noticed the watch

Frederic Fahey

I had given Edward for his birthday sat on her night table. I realized the likeness on the inner cover was also of her father as well as Edward's. Just as dawn started to crack, Her Majesty began to jostle.

"Dear sister, are you awake?" I said in a calm yet commanding voice.

"Is there someone here?"

"It is I, your brother Edward, sweet sister." At that, she turned her head and saw me sitting in the dark corner.

"Edward? Is that you?"

"Yes, my sister. I have been bothered that we parted on poor terms that afternoon in the courtyard last spring. I was touched that you left me with God's blessing. I am here to express my love for you. Thank you for the Mass you had celebrated in my honor. I am very grateful." Now she was sitting halfway in her bed as she peered through the darkness. "Father sends his love," I added.

"Your visit is a blessing, sweet brother," she finally managed.

"How are you, dear sister?" I asked.

"I am doing well. The weight of the Crown is heavy indeed. There is so much to consider in these times. But the affection of my subjects and the grace of God has helped me immensely."

"How is our precious cousin, Lady Jane? I fear I put her in a terrible position against her will." Her Majesty seemed a bit surprised by this inquiry but still addressed it directly.

"Frances has convinced me that Jane was a victim of the ambitions of the men around her, but my advisors insist that I cannot let a usurper, not even Jane, go unpunished. They fear it will encourage others to attempt to seize the throne. They say that she remains a threat."

"But she is not a threat," I said.

"I am not so sure."

"I am sure," I stated more forcefully. "She has no interest in your crown."

"I know she doesn't, but others around her might try to seize the throne in her name. I am under much pressure from the Privy Council and beyond. My cousin, Prince Philip, says that I must deal with Jane in the strictest terms. He says usurpers cannot be tolerated. I am trying. I really am. But I fear there will come a time when I cannot protect her any longer."

The Scoundrel's Son

I wanted to continue, but I was afraid that as her slumber further subsided, she would see through my ruse. So, I decided to end this ethereal discourse.

"Sweet sister, I must leave you now. Father and I beg that you show mercy towards Jane! You are a good and righteous queen. Know that we both love you with all our hearts. Now close your eyes and return to your slumber." She did as I instructed, closing her eyes, and soon was asleep. I very silently left her bedchamber, changed clothes, and exited the palace without incident. Maybe I was blessed with ghostly grace on that morning. Her last words stayed with me, however. "I fear there will come a time when I cannot protect her any longer." I had come worried about Jane's freedom, but now I feared for her life. Queen Mary was a spider with many pushing on her from all sides while Jane's life dangled from the most delicate of threads.

Chapter 31

Soon after, a trial was set for Jane, Guildford, two of his brothers, Ambrose and Henry, and Archbishop Cranmer. The archbishop was in his sixties, but the other four were all very young. They were being charged with high treason, the most serious crime in the land, and so a death sentence was a real possibility. Jane had always been single-minded regarding her religion but now her devotion was becoming all-consuming. Yet I was still surprised that she seemed to relish the opportunity to defend her actions and profess her faith.

"The people will finally hear what I have to say directly rather than my words being jumbled within the mouths of others," she said. She relentlessly practiced short and long speeches to use depending on what opportunity may arise. She also practiced answers to a variety of questions she thought might be asked of her. She was as determined and well prepared as anyone could be to say her piece. However, it occurred to me that she was more concerned about explaining why her actions were justified than making the case as to why her life should be spared.

"Do you think there may be some value in being more contrite in your speech?" I asked, trying to broach the topic as gently as possible.

"Absolutely not! I have been clear from the start that Queen Mary was the rightful heir to the Crown and that I was wrong to attempt to rule in her place. I continue to stand by that assertion. However, my motivation for what I did was righteous in the eyes of the Lord. I am strong in what I believe."

On the appointed day, I arrived early at the Tower so I could follow as the accused walked towards Guildhall where the trial would be held. Hundreds of onlookers had gathered on this fine November day. The air

The Scoundrel's Son

was crisp and clear, not adorned with the gloomy mist one comes to expect of the late autumn in London. The bright blue sky belied the solemnity of the moment.

At last, the accused, along with a number of guards and attendants, emerged from the Tower, striding with serious purpose towards their destination, about a mile away. The Constable of the Tower led the procession, holding an axe with its blade turned away from the prisoners, indicating they were yet to be convicted of the crimes of which they were accused. The archbishop was first in line followed by Guildford. Jane was third accompanied by two of her ladies, and then Guildford's two brothers.

Jane was dressed in a simple, solemn gown of brown covered by a black hooded cloak, a harsh contrast to the pomp of the royal robes she wore as queen just a few months before. The fair, pale skin of her splendid face and her bright red hair were accentuated by the blackness of her cloak. As the only female among the accused and flanked on either side by the strong statures of the Dudley brothers, her slight frame appeared even smaller. However, she walked straight, exemplifying her dignified manner and determination. She held the prayer book that now seemed to be always in her hands. She portrayed not one ounce of fear as she walked, resolute, almost rebellious, and not at all repentant as one might have expected under such circumstances. There was none of the jeering or mocking from the crowd that had accompanied Northumberland to both his trial and his later demise on Tower Hill. It appeared that Lady Jane and the archbishop continued to demand a certain level of respect.

Guildhall, with its towers and turrets, was a magnificent edifice. Although the current building was rebuilt a hundred years ago, older structures had stood on this spot going back to Roman times. The procession entered the Great Hall where the trial was to take place. The statues of the giants Gog and Magog, ancient keepers of the city, stood watch as the accused made their way to where they would stand during the proceedings. Ironically, I had attended a dinner as Edward during the masquerade in this same hall in the company of Jane and Edward's sister, Lady Elizabeth. Now that seemed several lifetimes ago.

A small number of commoners were allowed to view the trial from the gallery perched above the court. I headed directly for the staircase while others were still milling, and I found a place where I could see and hear the proceedings quite well. As hundreds of observers were there that day to witness the trial, I had to steadfastly stand my ground to maintain my chosen spot.

It was clear from the start that even though she was a member of the royal family, Jane would not be allotted any special treatment. I had heard that King Henry's wives, Ann Boleyn and Catherine Howard, were allowed to sit during their trials, but Jane stood with the rest of the accused. She was referred to merely as "Jane Dudley, wife of Guildford" without even the title of Lady. I thought that treating her in such a humble manner would actually suit her. The five were accused of proclaiming Jane as queen, and thus they were traitors against the realm and Her Majesty as the rightful queen. This was not a charge that Jane would deny. Since the night of Edward's death when she was first informed that she would be queen, she had asserted that Mary was the rightful heir to the throne. She also had been clear on this point in the letter she had written to Her Majesty. However, several letters and proclamations from the time of her brief reign were presented, which she had signed as "Jane the Queen." None of the accused were allowed to speak or present any witnesses in their defense. At one point, Jane stepped forward intending to make a statement justifying her actions, but she was rebuffed. Several times she went to speak and was promptly denied the opportunity. In the end, Jane and all the accused pleaded guilty to the charges as presented and placed themselves at the mercy of the queen. For all of Jane's preparation, the only words she was allowed to speak were her pleas of guilt. She could only express herself by the gracious manner she portrayed during the entire ordeal.

The punishments were then announced. The four men should be "drawn and quartered," which is to say they should be hanged and have their bodies lain out rotting on the ground with their organs openly displayed. Their heads should be cut off, their bodies divided into four quarters and placed where the queen wished.

"Jane Dudley, wife of Guildford, shall be brought to Tower Hill, and either be burned or beheaded, as it should please the queen." My sweet Jane stood with quiet dignity as the awful punishments were announced. Their grisly details were spoken as if they were the instructions on baking a cake. To me, each word was a brushstroke in the portrait of a nightmare.

The Scoundrel's Son

I don't believe a woman as young as Jane, only sixteen years of age, had ever been issued the punishment of death in the kingdom of England previously. At this point, the constable slowly turned the axe to face the guilty, who were then led from the Great Hall back to the Tower as the crowd exploded into a combination of hoots of approval and gasps at the gruesome nature of the sentences.

I stared down from my perch simply stunned. Even with all those crowded in the gallery, I was totally alone. Her reluctance, no her determination, not to turn from the new doctrine and embrace the old religion, made clear, in my mind, Jane's fate. At that precise moment, I knew that the spider's thread was unwinding, and nothing could keep it from ultimately snapping. The only uncertainty left was when.

That night, I was aroused by a terrible dream. Edward appeared to me sitting on his throne. He was as on the day of his coronation, wearing his most magnificent wardrobe, holding the Great Seal in one hand and the scepter in the other. He slowly faced me and, once again, made his final request.

"Would you rule in my stead?"

I snapped fully awake, in a sweat despite the frigid air of the autumn's dawn. I had hardly given it a second thought since my last visit with Edward. At the time, I had not even considered the request for more than a moment. But now it came rushing back to me, and I was wrought with tremendous guilt. What if I had agreed to his request? I could have ruled in his stead! I could have been the King of England! I could have saved the life of my sweet Jane. It was my fault! I could have saved her! Now looking back, I did not know all that would transpire. I did not even know that it would be the last time I would see Edward alive. I did not know that Jane would be proclaimed queen and all the misfortune that had befallen her. I did not know if my impersonation would even be successful. But none of that mattered.

"I could have saved her!" clamored in my guilt-ridden mind.

Maybe I still could.

Chapter 32

I rose early the next morning, stoked the fire, and sat in my chair to contemplate my next move. Jem had noted that I had gotten quite good at getting into places, even the mighty Tower of London. He said I had a certain "style." I started to ponder if it might be at all possible for me to secretly enter the Tower and rescue Jane from her captivity. Could I enter the Tower without Richard's help? Could I arrange to meet Jane at the precise right time? Could we both escape the Tower without notice? Could we leave the city together? What if everything fell into place like tumblers in a lock? Could it all be done? I decided that there were risks indeed but it was possible. And so, I began planning the rescue of Jane from the Tower, the most secure stronghold in all England.

I considered the scheme in phases. I assumed, up front, that I could enter the Tower and get to the Tower Green and to Jane. I had already accomplished this. This would likely be the easiest part. Then, from the Tower Green, how would Jane and I get beyond the wall of the inner ward? And then beyond the outer wall? How would we cross the moat? If we got that far, how would we escape the city and where would we go?

If my scheme was unsuccessful and we were captured along the way, I was sure that the consequences would be dire for myself as well as for Jane. I was certainly willing to put my life at risk, and, in my mind, Jane's fate was already sealed. The spider's thread was ready to snap. Thus, a rescue was her only chance for survival.

Even with all my skills, I realized that I could not do this alone. I needed someone with experience and guile to help in the planning and to assure that there was no aspect that was left unconsidered. I also needed help on the inside from someone almost as skilled as I with scaling walls and prowling in the darkness. I needed someone who could move silently and quickly without being noticed. I needed partners who were fearless and incredibly loyal.

I thought of a meeting place that was secret, secure, and away from the city. We met at the small cottage that was next to the barn where we had developed the musket. It was now mid-November, and the air was on the chilly side on the first day we met, so I built a good fire to heat the tiny room. The three of us sat around the table.

"Well, Tom," Lord Miles began. "Miss Alice and I have come as you have asked. I am guessing we are not here to go apple picking. What is on your mind?" Aly was nervously rubbing her hands together.

I warned them that what I was going to share with them was very serious, and if things went awry, there could be dire consequences for those involved. If, before I even started, they did not want to hear what I had in mind, they could leave now, or frankly at any time, and I would not think any less of them.

"I will let Miss Alice speak first," Lord Miles offered.

Aly looked at him and then at me. "Tom, you're my dearest friend. You look out for me. I know you've helped my family over the years with food when it was needed. You left toys for my brothers. You tried to keep it secret, but I knew it was you all along. You're the only person outside my family I trust. If you need me and I can help, I'll be there, no matter what."

I squeezed Aly's hand to express my thanks.

"Between you and my little friend," Lord Miles said, "I have already faced considerable peril over the years. And I am a better man for it without a doubt. Just say the word, Tom." He reached out and we all held hands, forming a circle about the table.

I took a deep breath. "I'm going to rescue Lady Jane from the Tower of London."

They both looked at me as if I had told them I wanted to sail to Spain in a rowboat. Aly sat frozen with her mouth half open. Lord Miles let out a long sigh and gestured with a wave of his hand.

"All right. You have our attention."

"Jane's execution date has not been set, and that might be to our advantage. Once the date is known, a rescue will be considerably more difficult." I presented the five phases of the scheme: entering the Tower, entering the inner ward, meeting with Jane, escaping the Tower, and lastly escaping the city.

I rolled out a large piece of paper on which I had drawn the interior of the Tower grounds. I figured I was the only one of us three who had ever been inside.

"As you know, the Tower is surrounded on three sides by a deep moat and on the south side by the river. You can see that the grounds are arranged as one quadrangle, the inner ward, inside a larger one, the outer ward. Jane is staying here," I said, pointing to a small structure located along the western wall of the inner ward, "at the cottage of the Gentleman Gaoler, Mr. Partridge, and his wife."

My finger traced the wall of the outer ward. "To reach her, we first will need to pass through the wall of the outer ward. There are two ways: by the well-guarded bridge that crosses the moat through the Bridge Gate." My finger then moved to the river side. "Or through the Water Gate. This is where the royal barge would dock if the king or queen were coming to the Tower.

"That's the Traitors' Gate, isn't it?" Aly asked as her fingers fidgeted under her chin.

"Yes," I answered. "High-ranking prisoners such as Edward's uncles, the Lords Sudeley and Somerset, also entered this way."

"Even if we manage to enter the outer ward, there is still the wall to the inner ward for us to cross. The space between the walls is narrow, ranging from thirty to fifty feet in most places. The wall to the inner ward is maybe forty or fifty feet high. It is not easy to scale, but Aly and I have climbed tougher walls." I looked at Aly and she smiled back. "And I can show her how to open the locks. Often folks come to Mr. Nobson's shop having misplaced a key, and so I have gotten quite good at dealing with practically every type of lock. Then we need to traverse both walls again to escape, and now Jane will be with us. I am still working on the best path for this." I went over the map in good detail. The clearer picture Lord Miles and Aly had of the Tower's interior, the better.

"The inner ward is dominated by the White Tower." My finger tapped on a large square in the center. "It is the colossal structure with turrets at each corner that all can see from practically anywhere along the river. The Tower Green is west of the White Tower and the Chapel of Saint Peter ad

The Scoundrel's Son

Vincula is just north of the green. Fittingly, I suppose, its name means Saint Peter in Chains. This is where I propose to meet Jane during the rescue.

"I know some things still need to be considered and certainly there are many holes in the plan at this point. We will see if we can identify all the holes and if we can fill most of them. We must decide if the scheme has any chance of success."

My friends were quiet for a few moments. Finally, Lord Miles said, "This plan has less chance than throwing a pair of ones with dice. And that is if the entire rescue goes close to perfectly. But compared to the chance for a stay of execution for Lady Jane, these odds are likely still better. However, one aspect of the scheme where we need help is escaping the city and finding a safe haven for the Lady." Lord Miles was right. This phase likely required additional help.

We decided we would plan one phase at a time. In general, Aly would help me on the inside and Lord Miles on the outside. We agreed to meet at the cabin again in three days' time.

As Aly and I rode back to Offal Court in a carriage I had borrowed, I noticed that she was deep in thought.

"What are you thinking?" I asked wondering if she was having second thoughts.

"I need to practice climbin' walls. It's been a while. And can you teach me about locks?"

"Yes, that I can do," I responded with a smile as we rode on.

I had arranged with Richard for a visit with Jane the next day. I had not seen her since her conviction. In the days immediately following the trial, the security around her had been markedly increased. But now a week had passed, and the oversight was a bit more relaxed. I decided this might be a good time to attempt to enter the Tower without Richard's help. I dressed in my Tower guard's uniform and easily entered the outer ward. Once inside, I decided I would do a little exploring to find a good place to escape the inner ward. I would need Aly's help and so I looked for a spot where she would be mostly concealed, but still with ample light for her to see. The gate to the inner ward, which I typically used, was close to both the Bridge Gate and the Water Gate and thus heavily guarded. However, I found a gate near Beauchamp Tower on the west wall, close to the Chapel and far from the river, that I thought might be a good option. I took notice of the lock on the gate. It was very solid, but one I knew I could train Aly to open.

Richard had informed Jane of my visit and so she was waiting for me at his cottage.

"It is so good to see you, Jane." She smiled at first, but her face was tinged with a bit of sadness. I wondered if the trial's verdict might still be on her mind. "I have been so worried about you since I heard the outcome of your trial," I added.

She waved my last comment away with a swipe of her hand as if it were nothing more than a bothersome fly. I was surprised that she did not seem at all concerned. Did she find the reality of her sentence overwhelming? Did she have faith that the queen would pardon or otherwise spare her? Did none of it matter to her? I could not judge, but on this day, she had other things on her mind.

"I am very sad today," she announced solemnly. "I have heard that my own father is considering renouncing his faith. He is the one who showed me the new ways and encouraged my studies, sometimes against my mother's wishes. I reluctantly accepted the Crown out of respect for him. Now he is willing to sacrifice his soul to please the queen. I pray every day that he will realize his folly and stay true to the Lord." Her fingers fumbled with the pages of her prayer book as she spoke.

"Have you heard at all from Her Majesty?" I asked, trying to change the subject.

"No, I haven't. My ladies say that all her thoughts are focused on her possible marriage to her cousin, Prince Philip of Spain. They say she has his portrait on her wall and is constantly gazing upon his handsome face."

"Is there concern that the prince could one day be king of both Spain and England?"

"I imagine so." She added "Although my concern is with her infatuation with the Bishop of Rome rather than the Prince of Spain." And so, the conversation again circled back to religion. With each passing day, the devotion to her faith seemed to be growing stronger.

***

The Scoundrel's Son

As arranged, Aly, Lord Miles and I met again at the cottage. Lord Miles suggested we discuss what would be a good night for our endeavor. He stated that we needed at least a month for planning. That brought us to the end of December. We wanted to find a night when the guards might be distracted. We briefly considered Christmas Eve, but with Jane's religious devotion, such a holy night was probably not the best choice. We finally settled on Twelfth Night, the eve of the feast of the Epiphany, twelve nights after Christmas Eve. There would be celebrations marking the end of the Christmas season with fireworks and plenty of distraction for the guards.

I again rolled out my drawing, and we discussed the early phases of the plan. The first phase centered on my ability to reach Jane. By now, my face was familiar enough that I did not think I would have any issues entering by the Bridge Gate and then the inner ward through the gate near Wakefield Tower as was my routine.

I would arrange to meet Jane at the Chapel of Saint Peter. Her dress tended to be simple these days, which was good as it would not garner any special attention, but I would bring a dark, hooded cloak to further conceal her appearance.

We also needed to get Aly inside. I pointed to Beauchamp Tower on the drawing and the gate I had decided would provide us with the best opportunity for escaping the inner ward. Lord Miles noted that the military leadership at the Tower traditionally hosted a Twelfth Night celebration at the lieutenant's quarters and that he might be able to pull some social strings to get an invitation for himself and a guest. No one would likely realize that Aly was ten years older than his real daughter, or maybe they would turn a blind eye to a noble gentleman arriving with a lady much younger than his wife. Once inside, Aly would find a dark corner to remove her dress for the celebration, as she would be wearing dark clothes for climbing underneath. She would make her way to Beauchamp Tower, scale the wall, and hide in a shadowed corner along the top of the wall to keep watch.

The next phase focused on Jane and me escaping the inner ward. Jane would don the hooded cloak and we would exit the chapel. I would signal Aly perched atop the wall, who would climb down and open the lock just as I had taught her. By the time Jane and I reached Beauchamp Tower, Aly would have unlocked and opened the gate, and we would slip through into the outer ward. We were all pleased with the plan to this point.

"One more thing today," I said as I took a deep breath and reached for my satchel.

"Lord Miles, I have something to show you. I am not sure, but it might be of use at some point." I opened the satchel and brought out the hand musket Robert and I had developed, and I handed it to Lord Miles. I had borrowed it from Robert's shop, figuring he wouldn't miss it over the next several weeks. At first, Lord Miles didn't seem sure of what he had in his hands but slowly he started to understand. He gave me a solemn look as he shifted it from hand to hand to get a feel of its weight.

"What's that?" Aly asked.

"A new kind of weapon," I answered. "Think of it as a small cannon that can be held in your hand."

"This may be better than the musket for this operation," Lord Miles added. "It is simpler to hide on one's person."

"That's true," I added. "But it's a bit less accurate, especially at a distance."

Lord Miles rose from the table, and we all left the cabin. I handed him some powder and the small balls that fit the hand musket's barrel. He loaded it, aimed, and fired at a tree. After a few more firings, he seemed to have a better feel for it. His accuracy was certainly better than mine when I tested the weapon.

"Yes, this smaller weapon can work with a bit more practice. I also need to learn to load it in the dark. This certainly could come in handy. But let's hope it won't come to that."

As we returned to the cabin and the warmth of the fire, I started to spout about many aspects of the scheme that had been scampering through my head like frightened hens these past few days.

"Everything needs to be perfect!" I shouted as I started to tremble. It seemed the awesome reality of what we were planning had suddenly overwhelmed me.

"Whoa, Tom," Lord Miles interrupted me holding up his hand. "Take a breath and try to relax. We will not have a sense if this scheme will work until we have discussed all phases."

Aly smiled at me and patted my hand.

The Scoundrel's Son

"Tom, it will be all right." I took a breath and tried to calm myself.

Lord Miles continued. "I am still concerned about getting Lady Jane from the city to a safe haven." He paused slightly, "If such a haven exists."

"I have been thinking of that since you mentioned it last time," I noted. "I think I might know someone who can help."

Chapter 33

I sat in the parlor trying to warm myself by the fire with a cup of warm cider when the Earl entered. When he saw me, he recognized my face immediately.

"Oh! You are that Master Thomas Canty! What brings you to me on this cold November day?"

It was not without risk that I decided to engage the Earl in our secret endeavor. If he was loyal to Her Majesty, it could lead to my imprisonment. Or he could even act as if he were sympathetic to our cause just to ensnare my conspirators and myself. But I had remembered him speaking quite strongly in support of Edward's religious reforms. He was our best chance for getting Jane safely out of the city. I had to take the risk.

"My Lord, before I start, may I ask you a few questions?"

"You can surely ask," he said as he sat back in his chair. "But I reserve the right on whether to answer."

"Do you know Lady Jane Grey?" I asked.

"I know the Grey family well. I have been invited and have partaken in several of their splendid hunts at Bradgate. I have only met the daughters of Lord Suffolk and Lady Frances on social occasions but Lady Jane's scholarship and dedication to Our Lord is renowned."

I paused before continuing.

"Do you still embrace the new ways of worship?"

He eyed me closely and pondered before responding. I hoped that I had made the right choice.

"I certainly do. It is the true way to the Lord our God." He paused for a moment. "I am very concerned with Her Majesty's return to the old religion. Where is this leading, Tom?"

I studied his face intently as I tried to judge the sincerity of his words.

The Scoundrel's Son

I took a deep breath and decided to continue. I did not go into detail regarding my relationship with Edward but explained that I had come to know Lady Jane quite well and that I was working with others loyal to Her Highness to rescue Lady Jane from the Tower. We needed a way of delivering her someplace safe. This could be beyond the kingdom, such as France, Ireland, or perhaps Scotland, or maybe even someplace in England where she could live her life in relative safety and obscurity.

The Earl gazed into the distance as he stroked his beard. I supposed he might be judging my true intentions as I had been his. After a short while, he sat forward and eyed me directly.

"There are many, and I mean many, within the kingdom who embrace the new ways. And they are very familiar with Lady Jane's plight. They may have believed that Her Majesty Queen Mary was the rightful heir all along, but they still feel that Lady Jane is the victim of Northumberland's ambition. I am very fond of her father, but he is not a strong man. He is too easily swayed by the whims of others.

"So, if you and your collaborators could somehow deliver Lady Jane from the Tower, I know a number of trustworthy noblemen who would be willing to help. The ports would be on high alert looking for a young girl with red hair, and many would be willing to trade her fate for a few pieces of silver. But I am sure we can find a good family that keeps to themselves, where a niece whose own family has experienced some misfortune might come to stay without attracting notice.

"Do you have a date in mind for this rescue?"

"Twelfth Night."

"Twelfth Night! I like that! It would be an interesting way to complete the celebration of Our Lord's birth."

We shook hands and I promised to soon return with more details. I could not wait to share the news with Lord Miles and Aly. Our improbable scheme seemed to be coming together quite nicely.

***

After several meetings at the cottage, we were ready to finalize our plan. We huddled by the warm fire and went through it phase by phase.

"I have been thinking," Lord Miles had suggested at an earlier meeting, "about how the three of you would leave the outer ward and cross the moat. Bringing Lady Jane through the Bridge Gate without her being recognized, or the three of you crossing the moat unnoticed, both seem close to impossible." He then pointed towards the bottom of the drawing. "I say you leave by the Water Gate."

"The Water Gate?" That option had not occurred to me. Maybe he was on to something.

"Yes. The guards at the Water Gate will be more concerned with persons entering the Tower than leaving. And there will certainly be fewer guards.

"Once I have escorted Miss Alice through the Bridge Gate, I will leave the Tower and go to a rowboat we will have tied at a dock close by upstream."

He then explained that he would arrive at the Water Gate in the boat acting as if he had already been celebrating Twelfth Night for several hours, even sharing some of his ale with the guards. He would pretend to fall asleep in the boat while he waited for a nobleman who was attending the lieutenant's celebration. Meanwhile, Aly, Jane and I would steal our way from Beauchamp Tower to the Water Gate by the longer but less congested path along the northern and eastern walls. We would silently traverse the gate, cross the landing, and enter the boat. If all went well, we would be heading down the river before anyone was the wiser.

"I met again with the Earl yesterday," I announced. "He has established several routes out of London with friends along the way. He has identified a family in Yorkshire that he is confident will provide an excellent haven for Jane. The family has several children under the age of ten who could benefit from the teaching by an educated sixteen-year-old niece whose family has fallen on hard times.

"I informed him that we would be escaping the city by the river, and he noted that he had a friend who lived near Poplar with a dock. He thought this would be an excellent place for us to meet. After leaving the Tower, we would head directly down the river to Poplar."

"Outstanding!" Lord Miles noted.

"I am going to visit Jane just before Christmas, and present the scheme to her," I announced. "All she needs to do during the rescue is follow our lead, but I want her to be prepared for what is in store. I don't want

The Scoundrel's Son

her to be surprised along the way."

"Very good!" Lord Miles concurred.

The rescue had really taken form. Like one of Robert's broaches, it still had some rough edges that needed to be "made lovely" as he would say, but, in general, each phase seemed doable. Of course, there were substantial risks all along the way, and we had figured in several contingencies and escapes, but we all agreed that it was all achievable. As far as I was concerned, there was no turning back at this point. We were all looking forward to an exciting Twelfth Night!

Chapter 34

The week before Christmas, I arranged to see Jane. I waited at Richard's cottage for her to arrive. His place was just as one might expect it to be. Small but quite tidy with everything in its place. I became fidgety as I sat knowing what I was soon to reveal to her. Every time my leg would start to quiver, I would take a deep breath and let it out slowly. I rose as she finally entered. She took her seat and invited me to do the same. We chatted for a few moments. She complained about the Masses being celebrated during the season which only heightened my concern for her well-being.

"I made a gift for you," I said, handing her a small bag. "I'm giving it to you now, as I won't likely see you before New Years Day."

"Oh, Tom. That is so thoughtful! But I am sorry I have no gift for you!"

"That is of no matter. I presume there are no Christmas shops within the walls of the Tower," I joked. Jane smiled as she opened her gift. It was a small locket with a likeness of Edward inside.

"This is beautiful!" she said as her hand went to her cheek. She looked at me with a grin. "Is this my sweet cousin, Edward, or is it you?"

"It is whoever you want it to be," I answered. "I also made a gift for myself." I reached into my pocket and withdrew an identical locket. I opened it and showed her that it contained a likeness of herself. She was touched by the thought that I always carried an image of her with me.

"That is so sweet!" she said as she blushed and reached to touch my hand. At her slightest touch, my heart leapt.

"Oh! I do have a gift! Please wait here!" She rose and hurried out the door of the cottage towards the Partridge's quarters. It had just begun to snow. Jane scampered across the Tower grounds as one of her ladies tried

The Scoundrel's Son

to stay with her to keep her from slipping. This break gave me a chance to collect myself. I quickly ran through my speech in my mind. At this point, I had gone over these words a hundred times. I was ready.

The door flew open, and Jane entered, frosted in snow and beaming.

"This is for you, Tom," she said, handing me a book. "It is a psalter, a book of psalms, written in English. It will light your way."

"Thank you so much, Jane," I said hugging it to my chest. "I will cherish it always." I opened the psalter to find a brief message:

Tom, your friendship has been a blessing in these challenging times. Jane.

I placed it in my satchel. I took a deep breath, and I began.

"Jane, I would like you to meet me on Twelfth Night at the chapel at precisely nine of the clock."

"Certainly, Tom. It would be lovely to pray with you on the eve of the Epiphany," she responded.

"It's not only to pray." I paused as I tried to quiet my spirit. "We have devised a scheme to help you escape from the Tower."

"I don't understand," she said with a quizzical look.

I spoke as slowly and as calmly as my racing heart would allow.

"I, with a small number of friends with whom I trust my life, have developed a plan." I described how I would meet her at the chapel, secretly move about the Tower grounds, pass through the wall of the inner ward and then to the Water Gate. I told her that Lord Miles would be waiting with a boat that would take us to the village of Poplar where the Earl would take her to safety. In our first meeting, the Earl had said that he had met Jane several times, and now she confirmed that she knew him to be a follower of the new ways.

"Where would I go?" she asked. Her voice was calm but the intensity in her eyes spoke differently as she attempted to grasp every detail of what I was relaying to her.

I explained that we had arranged with a family in the north of England to care for her. She would assume the role of their niece who had come to educate their children. I could tell from her look that she was very confused as she tried to make sense of all that I had lain before her. Maybe I had spoken too fast or shared too many details.

"We have given this scheme very much thought. We have planned to the finest detail. Jane, I know we will be successful!"

"You have my head spinning, Tom. I am trying my best to understand." She then asked a simple question.

"Why would you do all this?"

"Your life is in grave danger. You have pleaded guilty to the most serious crimes in the realm and have been sentenced to death. You are only alive by Her Majesty's mercy. However, the simplest turn of events could lead to her changing her mind. What if the Prince of Spain put pressure on Her Majesty to be rid of you? Or the Bishop of Rome for that matter? Jane, I honestly believe a tragic turn in your fate is only a matter of time. Your only chance for survival is to come with me on Twelfth Night."

Jane lowered her head and started to pray softly. I sat silently and tried to be patient, but I was as coiled as a fine horse ready to race.

"Jane, I need to go soon. Will you meet me on Twelfth Night and go with me?"

At last, she opened her eyes and looked at me.

"Yes, Tom," she said as she let out a long sigh. "I will meet you then."

My profound relief left me speechless.

"I wish you a happy and blessed Christmas, Tom," she said as she rose. She squeezed my hand, left the cottage, and disappeared into the falling snow.

***

Two days before Twelfth Night, we met at the cabin one last time. I told of my conversation with Jane and her consent to meet me at the chapel at nine of the clock.

"Splendid!" Lord Miles exclaimed. "This is for you Miss Alice." He reached into his bag and brought out a dress for the Twelfth Night celebration. "I told my wife's dressmaker that my niece was new to fancy affairs and asked if she could make a nice dress that was a bit looser so that my niece would have room to dance." The dress was pretty but simple and just loose enough to give Aly freedom to move. She slipped it over her clothes and looked up with a smile that seemed satisfied but maybe a little self-conscious. Even with its simple and practical design, I imagined that this was the prettiest dress that Aly had ever worn.

The Scoundrel's Son

"Let's have a drink," Lord Miles suggested as he opened a bottle of wine likely left over from his Christmas celebrations and filled a glass for each of us.

"This can work!" I pronounced with a voice on the edge of giddy. "It has to work!"

"Tom, I wanted to let you know," Lord Miles's tone turned a bit serious, "that there have been some rumblings in Kent regarding Thomas Wyatt."

"The poet's son?" I asked.

"Yes. It appears he is not happy with the prospect of Her Majesty marrying the Prince of Spain. He is starting to assemble some noblemen to lead an open rebellion." He paused and looked at me. "And Lord Suffolk, Jane's father, is involved."

I was staggered by this news as if shot by an arrow. Had Suffolk forgotten that his daughter's life was at risk? Maybe, like us, he also thought that bold action was necessary to save her. I did not know Thomas Wyatt, but I had little faith that Lord Suffolk could lead a successful rebellion. Northumberland's military abilities were no doubt superior to either man, and he had not been successful. I knew that this recklessness would surely snap the spider's thread.

"I say we go ahead. What say you?" I asked raising my glass of wine. First Aly and then Lord Miles raised their glasses.

"We go!" we all shouted in unison as we touched glasses.

Chapter 35

Finally, Twelfth Night arrived. The three of us had arranged that we would meet at precisely seven of the clock in the evening under the large oak tree in the square near Offal Court. Before I headed out, I grabbed the psalter that Jane had given me and quickly looked for some good words. My eyes settled on one of Father Christian's favorite psalms.

"Although I walk through the valley of darkness, I fear nothing for you are with me."

We had planned to the best of our ability. Of that, I was sure. Still there was much danger in what lay ahead, but I would face it without fear, by the grace of God.

"Are we ready?" Lord Miles asked. Aly and I nodded in agreement, and the three of us headed to the Tower. We were fortunate that it was a clear night with only a crescent moon, just enough light to see while keeping our actions hidden in darkness. As we walked along, Twelfth Night celebrations were beginning. The path we chose avoided busy streets, but we could still hear laughter, singing and a few firecrackers exploding a ways away.

We came to our chosen spot near the northern corner of the moat. It was in the dark while providing a view along the western wall of the Tower all the way down to the Bridge Gate.

"You two get prepared while I go down and see what is happening at the bridge," Lord Miles said, as he hurried into the shadows.

"Are you sure you are ready?" I asked Aly.

"I'm ready, Tom," she asserted. We both started to put on our outfits for the endeavor. Aly slipped the dress over her clothes and fastened a belt about her waist. She then commenced to arrange her hair in a manner more appropriate for the party she and Lord Miles were presumably attending. I

The Scoundrel's Son

turned away to afford Aly some privacy as I prepared and donned the guard uniform given to me by William back in the summer.

I was slipping my shoes back on when I heard a rustling, and Aly let out a gasp. I looked back to see Jem with his hand over Aly's mouth and a knife to her throat. My heart leapt in my chest.

"Now, I got your attention," Jem smirked. "If either of you move or even says a word, I'll slit her throat, here and now."

I raised my hands to show that I understood and, hopefully, to calm Jem down.

"All right, now that we understand each other, here's how this is goin' to go. We three are goin' inside. You as a guard, I guess from your uniform; Aly and me as your guests. Then, the fun begins! I'll be holdin' Aly's hand, but my knife will be right here in case someone does somethin' foolish."

At this point, the rescue was the furthest thing from my mind. All I was thinking was how could I keep Aly safe. Was there a way I could separate Jem and Aly? Could I somehow get the knife from him? I did not believe that the three of us could enter the Tower without incident. It just would look too suspicious. All my success in the past had been based on not causing attention. But I was not going to object to Jem's plan, at least not at this point.

"All right," I suggested. "Let's walk towards the bridge." I finished putting on my shoes and started to walk in a direction away from the bridge to give me more time to think.

"Why we headin' this way?" Jem questioned.

"I've used this path before. It's the way visitors arrive." I led the way as slowly as I could. Jem seemed frustrated by our slow progress and my chosen path.

"No," he finally said. He turned and pointed with his knife. "We need to go this way…"

Right then Aly took advantage of the distraction, stomped on Jem's foot with all her might and threw her elbow back into his ribs. He took a step back in his surprise. She started to run, but she tripped on the hem of her dress and fell to the ground. She tried to wriggle away, but Jem grabbed her foot and dragged her back raising his knife to stab her. Rage was in his eyes. I tried to come between Jem and Aly, but I was two steps away. I prepared to lunge anyway.

Frederic Fahey

"I warned y…" he started to shout when I heard a faint click and then a bang rang from the shadows. At first, I thought the noise was a firecracker, but then Jem fell backwards to the ground with a thud. Lord Miles emerged from the darkness with the hand musket still pointed at Jem. Smoke rose from the end of its barrel. I grabbed Aly and pulled her towards me. The ball had struck Jem square in the chest. He was bleeding badly. He placed his hands over the wound in bewilderment as he tried to speak, but soon he fell silent and still. Lord Miles hurried to Aly and me and put his arms around our shoulders.

"Are you two all right?" he asked, displaying an unbelievable level of calm. Lord Miles's experience as a soldier was serving him well at this moment. On the other hand, I could only nod as the incident had left me speechless. Aly's head bobbed frantically as her breath raced. He hugged the two of us to his chest.

Lord Miles then rose and walked to where Jem lay still. He put his hand to Jem's throat. "He is dead," he proclaimed. "Who was he?"

"Some thief from Offal Court," Aly said coldly, as I gave her another hug.

Lord Miles dragged Jem's body and placed it under a nearby bush where it was fairly well hidden. "I will deal with him later," he said. Firecrackers exploded in the distance.

"I do not think anyone will be alarmed by loud noises on this night," he concluded. He again draped his arms around Aly's and my shoulders.

"Now let's all take a deep breath and let it out slowly. Then count to twenty to clear our heads." We did as Lord Miles said. Twenty seconds seemed like an eternity.

"Are we ready to continue?" he asked.

I was still in shock, but Aly proclaimed, "Yes, let's go!"

I took another breath as Lord Miles looked my way.

"Let's go," I announced with resolve.

Aly straightened her dress and brushed the dirt from it, making sure it had not ripped in her fall or been bloodied, and then continued to fix her hair. I also tidied myself up. I had the cloak for Jane wrapped around my waist. We were now running late, but how late I could not tell.

"Miss Alice and I have a party to attend," Lord Miles announced. "Are you ready, my dear?" he said, offering his arm to her. Aly took his arm and

The Scoundrel's Son

tried to smile.

I turned to Aly. "I will await your signal. Jane and I will meet you shortly after nine."

"I will see the two of you then," she confirmed as she and Lord Miles headed towards the Bridge Gate.

I tried to collect my wits as I waited for my next move. For what seemed the thousandth time, I went through the entire scheme in my head. I kept thinking that I must hurry. I am late. How late, I didn't know.

As I approached the Bridge Gate, someone commanded, "Halt!" I turned to see a guard hurrying toward me from behind. He must have been on his routine rounds. "Why have you left your post?"

My uniform had worked. "I am reporting for duty, Sir," I answered, standing at attention. "I am not expected until nine of the clock. I am a member of the guard for Her Highness Lady Jane." I handed him the letter of my orders that Richard had given me back when Jane was queen. As he looked at my letter, I hoped he would not be able to read or maybe be in too much of a hurry to discern its finer details. Behind him, I could see Jem's foot protruding from under the bush where Lord Miles had placed him. I tried as best I could to look calm, but inside, my heart was hammering. The guard then looked back at me and regarded my face intently.

"I recognize you now," he said, handing me back my letter. "Get to your post. It is not long until nine, perhaps a quarter of an hour."

"Yes, Sir," I said and hurried through the Bridge Gate and to the inner ward without further incident. I slipped along the west wall of the White Tower, feeling my way across its well-worn stones. I hid in the shadows as I waited for Aly's signal before I entered the chapel. I peered in the darkness at the top of the wall, but I did not see her. I had expected she would have been there before I had reached the Tower Green. Where was she? What time was it? Had something happened to her? All that could go wrong started to bounce around my head. Was she lost? Was she captured? Did she fall trying to scale the wall? How long should I wait?

Then I saw her. A single wave indicated everything was all right. I returned the signal and headed to the chapel.

I was waiting in the back corner of the chapel when Jane arrived. The candlelight within the chapel highlighted her fair features and danced off her red hair as it flickered. She had a determined look. I let out a slow breath. Our scheme was working. We were almost there.

"Jane," I softly called. She turned and smiled when she saw me.

"Good evening, Tom. It is good to see you on this blessed night." I was struck by her calm given how much was in the balance. She then sat in one of the pews. I quickly approached and sat next to her.

"Jane, we must go. My friends are waiting for us. Their lives are in danger as we sit." She took both my hands in hers.

"Tom, listen to me," she said with composure and purpose. "I cannot go with you. I am very sorry, Tom. But I cannot."

I sat frozen by her words.

"What do you mean?"

"I must stay. I have thought and prayed on this many times since we last met. I must be true to God. I must be strong in my faith."

"But you will die!" I exclaimed. Her eyes started to tear.

"What does that matter?"

"It matters to me! I love you, Jane, with all my heart! You mean more to me than anything! I don't know if I can live without you! Come with me!"

"You are my closest friend, Tom. I love you dearly." Her voice hitched as she sobbed. She paused. "I am so sorry! But I am afraid this is not about you. It is not about you at all!"

"It is about your life!"

"But what would that life be? A life where I must run? A life where I must hide behind the mask of someone's forlorn niece rather than who I am? A life where I am afraid to be true to my God? As much as I love you, Tom, I cannot live that life.

"This mortal life means nothing to me if it costs me my soul. I need to be strong. I need to show the world what it means to be a person of true faith. It means nothing to light a candle. I need to *be* a candle." She started to cry. "Please try to understand!"

I released her hands, turned my back, and walked a few steps away. The pain in my heart was as deep as any pain I would ever feel in my life.

"I am very sorry! I do not want to hurt you! I am very sorry!" she said over and over again through her tears. I was at a loss as to what to do next. All I knew right then was that there was nothing I could say that would change her mind.

The Scoundrel's Son

"Jane, I cannot begin to tell you how much I love you," I said as I returned and knelt before her. "You are all that matters to me. I realize I have no choice but to respect your wishes. So, I will leave you here. Maybe someday, with God's grace, I will come to understand but until then, I vow to you that I will try."

Finally, the time came when I had to leave. Aly and Lord Miles were waiting, and every moment mattered.

"Jane, I need to go now." I then asked one last thing of her. "Would you sit and pray with me these last few moments?"

She raised her head, wiped the tears from her eyes, and took my hands in hers.

"Let us pray," she said to me. We sat silently looking into each other's eyes as we prayed.

***

I left the chapel and looked up to see Aly perched upon the wall. I waved my arm from side to side twice, which was the signal that the operation had been called off. She returned the signal and disappeared from view. As I came to the gate, she opened it, and I slid out.

"What went wrong?" she asked.

"She would not come," I simply replied.

"What?" Aly gave me a look of incomprehension. I waved off her second question without comment and started to walk around the outer ward towards the Water Gate. When the time was right, we slipped through the gate. Aly and I quietly walked to the dock and boarded Lord Miles's boat.

"Just go," was all I said as I settled in the stern. Lord Miles looked at Aly, who shook her head and shrugged her shoulders. He started down the river. Try as I might to control my emotions, I could not. The fatal scuffle with Jem along with Jane's decision not to come was too much for me to bear. What started as a few tears rolling down my cheeks soon turned to full sobbing. I tried to hide my weeping with my arm, but soon Aly embraced me, and I could no longer conceal my profound sorrow.

"She would not come with me. I pleaded with her. I begged until she was in tears, but still she would not come," I said between sobs. Aly and Lord Miles did not ask anything further of me. Lord Miles rowed the boat while Aly held me without a word. As we approached the meeting place near Poplar, Aly stood in the boat and waved her arm twice, again the sign that the endeavor had not been successful. Someone on the dock, perhaps the Earl, returned the sign as we continued to cruise on past to a second dock, where one of Lord Miles's men was waiting for us with a carriage. On the ride back to the city, no one said a word.

"I need to deal with the unfortunate young man at the Tower so I will leave you here," Lord Miles said once we came to Offal Court. "I suggest we meet at the cabin in a few days to talk about what happened. Tom, let us know when you are ready." I agreed but offered nothing more.

As I walked home, my deep sorrow was in blunt contrast to the Twelfth Night celebrations around me. There was shouting and singing all about. Once home in my bed, I kept asking myself the same questions. Why would she not come with me? Does she not realize how dire her situation is? Is it me? Did she not want to come because it was me? It was almost daybreak before slumber finally took me.

Chapter 36

A few days later, I met with Aly and Lord Miles at the cabin, and I described what transpired in the chapel.

"Do you think with time she might change her mind?" Lord Miles asked.

"I am sure she will not," I responded.

"I supposed that to be so," was his reply.

I told them that I had met with the Earl and informed him of what happened in the chapel. He affirmed that he would be there should the opportunity arise again.

"I want to thank the two of you. You put your lives in danger for me, and I will never forget it. I am very grateful."

"It was an honor for us," Lord Miles said.

"And we'd do it all over if we had to," Aly added in agreement.

I was blessed to have such good and loyal friends. Still, I was haunted by my thoughts of doubt.

"Was it all for nothing?" I asked.

"Not at all!" Lord Miles exclaimed. "In the end, we provided Her Highness with a choice, pure and simple. She could come with us and likely live, or she could stay and let fate be as it may. From all you have told me about Lady Jane, she painstakingly considered this choice. I believe she truly understood the decision she was making. I might not believe that with most people, but in her case, I do, even at her young age. She chose. She did what she thought was right for her, and, in turn, she did not put you or me or Miss Alice at any further risk than need be. Let's face it. If we had been successful, it is very possible that a look into her escape would have led back to us. So, I believe, she made the right choice for herself and, thereby, for us. We did our best, and we provided her with that

Frederic Fahey

choice. So, no, it was not for nothing. I have no regrets whatsoever." I rose and shook Lord Miles hand and gave Aly a warm hug.

By the time we returned to Offal Court, snow flurries were starting to fall. Aly headed home while I walked along the river towards the Strand. As I came to Norwich Place, I could see Whitehall up the river. I recalled spring afternoons in the garden with Jane and that very first day I met Edward when he rescued me outside the palace. The wet snow stung my face, and my fingers were starting to feel numb, so I stopped in a small church on my way back home. I said a prayer for Edward and for Jane. And I then said one for Jem. Lord Miles never told me where he had brought his remains. Thinking of him brought a tear. He was just a boy from Offal Court trying to get by in a painful life. But for one fortunate day outside Whitehall Palace, seven years before, that could have been me.

I was near Christ's Hospital, so I decided to stop by my mother's cottage. Her door opened as I approached. She must have seen that something was not right, as I was not met with her usual boisterous manner, but with a loving look and open arms. Her love engulfed me as she kicked the door closed.

"My little boy. Mama's here." She did not ask of my circumstances. It did not matter. I wept in her embrace as if I was a wee one afraid in the night.

A few days hence, a note arrived from Richard. At least, the envelope said it was from Richard. When I broke the seal and opened it, I recognized the handwriting immediately. It was from Jane.

Thank you for everything, Tom.
May God bless you.
J

Through the years, I have read this note over and over. Although the ink has faded, I still have it to this day. However, I could not bring myself to visit Jane after Twelfth Night, not out of anger but out of respect. What would we have to say? Maybe someday, we could see each other again, but I figured it would be a while.

I slowly returned to my routine. I went to the shop and tried to catch up on my work. I hoped that Robert would think I had fallen behind merely

The Scoundrel's Son

because of the Christmas season, but I suspect he knew it was something more dear. Father Christian asked me on several occasions if I was all right.

"Tom, you know you can talk to me about anything at any time."

"I know Father. Thank you," I responded but we never did speak of these things.

As Lord Miles had reported, Thomas Wyatt of Kent and his conspirators staged a rebellion. And, yes, Jane's father and his brothers were involved. Many among the rebels, including Wyatt himself, had fully supported Her Majesty's claim to the throne, but when in mid-January she announced plans to wed Prince Philip of Spain, the group decided to move forward with their rebellion. They could not abide by the thought that a foreign monarch may someday be King of England. The plan was to place Lady Elizabeth, not Jane, on the throne. The rebellion was launched during the last week in January and crumbled within a matter of days. Wyatt surrendered on the seventh day of February, and Lord Suffolk was arrested soon after.

On the night of Suffolk's arrest, I hastened to the Tower. It was overly fortified considering the rebellion. There had to be three times the usual guard at the Bridge Gate. It was getting late, but I decided to head to Whitehall to see what I could learn from William.

"You have not heard?" William asked with a bit of surprise. "The date for Lady Jane's execution has been set for two days from now. Lord Guildford Dudley is to die on the same day."

Blood rushed from my face as, I could swear, I heard the faintest crack as the spider's thread snapped.

"I am sorry, Tom," William said as he grasped my shoulder, "but I must go."

I don't remember walking but, somehow, I found myself in front of the Brown home. It was very late by now, so I did not knock. I just stood stunned. At last, Aly came outside bundled against the February cold with a blanket in her arms.

"Come inside, Tom," she said, handing me the blanket. "You'll freeze out here."

"Is anyone awake?"

"No, all gone to bed. It's past midnight. I happened to see you when I got up to stoke the fire. Come! Come! I'll fix you some hot cider."

We went inside and I sat by the fire. She handed me the cider and waited silently for me to speak. Finally, my words came.

"Jane is to die," I whispered, not wanting to wake anybody. "The actions of her father have sealed her fate. In two days' time, she will be gone." I started to weep. Aly remained quiet and let me talk.

"I have not seen her since the chapel. Maybe I should have tried to see her again. I did not know what I would say. I knew her death would come, but I still thought there would be time."

Aly moved closer and put her arm around me. "Oh, Tom."

"Why wouldn't she come with me?" I asked yet again. With that, my heart let loose. Aly and I sat there for quite some time.

Chapter 37

The winter sun was high in the sky when I eventually rose the next day. Father Christian was sitting at the table.

"Oh Tom, have a seat. I have something to share with you. Yesterday, I heard from my former student, Father Feckenham. He now serves Her Majesty as her chaplain and confessor. Her Majesty has asked him to speak to Lady Jane, and he called me to the Tower to consult with him."

My ears perked up as I was anxious for any news of Jane given that her execution was to be the next day.

"I told Father Feckenham that I had never met Her Highness, but that I had heard that she was exceedingly bright, thoughtful, and well read.

"I suggested that he refrain from telling her what to believe, and that instead he should use a more Socratic approach. He should ask her questions and let her express herself regarding her faith and her relationship with Almighty God. Trying to understand what she believes before attempting to convince her to choose a different path would be better. I did warn him that this may take more than a single day."

"She will not be told what to think on any subject, and certainly not about her faith which she holds most dear. But she will listen and express herself in straight terms. I could not have given better advice to Father… what was his name?"

"Father Feckenham. Oh, he listened to my suggestion and requested of Her Majesty additional time to meet with Her Highness. Her Majesty has agreed to three additional days. Lady Jane's execution is not tomorrow. It has now been moved to the twelfth day of February."

I am not sure why, but the three extra days gave me a sense of relief. Part of me held out the slim hope, very likely beyond slim, that Her Majesty would have a change of heart towards Jane and spare her. Father

Frederic Fahey

Christian gently reminded me that Father Feckenham's mission was not to save Jane's life, but her soul.

"Thank you for sharing this with me, Father," I said sincerely. "But I will say, in the end, Father Feckenham's efforts will be futile. She will not budge."

"We can only do the best we can do, and then leave it in God's hands," was Father Christian's response. This made me think back to my conversation with Lord Miles. We could only do the best that we could do.

"Yes, Father, I agree."

Over the days leading to the twelfth, I tried to go about my life. I woke each morning, walked to the shop, did my work, came home, had dinner, read by the fire, and went to bed. I tried to devise tricks to help me fall asleep. I would review my work for the next day, I would count to a hundred, I would recall old tales from my youth. But still my thoughts returned to Jane. I would try not to focus on her current situation but to recall our good times together. I remembered the first day I saw her and Lady Elizabeth during the masquerade. How pretty and precocious she was, spouting about things far beyond my ken. I remembered the little girl look on her face when the mechanical frog jumped. I remembered the time she recognized me as I sat upon Edward's throne. I recalled it all.

On the evening of the eleventh, I returned home to find that Father Christian had a visitor.

"Come in, Tom! This is Master Thomas Canty, the young man who shares my home," he said to his visitor. "Tom, this is my friend, Father Feckenham. Why don't the two of you sit in our reading spot while I prepare something to eat?" Father Christian suggested. I took my usual seat while Father Feckenham sat in Father Christian's chair. We made small talk about the weather for this time of year and might we see snow again. He asked about my work, and I told him of Robert's shop. I finally worked up the nerve to get to the point.

"Father Christian tells me you have been meeting with Lady Jane Dudley these past few days. I don't know if Father has mentioned it, but I have come to know Her Highness over these past few years."

"No, he had not mentioned it," Father Feckenham said, surprised. "How is it that you have come to know Her Highness?"

"It's a long story. I was named a ward of King Edward and, as such, I

The Scoundrel's Son

had the opportunity to meet Lady Jane on several social occasions."

"Interesting. Yes, Her Majesty has asked me to provide Lady Dudley with spiritual guidance in this special time. I find her to be a remarkable young lady. Because of my priestly responsibilities, I cannot share the specifics of our conversations, but I can say that she had an answer for all my queries without hesitation. She is truly grounded in her beliefs which are fundamentally based on her understanding of the Almighty.

"As stimulating as our discussions were, I am afraid I failed in what Her Majesty asked of me. I had hoped that our conversations would open the opportunity for Lady Dudley to see her way back to the true faith. But alas, we did not get there. I was grateful that Her Majesty granted more time, but I understand now that whether it was three days, three weeks, or thirty years, I would not be able to sway Her Highness from her beliefs. And her beliefs are wrong, and so I am gravely sorry that I was unable to save her eternal soul. She has made all the wrong choices for all the right reasons.

"After the time we have spent together, I have come to have great respect for Lady Dudley. I believe she has come to respect me as well. She has asked me to be with her during her last moments tomorrow, and I told her that it would be my honor."

"Is she afraid to die?" I asked.

"Not at all, as far as I can tell. She has told me that the day of her death is more precious than the day of her birth, and she has decided that this is her time to die. I will pray for her until the moment of her death and beyond in the dim hope that her soul can be saved by the mercy of God."

Father Christian invited Father Feckenham to stay the night, so he would be closer to the Tower, and he agreed to stay. Father Christian slept in his chair, which was often his custom, while Father Feckenham took his bed. That night, I laid in bed thinking about Lord Miles's conclusion. We provided Jane a choice, which was all we could do. She was not merely a victim of circumstance; she was someone who made the solemn decision to place her fate in God's hands. But when she made this choice, did she truly, not just philosophically, appreciate that this most likely meant the loss of her mortal life? Father Feckenham confirmed that yes, she did realize this and fully accepted it. My gift to her was that I made this choice, a choice she fully grasped, available to her.

Frederic Fahey

***

When I rose the next morning, I was pleased to find the two priests still asleep. I quietly stoked the fire as not to wake Father Christian, who laid nestled in his chair. I prepared myself a cup of warm cider. As I waited for it to warm, I wrote a note for Jane that simply said:

I now understand. May God bless you.
        With love
                T

When Father Christian finally arose, he was surprised to find me already up and about in the kitchen.

"Well, Tom. Did you wake to rouse the rooster?" he joked.

Father Feckenham came into the kitchen soon after. The two priests did not eat as they were going to attend Mass before Father Feckenham headed to the Tower. When Father Christian was getting ready, I handed Father Feckenham my note.

"Father, I have a great favor to ask of you. Would you be so kind as to give this note to Lady Dudley if you have the chance? It would mean very much to me."

He took my note, folded it without reading it, and offered me his hand.

"I certainly will. It was a pleasure to meet you, Tom. May God bless you."

By then, Father Christian had returned, and the two priests headed to Mass. After they left, I made myself some toast and jam to break my fast. I sat still for a moment after swallowing my last bite, and then slammed my fist on the table. "I need to be there," I said aloud, although no one was there to hear me. I would attend the day's events and bear witness to this most sacred point in Jane's fateful journey.

First, Lord Guildford would be executed on Tower Hill, just north of the Tower. As a member of the royal family, Jane's execution would be a more private affair within the Tower walls. Her Majesty had decided that both prisoners would meet their ends by simple beheadings. Lord Guildford would not be drawn and quartered, and Jane would not be burned.

The Scoundrel's Son

I packed my guard uniform and headed to Tower Hill. The sky was cloudy and the air cold on this February morning. I slipped into my guard uniform and stayed hidden until the procession with Lord Guildford approached the hill. The scaffold stood on almost the exact same spot where his father's life had ended months earlier. The delivery of the sentence was not delayed as Lord Guildford had no words to say. I had heard that he had also refused to convert to the old religion, unlike his father. I wondered if, perhaps, he and Jane had come to some understanding as the end neared.

I fell in with the guard as the procession was formed to return to the Tower. As I marched behind the wagon carrying Lord Guildford's body, I could see the red trail formed by his blood dripping from the wagon onto the frozen ground.

Once we reached the inner ward, I changed back to my street clothes, which I had wrapped about my waist, since I was not sure a common guard would be allowed to witness the solemn event. I found a place among the few who were assembled. The scaffold that had been constructed on the Tower Green simply consisted of a small, raised stage with a large wooden block towards the front. The executioner was already waiting along with the Lieutenant of the Tower. I gazed up at the various towers that rose above the green. I had heard that Jane's father was being held in one of these towers and wondered if he knew what was happening today, that his eldest daughter was about to lose her life.

It was not long before the procession from the Partridge's quarters to the scaffold began. Father Feckenham led, followed by Jane, two of her ladies, and Richard. Jane was wearing a simple black dress. She carried the prayer book that she had held almost constantly during her imprisonment. She walked with grace and a sense of purpose, holding her head high with her eyes straight ahead. Her delicate face exuded strength and determination. After climbing the scaffold, she walked to Father Feckenham, who took her hands as they exchanged a few words. He handed her what appeared to be my note. She unfolded it and read it before slipping it into the pocket of her dress.

She came to stand directly behind the block and surveyed the crowd. Then she looked right at me. Her gaze lingered and the subtle change in her expression was likely imperceptible by everyone but me. But I knew she had read my note and that she was pleased. She looked directly into my eyes and touched my heart. I could feel a sense of warmth travel up my spine to the back of my head. Then her gaze moved to the next person, and she started to speak.

"Good people, I have come here to die. My actions against Her Majesty and her rightful reign were unlawful. Though it was not my plan nor my wish, I knew what was right in God's eyes and acted otherwise, so I gladly receive this punishment for my sins. Today I cleanse my hands before you and before God. I pray that you bear witness that I die a good Christian woman looking only to be saved by the mercy of God. I thank Almighty God for giving me the time to repent. And now, good people, while I am here, I ask you to pray for me." She turned to Father Feckenham. "Shall I recite the psalm?"

"Yes, my lady."

"Dear God, have mercy on me out of your loving kindness that, in all of your tender mercies, my sins can be forgiven."

She handed her gloves and scarf to one of her ladies. She gave her prayer book to Richard who, in turn, presented it to the Lieutenant as a gift. Her ladies assisted her in untying and removing her dress leaving her in a white, linen gown. She let down her hair.

She addressed her executioner. "I ask, kind sir, that you dispatch of me quickly." He remained motionless.

She knelt before the block and was handed a piece of white linen to cover her eyes. As she reached for the block in her blindness, she could not find it. For the first time since the procession began, she grew anxious.

"Where is the block? What should I do?" she asked. Richard stepped forward and gently guided her hands.

At that instant, I decided I could not watch my sweet Jane's last moments. I did not want that to be my last image of her on this Earth. I turned and walked toward the gate next to Wakefield Tower, as I heard Jane's last words.

"Lord Jesus, I commend my spirit into your hands."

As I passed through the gate, I barely heard the swish of the axe or its sound striking the block. I did not hear another sound that morning as I stumbled back home to find Father Christian waiting for me.

Epilogue

Tom paused and took a sip of ale before continuing.

"Father Christian had some warm cider on the stove and poured me a cup. We made our way to our reading nook without a word. He sat in his chair and I in mine. He was right there if I wanted to speak of the day's events. However, a quiet time by the fire was all I needed. I did not speak to Father Christian about my sweet Jane that morning or on the following day or the day after that. Truth be known, I have not spoken of these events to anyone for over twenty years. Not to Aly nor Lord Miles. I have never spoken of Jane to my dear Margaret, my loving wife of these past ten years. I have kept these things locked inside me for a very long time. Only now, my lady, do I share this tale with you."

Tears ran down her face, and her tiny hands reached for a hand linen to wipe them away.

"But I tell you," Tom continued, "there has hardly been a single day that I have not stopped to recall the memory of your sweet sister. A rose reminds me of her hair, a sunrise of her smile, a passing child's giggle of her laugh, a warm breeze of her touch. She was with me as she looked into my heart on that last day, and she has been with me every day since."

Lady Mary sat forward in her chair, one that had been constructed especially for her small stature, built high so that she could look her guests in the eye with a rung to place her tiny feet. She beckoned Tom to move his chair closer so she could take his hand.

"Tom, you have been kind and respectful to me since that first day we met at Norwich Place when I was what, four years old? Others treated me as either a precious toy or a pet because I was so small. But you treated me as a person even then. Perhaps you were the only one to speak to me on the day of my sisters' weddings.

Frederic Fahey

"When you arrived at my door a few days ago, you may have mistaken my look of surprise for one of not recognizing you. No, I knew exactly who you were, after, lo these twenty years." She wiped the few remaining tears from her cheeks and took a deep sip of her wine.

"I was almost nine years old when my sister went to join Our Lord. But I too have sweet memories. I remember her reading to me when I was very young. She gave me my first book, one on animals, which I still have and cherish. She helped me with my lessons when my teachers did not know what to make of me. Jane, on the other hand, was somehow patient and demanding in the proper balance. I remember walks with her and Katherine in the garden. Katherine would tell me which flowers looked best in her hair while Jane told me the names of those flowers. Yes, I also remember Jane fondly.

"But over the years, those sweet memories became mixed with the legend and the martyrdom of Jane. I would hear of how serious she was, how intelligent, how pious, how holy and how tragically she lost her life for her undying faith. Her humanity became lost in her sainthood. She became one of those statues she so despised, made of stone and lacking all warmth.

"You, Tom, bring me a different story. You bring me back the spirit of the sister I remember in my heart. You bring me a girl who laughs." Mary paused for a moment as if something had just struck her.

"Wait right here!" She climbed down from her chair. A bright red petty coat shown from underneath her black dress as she hurried into another room. She returned a few minutes later with a box.

"I love this so much, as does my godchild when she comes to visit me!" She opened the box to reveal the mechanical frog Tom had given to Jane all those years ago. She placed it on the floor before her. Tom had to smile as her face lightened.

She rescaled her chair and took another sip of her wine as she sat quietly for a moment. At once, a tear formed in the corner of her eye and a smile rose to her face. She looked back at Tom.

"I am a woman who is blessed to know what true love is. My darling husband and I were married but for a brief time. He is gone now, but I cherish those days we had together.

"So, I cannot tell you how much it warms my heart to hear of your

The Scoundrel's Son

love for my dear sister. When one dies so young, we are left to lament all that she missed in her brief life including love. But now my memory of Jane will always be bathed in a warm glow. Thank you, Tom, for loving my sister."

Tom took the last sip of his ale as he let Lady Mary's words wash over him. He sat silently for a while before responding. Then he spoke.

"Thank you, my lady, for patiently listening to my tale. I feel as if a weight has been lifted from my spirit." Tom reached into his pocket, brought out a small locket and handed it to Lady Mary. She opened it to find Tom's rendering of her sister's lovely face that he had shown to Jane on their visit just before her last Christmas. Tears returned to Lady Mary's eyes.

"I have carried this in my pocket for more than twenty years," Tom said. "Now I want you to have it."

She smiled and clutched it to her breast. The two of them sat for quite some time without saying another word. None was needed. The bond of their shared love for sweet Jane was enough.

Author's Note

When I was around nine years old and I would come home from school, one of the local television stations would be showing old movies. This one afternoon, I curled up in my father's easy chair and watched the 1937 movie version of *The Prince and the Pauper* starring Errol Flynn with the Mauch twins playing Tom Canty and Prince Edward. I was riveted to that chair as the story unfolded. After "The End" flashed in the snow of our little black and white TV connected to the antenna strapped to our chimney, I ran to our twenty-volume *Collier's Encyclopedia* to see if Edward actually existed. And, sure enough, King Edward VI of England was truly crowned at nine years old, the same age as I was! Later when I read Mark Twain's wonderful tale, I was not only struck by the idea that Tom Canty, an ordinary boy, got to be prince, but also by the harrowing adventures of Edward out on the streets of London. If not for the gallant and often patient Miles Hendon, the Prince of Wales would likely not have survived!

I then asked myself, "What happened next?" Did Tom and Edward remain friends? Twain only said that Tom lived to be an old man, and the encyclopedia said that Edward did not. And what of the other members of the royal family in the story, Edward's half sisters, Mary and Elizabeth, and his cousin, Lady Jane, of about his same age. A new story rattled around in my head for years, one of the precious friendships we form when we are eleven or twelve, sometimes more steadfast than any for the rest of our lives. As we start to face who we are and who we want to be as teens, these friends are the only ones who seem to understand us. Life can take wicked turns, and sometimes we must face seemingly intolerable tragedy even at such a vulnerable age. *The Scoundrel's Son* is that story of what happened next.

I am not a historian by training or profession, and so gaining a better understanding of the real people of my story and the times in which they lived took a bit of work. Still, I am sure I didn't get it quite right. I am grateful for Megan Cook, Associate Professor of English at Colby College, who pointed me towards many valuable resources such as the *Oxford*

Dictionary of National Biography and informed me regarding the availability of printed books in the 1550s. Online podcasts of the early modern era such as *Not Just the Tudors* with Suzanne Lipscomb and *This Shakespeare Life* with Cassidy Cash informed me of other references on aspects of the time such as the card game Primero, the state of the technology of guns as well as the clothes, foods and what folks drank.

Some of the references that I found particularly helpful were the biography of Lady Jane Grey entitled *Crown of Blood: The Deadly Inheritance of Lady Jane Grey* by Nicola Tallis, *Edward VI: The Lost King* by Chris Skidmore, a biography of Edward VI, and *Tudor Church Militant* by Diarmaid MacCulloch touching specifically on Edward's role in the English Reformation. I found *Weapons and Warfare in Renaissance Europe: Gunpowder, Technology, and Tactics*, by Bert S. Hall, a very useful work on the history of guns and gunpowder as well as *The Book in the Renaissance* by Andrew Pettegree, a wonderful reference on the early printing of books. I also appreciated *Power and Politics in Tudor England* by G.W Bernard which discussed the roles and demise of the Lords Somerset and Sudeley. I was fortunate to happen upon several sources of the time: *Edward VI's Chronicle* a terse history written by Edward himself with a useful forward by Ben Egginton, *The Chronicle of Queen Jane* by an unknown author of the 16th century as published by John Gough Nichols and *Foxe's Book of Martyrs* by John Foxe which tells of Jane's last days. Along the way, I also enjoyed the good works of my fellow historical fiction writers covering the same times and people such as Philippa Gregory's *The Last Tudor*, Alison Weir's *Innocent Traitor*, and Janet Wertman's *The Boy King*. Lastly, thank you to Mark Twain for your wonderful *The Prince and the Pauper*. I pray my humble endeavor captured at least a hint of the charm and spunk with which you endowed Tom and Edward.

The Scoundrel's Son is a historical fiction with Tom telling the story of his extraordinary and heartbreaking young life. The conversations including the thoughts and hopes shared by the historical figures are of my imagination, hopefully tinted by some whisp of what I had learned about them. Otherwise, I have tried to be true to the historical events as they occurred. However, I did take some liberties for the sake of the story. I likely have Edward spend more time at Whitehall Palace and Jane at

Norwich Place as these were convenient for Tom's visits. I also had Edward's death occur at Whitehall rather than in Greenwich for the same reason. For Tom to head to Windsor by way of Kent at the time of Edward's abduction was certainly not the most direct route, but I wanted Lord Miles to be part of the adventure. The visit to Whitehall by the Ladies Mary and Elizabeth in the spring of 1553 was totally imagined by me. Father Feckenham's interactions with Jane in her last days are reported to be true, but, obviously, how he spent the night of 11 February 1554 is pure fiction. I hope that these and other unintentional mistakes of places and facts of which I take full ownership did not detract from your enjoyment of Tom's tale.

Acknowledgements

I would like to acknowledge my writing coach and developmental editor, Stephanie Feldman, who has guided me through this entire adventure. I am also grateful for Deborah Benner and my friends at Goose River Press for making this book happen and a dream come true. Thank you to Douglas Smith and Scott Nash for their help with the cover and art design and making the book look so fabulous. I would also like to thank my readers including Beth Harkness, Taylor Engdahl, Lynn Lak, Catherine Dent, Brenda Buchanan, Jeff Billig, Maureen Hall, and Julianne Arden Lee who gave me honest and invaluable feedback. I greatly appreciate the encouragement I received from my Wilmington Memorial Library writer's group, Barbara Alevras, Mark Ryan, Ralph D'Angelo, Meghan Ryan, Amber Kovach and Lynn Koontz. Thanks to Megan Cook, Associate Professor of English for pointing me towards wonderful resources along the way and Emily Rowe who strove to minimize as many anachronisms in my work as possible. My family, including my children David, Bob and Dustine as well as my grandchildren Chase, Cole, Ciella (my teenage expert) and Aezra, has provided me with marvelous support. And, of course, I send my deepest affection and gratitude to Chris, my beautiful wife and partner in creativity, who received the daily audio versions and listened to me rant about what those crazy kids in my head did each day. Chris also contributed the marvelous artwork at the beginnings of Parts I and II. Thanks so much to all of you.

Frederic Fahey is a writer of historical fiction. He received his Doctor of Science from the Harvard School of Public Health in Medical Radiological Physics leading to his career as a medical physicist, most recently at Boston Children's Hospital. He is a Professor of Radiology Emeritus at Harvard Medical School. Fred was born and raised in Massachusetts and now lives with his wife on Peaks Island, Maine.

www.fredericfahey.com